Across the
Mystic Shore

Suroopa Mukherjee

Across the
Mystic Shore

MACMILLAN NEW WRITING

First published 2006 by Macmillan New Writing,
an imprint of Macmillan Publishers Ltd
Brunel Road, Basingstoke RG21 6XS
Associated companies throughout the world
www.macmillannewwriting.com

ISBN 0230 000509 (hardback)
    0230 007325 (paperback)

Typeset by Heronwood Press
Printed and bound in China

For Gautam
who first took me to Varanasi,
the sublime city

Avimukta,
the Never Forsaken

CHAPTER ONE

The Arrival

The boy arrived on a Sunday morning in the midst of a great deal of din and clamour. As the rickshaw skidded into the broad-avenued lane in front of the Sengupta residence, something truly extraordinary happened. Its front wheel hit the road divider, and sent the two occupants flying in the air. They landed on a pile of mud that the municipality had dug up in order to lay the telephone cables.

"Thank God for small mercies," said Abhishek, long after the boy had taken a bath and had his breakfast, "imagine what would have happened if he had fallen headlong on the pavement."

Mira suppressed a giggle, trying to ignore her mother's frowning glance. Just then the calling-bell rang and the neighbours trooped in, led by the indefatigable Mrs. Chopra. Her double-layered chin was hobbling with excitement, and her eyes were round like two large-sized saucers. Her breath was coming in little gasps.

"Dear me, Vandana, dear me. What a calamity! Is the boy hurt?" she hissed in a high-pitched tone.

"No, not really," Mrs. Sengupta replied in a distraught voice. She did not want the boy to be frightened by the presence of this woman. Abhishek gave Mrs. Chopra a knowing look, and propelled her into a tiny covered verandah. "Wait here," he said in a whisper, "I have something to tell you."

Mrs. Chopra felt a thrill course through her veins. She had been lucky today morning. Just when the little accident had taken place, she had pushed her head out of the window and seen the whole thing with her own eyes! "Who is the boy, Abhi? A poor relative? I know how philanthropic your parents are," she said dramatically.

"Oh, no!" Abhishek replied, ready to torture the woman by suppressing information. "No one really!"

"No one? How is that possible?" Mrs. Chopra shrieked. "And Abhi, why does he look so odd?"

From the corner of his eyes Abhishek could see the boy sitting solemnly on a large sofa, surrounded by a gaggle of ladies. He looked tiny and helpless. He had beads of perspiration on his forehead, which he kept wiping with the back of his hand, leaving bright red traces on the delicate skin. His eyes, large and liquid, were serious beyond his age. Even when Mrs. Sengupta had extricated him from under the pile of luggage scattered on the roadside, and dusted his mud-covered body while making a clucking, sympathetic sound with her tongue, the boy had not cried or let out so much as a whimper. It had made her heart reach out to him. Poor, dear child, not a day older than her own Mira, and already separated from the only family he had ever known!

She had rushed out to the pavement her slippers flying, the early morning newspaper fluttering in the breeze, the reading glasses sliding down to the tip of her nose. As she bent down to pick up the boy, she stopped for a fraction of a second. He looked so ridiculous with his tiny frame covered with mud. And then she noticed how the large, spoked wheel of the cycle rickshaw was moving with a slow, clanking, dizzy movement close to the boy's head, and it made her cry out in sheer panic. The head was round, clean shaven except for a little tuft of black hair that was tied in a neat plait at the base of his skull.

Dr. Sengupta, who was sitting in his chamber working out the medicines he would prescribe to his patients, had rushed out as well. The boy was unhurt and so was his companion, the man who was accompanying him from the ashram. After the doctor had yelled at the rickshawallah for his carelessness, he asked his wife to take the boy in, for they were drawing too much attention. He had wanted the arrival to be low key, but that of course was not to be.

Later, Mrs. Sengupta led the boy to his room, the spare one next to the dining hall. It was a tiny room, with a high skylight, and space enough for a bed, a straight-backed chair and a narrow, wooden cupboard. The boy had arrived with very few luggages, just a tin case and a slim brown rexine bag. Both were pushed under the bed, for Mrs. Sengupta disliked a room to be unduly cluttered with things. And then she showed him into the bathroom.

"Clean yourself properly, son," she said, trying to sound as normal as she could. He was pale, pitifully thin, the bald pate framing a sweet, harmonious face. Only the lips were not smiling, and the eyes were remote as though they were looking through a window at something distant. She pointed to the bucket filled with clean, glimmering water and a tiny cake of soap and repeated her instructions. She wondered whether the boy could understand her dialect. At last he nodded dutifully, and as she kept an anxious eye on the closed door, she heard the sound of water running down the drain.

For Mira the events of the past few weeks had been peculiar indeed. As she and her brother Abhishek hung out from the upstairs verandah and watched the entire scene with open mouth, it was almost as though they were expecting something like this to happen. "Drat," said Abhishek, "this is going to upset mom. You know how much she likes everything to be under control."

"He's cute," Mira giggled.

"Cute? What! He'll have to do something about growing his hair. He can't meet my friends with that ridiculous ponytail! It would be so embarrassing."

"Do you think it is some sort of rule at the ashram?" Mira asked.

"Heaven knows," Abhishek retorted, "and not interested either. Loony growing up in a place like that."

"Don't you think you should be rushing down to help?" Mira inquired anxiously.

"And add to the chaos? No, thank you! Enough people to help. I prefer watching things from a distance. It gives a perspective you know."

Mira watched. The boy was lying flat on the road, his head upturned, as though he was granted the vantage point from where he could see the entire neighbourhood ogling at him. For a split second her eyes locked on to his. There was amazement in them, but just about that. Even from this distance she could see the dark orbs brimming with unshed tears. But as she was to discover in the months to follow, the boy rarely cried; just as he rarely laughed.

"Mira, come here darling," her mother called, "show him around the house."

Mira grabbed the boy's hand and took him upstairs. "What is your name?" she whispered on the staircase landing. When the boy did not answer, she repeated the question with a gentle insistence. She came to a halt mid-way. Somehow it seemed important to pass this first barrier of communication before she could show him her room.

Initially she had been reluctant to allow this stranger into their lives, but there was nothing unusual about the situation. It was part and parcel of her life, the way she had been brought up. She understood with almost a disapproving clarity why her father's profession involved strange experiments of this kind. When her mother had explained the situation to them, brother and sister had accepted, though not without some argument from his side and tears from her. After the two children had returned to their room, Mrs. Sengupta sighed with relief. It had not been easy providing an explanation. But she was a kind woman, and having taken an oath as a doctor almost twenty years back, she believed in service to the needy. But there was a curious tremble in her heart, as though deep inside she was afraid.

"Do you understand Bengali?" Mira tried again. She shifted to Hindi. "What is your name?" A flicker of understanding brightened his face. "Avinash," he answered, in a soft musical tone, like the chime of temple bells.

"Wow!" she cried out, laughing spontaneously, "Do you know what it means?"

"Yes," he answered, his brows deepening, "It means The Indestructible One."

Mira could feel the hysteria rising from the pit of her stomach. "Boy," she chortled, "you are a scream! I don't care what Abhi says, I think we are going to have a lot of fun having you around."

She moved upstairs and throwing open the bedroom door, she said with a great deal of flourish, "Our room!" On seeing the boy lingering at the door she pulled him in impatiently. She had this unreasonable urge to boast, to open out her cupboards full of books, toys and clothes and display them all before this boy's hungry eyes. There was something so incongruous about his presence here, like Aladdin in a cave full of treasures. But the boy stared at everything with no desire. It was a part of him that Mira would grow to cherish, but today she felt dimly disappointed.

"Do you like it here?" she asked, pausing a little as though she was hesitant to hear his answer. Avinash went slowly to the window. He nodded yes, but it was visible to no one.

~~~

Mrs. Sengupta brewed two cups of hot coffee and went down to her husband's chamber. This had become a kind of routine that she did not want to change. She knew she would find him at his desk, poring over some case or the other. He was a quiet, introspective man, given to long hours of reading the latest medical journals. In the daytime he was a consultant at one of the leading hospitals in the city, and in the evening he saw his patients at home. There was always a long line of them, sitting on the wooden bench in the portico outside the room. Ever since his practice had picked up momentum, he had hired a young man who helped him with the nitty-gritty of running the place. The man, his personal assistant, sat on a small chair at a table provided for him, and ushered in the patients. The chamber had been cordoned off from the rest of the house by a low wall and a separate gate, through which the patients could come in without disturbing anyone. A board announced, *Dr. S. Sengupta, M.B.B.S., M.D. Psychiatry*. The children's bedroom upstairs overlooked the small gate, and Mira's favourite pastime was to check on the people who walked in. "I can tell how ill they are from the way they walk," she said to her brother.

"Rubbish," he retorted, "their illness is in their head and not in their bodies." It was a statement that brought a solemn look to Mira's face, as though she was confronted with a truth that was somehow inevitable and frightening. Abhishek did not want to become a doctor and follow in the footsteps of his parents. He wanted to be a physicist instead. "I like dabbling in matter. The human mind and body is too narrow a sphere of study. I want to grapple with the fundamentals of things," he said to his sister.

Mira had wanted to be a nurse ever since she had read about Florence Nightingale. On the nights that the electricity went off, she carried a candle into her room and imagined herself walking down a long, white corridor, wearing a white uniform. Like her mother, she felt a strange bonding with Avinash, as though he needed her to tend and care for him. She kept a close eye on him, and protected him from the curious onlooker.

Mrs. Sengupta set the coffee on the table. She looked exhausted, but it was the kind of tiredness one acquires at the end of a long, meaningful day. Ever since the boy had arrived her days acquired a new kind of preoccupation. There was a strange quietness in the night air, and the only sound that could be heard was the constant whirring of the fan. Her routine was very different from her husband's. As a paediatrician she visited a nearby primary health clinic run by the Delhi Municipality for a few fixed hours in the morning. She was back home by noon to oversee her family. This kind of job suited her better, and she never thought of changing it for something more profitable. When Mira returned home from school she always found her mother there, ready to fuss over her, and hear her recount the day's happening in school.

Today her husband noticed the creases of worry on her forehead. She flopped into the cane chair ("my chair" she called it) with a sigh. "I am tired!" she muttered.

She had an expressive, mobile face, across which flittered

a myriad of moods, like the quick, shifting sun falling on the landscape. Her eyes would frown, hesitate, smile and brood, all in rapid sequence, and accordingly her hands would rotate in tiny movements with the grace of a dancer. She was slim and agile, and yet not restless. There was something gentle about her face that merged well with the energy she exuded. As she sat down, she frowned, a trifle angrily.

Dr. Sengupta noticed this and said warily, "Do not worry yourself too much, Vandana. His upbringing at the ashram was good."

She gave him a sharp look. "I am hardly worrying about that," she said vehemently, "but you know how people talk. Mrs. Chopra actually had the audacity to ask me whether the boy's background matched our own. You have to think of its influence on the children," she said. "Imagine!"

Dr. Sengupta laughed. "Are you surprised?" he asked jocularly. "You saw the way she searched for a bride for her son. How many horoscopes went down the drain, how many ill-starred matches were pushed aside? Did you expect anything better from her?"

"Well, she talks too much and I don't like the way she sidles up to Abhi. The boy is growing up, you know, Sameer."

"That's absurd," Sameer retorted, "nobody can influence children that easily. They have firm minds of their own, specially our two."

Yes, thought Vandana, but she did not feel optimistic. "And would you believe it," she said, raising her eyebrows, "Mrs. Menon actually seemed to think that falling off a rickshaw was an ill omen. She kept saying we should have brought him on an auspicious day."

Sameer's face turned serious. "Really, Vandana, I don't think you should worry about such trivialities. The entire arrangement is temporary. You understand that, don't you? Six months at best. The boy has been through a great deal in the last few months. Besides, he needs acclimatization to life outside the ashram. Then we will discuss with Abha about what our next step should be. Abha said she will come down to Delhi and discuss matters with us."

Vandana sipped the coffee silently. I hope we are doing right for him, she thought fearfully. But it was an idea that she kept to herself. Only her fingers moved to her forehead and she brushed back the few strands of hair. In the halflight of the room her face looked secretive and sad.

Sameer closed his books and retired to bed earlier than usual. He slept fitfully through the night.

~~~

Abhishek was used to studying through the wee hours of the night. Their room was L-shaped, so that his study corner was secluded and he could keep the night-lamp lit without disturbing Mira. Once in a while he would turn to see her curled up in bed, a pillow held firmly in the crook of her legs. Her face was always serene, as though she had happy dreams. A streetlight nestled close to the large window next to her bed. Some of the light filtered into the room and fell in a trajectory close to her mouth and chest; he could see the undulating movement of her breath. Then, almost with a sense of shock, he noticed the moon, large and bright and brilliant.

He returned to his book, and absorbed himself in his reading. Scientific facts fascinated him. Science unravels and clarifies the mysteries of life, he thought with a sense of thrill. When he turned again to look at the sleeping face of his sister he saw that the play of light had shifted – now her face was luminous, moon-like and delicate.

He was in the final year of school and, though he had heard fearsome accounts of board exams, he suffered little of the anxiety. He studied steadily, taking in facts with a kind of easy penetration. He had a steady hand so that his diagrams were adjudged the best in his class. "Well, he has the calibre to join one of the IIT's," his teacher said to his parents. Abhishek felt the security of one who knew his future.

But for the past few days a strange sense of displacement bothered him. It was as though each member of his family was coping with a new experience. What was it about Avinash that disturbed him? Was it the touch of the unfamiliar, or was it an identity that did not quite fit in? Abhishek felt a strange urge to verify. He switched off the table lamp and tip-toed downstairs to the room where the boy was sleeping.

The large drawing-cum-dining room seemed strangely unfamiliar. The door leading into the tiny room next to it was ajar, a pair of brand new curtains hanging across. The room was occupied, and despite himself Abhishek felt a shiver run down his spine. They had guests every year around puja, but this room was never used. It had the air of a place distant from the rest of the living space, as though it could only be brought into use in very special circumstances. To Abhishek, Avinash was an oddity, creating strange ripples and disturbing the even pace of their lives. He felt the embarrassment of having to explain to his friends who Avinash was and why he had come to live with them. "Imagine, mom, he has never gone to school in this day and age," he'd said with incredulity, "what do we do now? Let him continue with his illiteracy?"

"Well, he is not exactly illiterate," his father had intervened. "He was taught by several masters at the ashram. What he lacks is formal education. He is well-versed in the religious books."

"Pah! Mighty good that will do him!" Abhishek cried out, irritated at his father's undue support of the boy. Mira shuffled her feet, uneasy at the intensity of the exchange. They were at the dining table, and somehow she felt that Avinash should not be discussed so openly in his presence. Nothing seemed to suggest that the boy was following the tenor of the conversation, but Mira could feel her ears burning. She gulped down her food, and asked her mother permission to take him upstairs to her room. Avinash followed her dutifully, just as he had polished off his plate mechanically without any indication that he had enjoyed the dinner. He ate without hunger, and he followed the girl without intention or will.

The argument had continued for a length of time after Avinash had let the table, but Mira had shut the door firmly so that the voices did not float upstairs.

Abhishek found himself now, standing in the same dining hall, and in the silence of the night his earlier loud protests seemed strangely out of place, as though in the larger scheme of things they did not really matter.

He pushed aside the curtain and stood at the doorway, uncertain of what he expected to see. He could see nothing, the room was so dark. A dank, musty smell of unlived quarters hit his nose. The room was oppressively small and airless, and the difference made him stagger a bit and move back. There was a skylight through which the moonbeams slid in, but they were suspended in mid-air as though they could not penetrate the darkness beneath. The opaque, crusty glass pane covering the skylight hid the moon from sight. Was the boy sleeping? There was no way of knowing, as though sleep and oblivion had merged, becoming one continuous activity.

Abhishek rushed upstairs, panting slightly. Mira was awake, sitting up on her bed. "Abhi," she said, "can I go downstairs and check out on Avinash? Do you think he is frightened of sleeping in a new place?"

"Go back to sleep!" Abhishek cried harshly. He did not return to his studies. Outside the window the moon glimmered and glowed, swamping the room in its ghostly light.

≈≈≈

Avinash was back in Varanasi, in the ashram from where he had come. He was drowning in a large pool. The water was dragging him in and, though he was struggling very hard, the swirling darkness was pushing him from all sides. It was an unequal battle for survival, and however hard he tried he was unable to cry out for help. He closed his eyes and tried to repeat the prayer they had been taught at the ashram. It was a slow chant, said with a kind of intense piety. The words had never meant much to him; he repeated them out of obedience. Now, sucked under water, they eluded him. He felt helpless, very helpless.

The water was dark and thick, stagnant with the growing hyacinths. Where did the strong undercurrents come from? He moved down, down until he hit the bottom. It was a gravelly waterbed, the sand loose and moist, curled around his toes. He felt comfortable, ready to die. He allowed himself to be drowned.

They had saved him, this house full of strangers. They had cleaned his body, given him fresh clothes and food to eat. Just before he had gone to sleep the lady had stood over his bed and said in a kind voice, "Drink your milk, Avinash. These are some of the rules of this house. Remember them."

Her hand had reached out to touch his forehead with the light touch of someone imparting a blessing. He had drunk the milk, allowing its lukewarm taste to swirl against his palate.

He remembered the river then, its banks so wide that from the end where you stood only the twinkling lights were visible. This river, the Ganges, had its source in the high mountain ranges, and as it meandered down it carried the rich alluvial soil to the sea. His early morning prayers were tied up with the river. But the touch of the icy cold water never ceased to shock his skin and make him recoil. His prayers got frozen on his tiny lips.

Later, he sat at the tea stall sipping a small earthen cup of hot, delicious milk. It was fragrant with slices of green cardamom seeds, and large sugar granules that crunched in his mouth long after he had drunk the last sip. A young woman was with him, keeping a sharp eye. She drank tea in little sips. Her eyes wandered across the river now and then. Her body was wet, the river water running in little rivulets down her back from the nape of her neck. She wore a white sari with blue border that clung to her body. It would dry in the course of the day as the sun moved overhead. In this Holy City, Varanasi, men and women carry the river in their bodies until the day they die. And when they are burnt on the ghats adjacent to the river, their bodies merge with the rich soil. It is a continuous circle, without break, ceaseless like the flow of the river.

"When you enter the river you must remain on the surface, floating forever," the woman was telling Avinash.

Avinash looked at the dark still surface of the water. He felt the swirling currents sweep over him. He closed his eyes, ready to drown.

Mira waited for Abhishek to go off to sleep. Then, very quietly so that she would disturb no one, she went down to Avinash's room.

"Listen," she whispered, "don't get frightened. It's me."

Avinash was not sleeping on the bed. He had shifted to the floor. Mira noticed that he had taken neither the sheet nor the pillow. He was lying on the cool, mosaic floor, his eyes wide open. He looked a little scared, as though the recent happenings had been quite overwhelming for him.

"You are awake," Mira said kindly. She squatted on the floor next to him. "Aren't you surprised to see me?" she asked. Sometimes she found the boy's lack of response exasperating, at other times it amused her no end. In the dead of night there was something exciting about finding herself alone in a room with the boy. This boy is going to change our lives, she thought, and somehow, despite herself, she felt glad.

The floor was bare and hard and cold. It was so different from her room, strewn around with thick carpets. She could get the faint smell of phenyl with which Shantabai swept the floor, and she felt the strange urge to lie down next to the boy. She prodded him instead and said, "Come, I will take you to the terrace."

On the way, she stopped at the kitchen. "Are you hungry?" she whispered. Then entering the larder she took out some pickle and led the boy up the stairs.

The terrace was flooded with moonlight. They sucked the peels of mango, the boy grimacing as the tangy taste hit his tongue. "I love mango pickle, don't you?" Mira asked.

"Yes," the boy answered, "my mother used to make pickle and keep it in big glass jars."

"Your mother? Where is she?"

"I don't know," Avinash replied, "she got lost."

"Lost?" Mira asked incredulously. "Where?"

"In the river." He did not say anything further, and the trail of conversation was lost. They ate the pickle silently.

At last Mira broke the silence. "See! See the moon. It looks like your bald pate." She began to laugh uncontrollably until the tears ran down her face. He watched her silently, a solemn look in his eyes, his pickle-stained mouth quivering like a red, angry gash.

CHAPTER TWO

The River

Ramakant, Dr. Sengupta's Man Friday, was pottering around in the chamber, arranging the files in some sort of order. He eyed one closely. It was a nondescript brown file with number 24 scrawled on top in the doctor's own handwriting. Ramakant recognised the file; it belonged to Uma.

Ramakant sensed that the doctor was deeply involved in Uma's case. There was something unplumbed and uncharted about the file, just like the mind of the patient that Dr. Sengupta was treating. Ramakant straightened the desk calendar, and checked whether the flowers arranged in the vase were fresh. It was not part of his duty, but he liked doing these odd jobs. It gave him a sense of belonging.

He had entered this job almost five years back. He was then a fresh science graduate without much ambition. He needed a footing somewhere, and when the doctor advertised for an assistant, he applied. He liked the man who was employing him. In his mid-forties, Sameer had the dignified bearing of a man who listened carefully to the needs of his patients. He spoke in a quiet tone, peppered with the sort of muted humour that made you smile rather than laugh out loud. He never raised his voice, or allowed anything more than a sparkle to lighten up his eyes. Five years later he had greyed gently around the temples, but the face was mild and young still. Ramakant had not once contemplated changing his job. When he got married the doctor raised his pay packet without asking. Sometimes, Ramakant's wife did grumble about the job being too menial, but he shushed her up without so much as giving a second thought to her arguments.

He heard the bell ring, the 'dinner gong' as it was called in the family. He smiled. On Sundays the bell summoned him to join the family for lunch. Usually he was off on Sundays, but he came over on one pretext or the other. On such days he was ushered into the inner circle of the family, and sat down to lunch with them. The meals were simple, but Ramakant enjoyed every bit of what he ate. Mira and Abhishek were at their boisterous best in his presence, often wheedling him to enter into a heated debate. Vandana was, of course, the adjudicator, never allowing the discussion to go out of hand. She would strategically change the topic, or serve the sweet dish to bring matters to an end.

For the past few months, since the boy had arrived, the discussions were becoming a little uncomfortable. More often than not Abhishek ate his meal quickly and silently, and left the table. Mira lingered on, her eyes probing the faces circling the table. When it came to Avinash there was a curious pain in her eyes that no one else quite noticed, least of all Avinash himself, though he had grown dependent on the girl for every little chore that he did. He followed her dutifully, with a slight frown on his forehead, and when she chided him for his lack of friendliness he looked at her with a certain unstated hostility.

The bell was part of a ritual that herded the family together. As it jangled impatiently that afternoon, Ramakant knew it was Mira who was holding it over her head and shaking it vigorously. The bell had been a family heirloom ever since the Sengupta's could remember. It had come from Varanasi almost twenty years back. There in the ancestral home, it had belonged in the family prayer room, and Sameer remembered how his grandmother and then his mother would frisk it gently to usher in any important event. Thus his wedding, the rice ceremony announcing the birth of his children and their birthdays were accompanied by the sound of bells. But now the children had grown and the bell served a more practical purpose. Vandana firmly believed that meal times were family affairs, when they should sit down together and share their troubles and joys. She insisted that the bell act as a kind of summons, enforcing a discipline that everyone had to follow.

But Avinash rarely heard the bell. This was the reason why Mira shook it hard, bringing the rest of the family scrambling on their feet. 'What's the matter, idiot?" Abhi called out. "Is this some sort of a fire alarm?"

"Mind your language, Abhi," Sameer said firmly. "And stop it, girl. That's enough."

"Why can't we serve him meals in his room?" Abhishek continued, to no one in particular. Ramakant stopped in his tracks. Why did he get the feeling that his presence was unwanted, particularly at such moments? He sat down heavily.

Mira fled from the room, tears of pique rushing to her eyes. She went straight to Avinash's room. He was not there. She knew where to find him. He was up there most of the day, even in the afternoon when the sun was hot and over-head. He would walk barefoot on the empty terrace, allow-ing the spiralling heat to seep through his body. At night he would lie down under the open sky, his loose-fitting shirt damp with perspiration. The day's heat would rise from the rough-hewn stone of the terrace floor, burning into his skin.

"Are you deaf? Can you not hear the bell?" Mira cried out angrily.

"I am not hungry."

"You are never hungry. You fill your stomach with empty air."

Avinash's ponytail had been cut off. His hair had grown into a close crop. He looked handsome. One noticed the fine bone structure of his chin and jaws, and the slight slant to his eyes. His face was oval, and his skin fair.

He turned to face Mira. He saw the swelling tears in her eyes. He moved close to her and reached out his hand to brush the tears from her face. It was a strange gesture, passionless – as though he was getting rid of a bit of grime. She lashed out her arm, hitting him hard, "Get lost. Get lost," she cried out bitterly. They were locked in a vicious combat, each unable to move, to get away from the scene that held them together.

Mira used her trump card. "Mother will get really angry if you don't come down for lunch. The whole family is waiting for you." Avinash never disobeyed Vandana's instructions. Her annoyance seemed to draw from the boy an instinctive compliance. He followed her often around the house with a strange expression on his face. It was a kind of yearning, childish and yet disconcertingly sombre.

~~~

There were times of the day when Vandana felt she needed to retire from the hurly-burly of daily routine and simply "be", as she called it. But such times were difficult to give shape; they had to be gleaned from a kind of constant negotiation with the exacting demands of the clock. Returning from her clinic in the afternoon meant browsing through the letters, finishing off the chores in the kitchen, checking on Avinash, and waiting for Mira's return from school. It was simply an underlying anxiety that kept her attention diverted from herself. But she found the moment before she retired to her room strangely exciting, as though she was entering a hallowed space, intimate and deeply private.

Today, she found a letter addressed to her. It had arrived by the afternoon courier service. "A letter by courier?" she thought briefly. The envelope lay in her hand, heavy, moist, wilting in the heat, and as she held it close to herself she could smell the faint trace of old, rotting glue. She let it drop on to the desk.

She was not in a particular hurry to open it. She put her head down on the pillow, closed her eyes, and allowed the tiny noises of an empty afternoon to seep through her body. It felt good, and she found herself drifting through a sort of space travel, the kind that is neither sleep nor waking.

Her life had been happy in an untroubled, neutral way. She and her husband had made enough money to lead a comfortable, middle class life. And Sameer was caring and understanding in a way that suited her well. She smiled mistily, remembering the early years of marriage, when she was just beginning to fall in love with her husband. But Vandana had been clear that she wanted motherhood. So her true happiness began from the day she conceived Abhishek. In no time, a second conception followed, and her family was complete. The transition had been simple and matter of fact. Now all her attention was given to maintaining that family. If she had had any other desires they were irrelevant to her now.

She got up to draw the curtains. Usually she liked her room to be bright and airy, but today the sun was a trifle too strong and it hurt her eyes. They lived in an upwardly-mobile neighbourhood in one of the newer colonies in New Delhi. Though the block where they stayed had rows of

houses on smaller plots, their own house tastefully occupied
a corner plot, which gave them the added advantage of extra
space. Her bedroom was constructed in a semicircle covering the corner and overlooking the street. A door led to a
large balcony that was decorated with low settees and cane
chairs and a Rajasthani coffee table with tiny, rounded legs.
She had put up wall hangings they had picked up from different parts of India.

She sat down on the armchair kept next to her bed and
opened the letter.

Dear Vandana,

*Sameer has sent me an email confirming Avinash's stay in
your house. I am forever grateful for the decision that you
have taken. I am thinking of returning to Varanasi after a
gap of many years. I believe you have two children now.
There is so much catching up to do. Frankly, I don't know
where to begin. I will, when given a chance, visit you and
your family in Delhi. I have an open invitation from
Sameer, the good doctor.*
I sign off now,

Yours, David.

*P.S, I am enclosing all the necessary papers from the
ashram concerning Avinash's release. Abha sent them to me
in duplicate. They are for your close scrutiny. If there are
any formalities left to be completed, please let me know; I
will be more than happy to help.*

Vandana sat quietly as though the slightest movement would
break her equanimity. She checked the postage stamp. It was
from Varanasi. The letter had been sent through Abha.

David? A tall, lanky man emerged from the shadows and loomed over her chair. He had always done this – in a kind of swamping, overbearing way, as though his great height was an advantage that he had earned over her. She had felt petite and vulnerable in his presence. He had curly brown hair, the colour of honey, falling over his forehead in tight locks that she found decidedly girlish. But his face was mannish, flat and square with big features. The eyes were covered with heavy lids, but when he looked up at her she saw the most brilliant, piercing, pearl-green eyes she had ever seen. The white was freckled with spots of dark green, like foliage after a storm. The eyelashes were translucent, delicate, falling over the mounds of his cheek in an indiscreet pattern. The smile was electrifying, beguiling, and dangerously innocent.

This was the face that Vandana had learned to forget, wilfully and completely, so that her life could move on. Was her memory playing a trick? How was it that the face returned to her with a clarity that made her cringe? As though she could feel his breath close to her face, feel the crook of his arm brushing gently against her moving hands, and hear the soft crunch of their shoes pressing over the grass.

≋≋≋

It was the mid-seventies, and she stayed in the campus of Banaras Hindu University where her father was a Professor. They had been allotted a big, sprawling bungalow with green jaffri work done on the verandah. It was a circular verandah that went all around the main building, except for the part where it met an open corridor leading to an outhouse. The outhouse consisted of a large room that was used for storing firewood, cow-dung cakes and huge earthen stoves, for it was still customary then to use stoves for heating water in winter. As the water boiled in large, blackened aluminium utensils, the servant boy hummed a love song from a Hindi film. Later, he carried the handi to the bathroom, placing it carefully on the red floor. The Professor's bungalow lacked fencing, as though the greenery was all part of a continuous stretch. Trees grew everywhere, as did the plants and weeds, sprawling over trellises and climbing bamboo rafters in a spilling-over of nature's bounty.

It was one such green rafter over a tiny portico that David had to negotiate before he could enter Vandana's house and, as he sauntered along, he always hit his head against its low edge. "Phew!" he grinned carelessly, "does this darn thing have any role to play except act as a barrier?"

"Be careful, David," Vandana said anxiously. She was a medical student, studying in the University Medical College. She had met David through her friend Abha. He was a research student from England on an exchange programme in the Department of Indology. She found his work obscure and abstract. "How are you ever going to use it for anything pragmatic?" she often asked him. He was studying Bengali and Sanskrit from her father, and that brought him over to their house everyday.

"It all depends on what you mean by pragmatic?" said David. "What's this with you women, constant talk about pragmatics! Abha too insists that her role as social worker keeps her in touch with the practicalities of life. Ladies, ladies! Have you not learnt the art of relaxation?"

Their conversation was always in snatches, in stray moments that they could find together. But there was a strange continuity, as though they were reaching out through the very distance that separated them. David found himself walking the narrow by-lanes of Varanasi, trying to absorb details that he could then relate back to her. He paused in front of shops, staring at the saris kept in neat folds behind glass cases, or the twists and turns in the salwar kameez and the kurtas displayed on the walls. They did not quite remind him of Vandana, for she had a more or less Western upbringing that was increasingly common in the cities. On special occasions she wore a sari or the usual salwar kameez.

But her body language was intriguingly different: the way she bent her head or tilted it to laugh, the way her arms crossed on her lap or the way she held herself at a little distance from him. It was the unfamiliar that drew him to her, but she was never available for him to view in isolation. She carried the vast ambiguity of an alien culture in every part of her being. Sometimes it frustrated David enormously that there was not a moment of privacy in their relationship. She was never alone in the true sense of the term.

Vandana, in turn, was not quite serious about David. He was much too casual for that (you are lazy and laidback, she said to him with cutting intensity). He was like a character she had read about, say in a Somerset Maugham novel. He was becoming conversant in Bengali, and when he drawled out a phrase here and there in his thick accent, she went into gales of laughter. "Stop it, David, stop it. You are murdering my beautiful mother tongue!"

"And to think you accuse me with such ease in my mother tongue!" He loved the way she spoke English, with a kind of startling fluency in a sweet, perfect accent that made the language sound so different. It was only when she was worried or thinking about the future that she stuttered a bit and groped around for the right words. He wanted to speak at length then, to hold her hand in assurance, but where in this vast campus could they be together without drawing attention?

~~~

David's hostel room overlooked the extreme fringe of the University campus. The presence of the river was always felt, even when it was not visible to the eye. The evenings brought in a cool breeze that carried the moisture of the river. It was there, cutting across the city, slow and meandering, carrying down in its thick, muddy depths the heritage of India.

It was David who brought into their relationship his knowledge of the river. Ganga, he said in a singsong way in the local dialect. He always rolled the name on his tongue as though he was referring to some mystical woman. There was a sensuousness about this man and the way he negotiated her culture that troubled Vandana.

They were returning home in the evening, strolling along casually, the way that Vandana was compelled to do in the company of David. She preferred to walk briskly, as she always did when she was alone. "You are forever loitering," she said. "Loitering?" he laughed, a quick innocent laughter that made Vandana nervous. "It is loitering that carries the art of possibilities . . ."

He had this strange habit of reaching out and plucking the leaves from the overhanging branches in a short skip-and-jump movement that startled Vandana. He was writing a major research paper on the mythical source of the Ganges, and he spent most evenings clattering away on the small white Remington typewriter that he had brought with him from England. But Saturdays he spared for Vandana, for he knew she would be returning from the hospital in the evening. This compulsion was not what he had planned, least of all on the day that he first saw her at the Professor's bungalow. There was something compelling about her small, compact frame, a litheness that was mysterious. Her hair fell wavily just below her shoulders and she tied it in a plait. But it was the intelligent play of expressions on her face that kept David riveted. She was reserved with him, but he noticed the jollity with which she interacted with her own family. He felt a strange urgency to cut across her quietness and reach out to the inner part of her being. It became as important for him to do that as to crack the mystery of India that stared him in his face at every corner.

What had brought him here to these unknown shores? It was a question that Vandana put before him whenever she got a chance. He tried answering her playfully. It made her curiously disgruntled, as though he had made such a momentous decision based on a non-reason. She felt in a vague, undefined way that he was not respecting her culture enough. Somewhat like his ancestors, who had landed by mistake at Calicut yet stayed on to rule for the next two hundred years. You can't change the course of history so casually, she thought to herself.

The history of the Ganga fascinated David. "It is a slice fallen from heaven," he told her. It was the curiosity of his narratives that drew her to him. They were borrowed from the tomes of literature that he was reading, or from the explanations that her father was providing him. But his rendering of it had a touch of the mystical, as though he was assimilating knowledge at a subliminal level, neither emotional nor rational. When he spoke about his work there was nothing non-serious about David. His eyes acquired a strange, hooded quality, like a chameleon in the grass.

He loitered then more than usual, not at all willing to let

go of the evening, or to return to his room in the foreign student hostel. Vandana often coaxed her mother to let David
stay on for dinner. He ate the fish cooked in thick coconut
gravy with a fork and spoon. He had learnt to eat dal and
chapatti, and the steaming hot rice that accompanied the
main course. At meal times the Professor entered into a long
discourse on the river. Later, they sat out in the verandah
and drank tall glasses of shikanji, green with the bittersweet
taste of unripe mangoes. David watched Vandana intently
over the rim of the steel tumbler. Her face was shy and alert,
as though she was following the course of the conversation
with an unstated excitement. Her father in contrast was
relaxed and expansive. David was his favourite student. Her
mother remained in the background, a little too shy to enter
into any conversation with a foreigner in her broken English.

There was an intrinsic sense in which David remained
outside the inner circle of her family. Yet he lolled around
with a kind of easy familiarity that made Vandana tense and
jumpy.

And then one day the realization dawned on her that she
was falling in love with David. It came to her as surely as she
knew that in a few months from now she would finish her
internship and acquire her medical degree. She felt the bittersweet taste of happiness like the breaking of some
unknown barrier. She knew she had to let her future flow in
whichever direction, like the river.

She confided in Abha. "It's just a piece of indulgence
that you have to get rid off, the sooner the better," Abha
advised her in all seriousness. "There is no future in this
relationship."

Vandana felt the tears stinging her eyes. Though she was
concentrating on her approaching exams, a tight, painful

feeling never quite left her. "Please Abha, say something more encouraging," she pleaded. But Abha was relentless. She shook her head firmly. "I hope you have not given him any indication of your feelings. Remember he is just a tourist. A vague curiosity about our culture brings him here. He sees, he writes about it, and then he returns. How do you fit in?"

"No, Abha you are wrong," Vandana said. "He is serious about us. I think something larger than mere curiosity brings him here."

"I know, I know, academic interest!" Abha retorted. "I tell you, avoid these academics like the plague. They make love to words, and for them people matter very little. I am scared for you Vandana. I don't want you to be hurt."

"I am hurting anyway. Besides, I believe in destiny. Why else should I feel like this for David?"

The coming Sunday David had organised a boat ride on the Ganges. The two girls were invited. They were to leave a little before sunrise, catching the river in its early morning splendour. "The time for contemplation," David said. "They say the Ganga brings you back to her bosom – to die. Holy release which is also an allurement."

When the three of them were together, David always addressed himself to Abha. Abha nodded absent-mindedly. She found much of his talk boring. Abha with her matter-of-fact ways, her tiny crop of hair tied in a careless ponytail, and the round specs perched on her nose. She carried herself with an air of business, like a squirrel frisking from branch to branch. It was not surprising that after doing an under-graduate course in history, she had switched to a postgradu-ate in social work. As part of her fieldwork she was living in close proximity to an ashram. Much of David's research was tied up with her, and one of his papers was to be written in collaboration with her. She acted as a mediator between the two lovers, a rôle she often found wearisome.

They had hired a boat, and after much haggling they had settled on a reasonable sum to take them from the Asi to the Adi Keshava Ghat, covering practically the entire stretch from the southern to the northern part of the city. They had the boat to themselves and this exclusiveness came at a price. David carried his notepad, scribbling down furiously little details that caught his attention. The boatman watched him with suppressed amusement. In this city of pilgrimage he was used to the odd man out, the "white skin" with a "mad desire". When Vandana translated the word for him David laughed merrily. The dark-skinned boatman pulled at his oar, his wiry muscles rippling in the cool breeze, his eyes beadily ancient, his mouth stretched in a leering grin.

The morning light was breaking through, first softly, in dark and light shades. Then a sharp crimson transformed the horizon and the ghats with their majestic steps caught the glow, revealing the first break of life. But by then the boat had moved away from the shore, leaving the bustle of the morning behind. The river stretched endlessly, its water lapping peacefully in green furrows. David bent sideways and scooped up the cold water in the palm of his hand. As it slid through his fingers he felt the infinite ache of yearning.

He opened the pages of his notepad and began to read what he had gleaned from listening to Vandana's father, "Listen to what the sacred lore says about the Ganges. I have put it in my own words. *The Ganges is the river of heaven . . . it flows on earth only after Lord Brahma agreed to the plea of King Bhagiratha. 'Oh, Great One,' said Bhagiratha. 'Grant me this single boon! An angry ascetic has burnt my ancestors, sixty thousand of them, to ashes. Our entry to heaven is forever barred.*

*Only the holy waters of the Ganges can wash away the curse.'
Brahma relented, for Bhagiratha was a pious king. He instructed
the Lord Shiva to catch the Ganges in his hair even as it hurtled
on earth with torrential force. So the Ganges flowed to the
Himalayas caught in the tangled locks of Shiva; and, once tamed,
flowed down to the plains. There at Ganga Sagar she entered the
sea, plunging back into the netherworld, thus restoring the ancestors of Bhagiratha. She is the triple-pathed river, flowing in three
worlds: heaven, earth and the netherworld."*

David was watching Vandana. Her eyes were slightly
averted, as though his words were piercing her skin, making
it crawl in shame. They were sitting close to each other on the
wooden benches placed symmetrically across the two sides of
the boat. Underneath them the wood was warm and rotting,
yellowing with age and slime, and yet the strong undercurrent
of the river kept the beams afloat, making a creaking, rhythmic noise that merged with the slow lapping of the oars. The
planks were held together with invisible iron screws, the cut
edges rough-hewn and wet from the water seeping through.
The river was beneath their feet, holding them in an embrace
that made them acutely conscious of each other.

Abha felt self-conscious too, but for a different reason.
She was concerned for both of them. Vandana was her childhood buddy and a dear family friend, and David had first
come to India through her family ties. Abha's father had
taught Comparative Religion at the University of London.
He had met David then, a research student working on
aspects of Hindu faith in relation to the ancient city of
Banaras. A friendship was struck and, when David expressed
a desire to visit India, a tie-up was fixed with the help of his
friend, Professor Dasgupta of Banaras Hindu University. Yet
what had started off as a happy sequence of events ended in

tragedy. The very month that David set off for India, Abha's father suffered his first heart attack, in an alien country. He was brought home to Varanasi where, eventually, he succumbed to a third attack. Abha's widowed mother shifted out to stay with her son in another city. Abha remained behind with her friends and work to take care of her.

Now, two of her best friends were in trouble. She felt concerned. She had not bargained for this to happen. Vandana was much too level-headed, a student of science, not taken in by the kind of abstractions that David dealt with. And David, surely he was much too casual and lazy for something as intense as love? She felt puzzled and mildly irritated.

"Ahem!" she began clearing her throat. "Well, Vandana, don't get drawn in by all this mythical claptrap! Ganges might be a vital part of our civilization but she is not beyond history." She sent the packet of roasted peanuts around, tossing a few into her own mouth.

David loved arguments of this kind. He relaxed and turning to Abha he said, "The City of Kashi is even more ancient than the Ganges. They say the city was there long before Bhagiratha brought the Ganga on earth. Hold your breath, what you are witnessing now is the silent footfall of time emerging from a source that is timeless. This is the Ganga in her brief sojourn through earth!"

"Nonsense," Abha cried. "Kashi or Varanasi, call her what you will, is steeped in history. This preoccupation with myth is eyewash. A purely Western construct meant to undo several pages of our history."

David turned to Vandana. "Like a loved one, Varanasi has many names. You roll them on your tongue and they spell magic. Kashi or Kasha, the ancient king; or Kasha, the tall, silver grass growing on the riverbank, whispering lovesick lore to the wind; or Kashi, the City of light, its roots in Kashika the luminous one, like the light of enlightenment." Vandana listened transfixed. He continued. "There are others, even more intriguing. Varanasi, the confluence of the river Varana and Asi. The Pali version of this name was Banarasi, from which came the corrupted form Benaras, the name that was prevalent in both Muslim and British India. But after independent India dear old Varanasi became official."

"Stop, stop," said Abha. "See how history creeps into your account! Can we underplay the role of the British? How intrinsically it is tied up with the story of our civilization."

Vandana was suddenly tense. Why was Abha doing this to them? As for her, she wanted David to go on endlessly, just as she wanted the boat never to stop. When her father would discuss all this with David, she had not listened to the words with any degree of attention. But now in the quietness of the morning as they floated over the silver sheen of water, the words poured into her ears like melody.

"David is right," she said. "History has corrupted the Ganga."

"I like that," Abha retorted angrily. The sway of the boat had made her doze off in snatches earlier, but now she was wide awake, bristling with indignation. These two had ganged up against her. "History is the corrupting force, ha! I like that. History alone speaks the truth. Can we separate the Ganga from the people who have lived for centuries on her bank? Is their story any different? For over five hundred years the entire Ganges valley was under Muslim domination. The city was sacked by Muhammad Ghori in the 1300s. It was in the late eighteenth century that Banaras came under British administration. This city contains the history of the Marathas too and Shivaji's resistance to the Mughal power."

"The silent footfall of time . . ." David intoned teasingly. He liked Abha when she became intense. Her hair would bristle and stand on end and her eyes, otherwise laconic, would sharpen and focus into tiny pinpoints of light. To David, Abha was more like her Western counterpart – her attractiveness was overt, not hidden in mysterious folds like Vandana's. He found Vandana intriguing, and his love for her kept spiralling its way through a vast, bottomless space, filling him with a sense of bewilderment.

He was conscious of her now, a presence to be reckoned with, an urbanity and sophistication that belonged to the here and now, not shifting and evanescent like the flow of the Ganga. The contours of her body were firmly etched, and though the early morning light created shades that fell across her face in a delicate pattern, there was something acutely intelligent and knowing about it. He wanted to run his fingers through the thick black strands of hair, down the skin at the nape of her neck to the point where her body fleshed out. A dupatta, 'yards of modesty' as he called it, covered her bosom, and yet the narrowing waist and the folds of the fabric falling like cascading water made him shiver with an undefined thrill.

"Don't get taken in by all this rhetoric," Abha was saying emphatically, "he is enticing you into a collusion—" She stopped, not quite sure what she was going to say next.

"Please David, continue. What other names?" Vandana said, ignoring Abha. She had to succumb, the strong under-current of the water was drawing her into its vortex.

"Such names . . . When you roll them in your mouth they emerge crystal clear. Avimukta, the Never Forsaken Land – by Shiva; Anandavana, the Forest of Bliss, where the lingas of Shiva sprout in sheer bliss in springtime; and, of course, Rudravasa, the permanent Abode of Shiva." David began to quote softly, in that quaint foreign accent of his, "This is the *Kashi Khanda*: 'Whatever touches Kashi, the thing becomes her, just as a stream of wine poured into the River Ganges becomes like the Ganges. Just as iron touching the philosopher's stone becomes gold, so does one obtain the very form of Brahman, which is the form of Shiva in Kashi . . .'"

~~~

They were approaching the Dashashvamedha Ghat, the mid-point in their journey. The boat was coasting towards the bank. Suddenly the silence was sucked into a continuous drone of noises, so persistent, so immediate that the three moved out of their reverie. The boat would anchor here for a while, allowing the occupants to disembark.

Of all the ghats that made up the majestic riverfront, none was busier and more commercial than the Dashashvamedha Ghat. It was considered the most sacred as well. The road that approached it from the city side wound its way through the most vibrant market of Varanasi. It was here that the city dwellers stopped to buy their share of offerings to the gods – flowers, incense and sweets. The shops displayed their lamps made of brass; idols and clay animal figurines, painted over in garish hues of red, orange and inky blue. Nestling close by were tiny stalls selling a wide variety of snacks, delicious ware ranging from sweets made of thickened milk and covered with delicate silvery paper to the freshly fried kachoris, puris served with fragrant potato curry and spicy mint chutney. And, of course, the green pan leaves filled with betel nuts and a rich array of condiments, so intoxicating that they say the extravagance of Banarasi life style is contained in them. One who partakes of this pan, and allows its red stain to smear their lips, will return to these lanes or 'gallis' to be intoxicated again and again!

This was part of old Varanasi, where the streets were narrow and labyrinthine, where ageing houses seemed to lean over like a canopy that replaced the sky. There was little sense of space. And yet men, women, bicycles, hand-pulled and motorised rickshaws, horse-drawn tongas, the sacred cows and buffaloes treaded their way with a sort of dexterity that never ceased to stun David. Despite the ceaseless flow of traffic, there was a sense of peaceful co-existence and sharing. It seemed to permeate the street corners, giving it an air of grace. The only way to negotiate these streets was to walk, and David did precisely this. He felt an urgent need to absorb an alien culture, both as part of his research practice and a simple way to survive. He was getting used to the relentless summers, the heat burning his skin to an even tan.

They walked up the stairs that rose from the edge of the ghats, rows and rows of them like a symphony pointing skywards, the notes reaching a crescendo. The water of the Ganges was dwarfed by the sight of these stairs, symmetrical, poised, sacred and timeless. The stairs led up to the foot of the temples, the myriad places of worship that seemed to fill the air with the chant of hysteria. This was unabashed surrender to divinity, a power so frightening, so overwhelming that Vandana felt faint. Almost unwittingly she clutched David's hand. He held it firmly, his large palms squeezing her fingers tightly, propelling her through the mass of devotees. Nothing seemed out of place, even for Abha, who quickened her pace and led the two into a small eating place.

There they were served breakfast in clean stainless steel plates and bowls. They drank the thick lassi with the white liquid curd frothing at the brim. It felt cool and nourishing.

The place was crowded, but they were given a tiny corner that was curtained off by a light grass-matted screen, a fine filigree pattern that kept out the noise as well. In one corner a table fan whirred and cackled, spilling out gusts of hot air. It felt claustrophobic after the wide expanse of the river. Vandana was silent, sick inside her soul.

She had never liked coming to the ghats. The noise, the throng of devotees, the priests sitting on their low wooden chaukis under bamboo umbrellas, instantly ready to minister to the needs of the pilgrims, the masseurs working on the well-oiled half-naked bodies, and the barbers snipping away the remnants of hair – these sights pressed upon her consciousness with a kind of oppressive urgency. This was not a part of India that she wanted to show David, and yet he revelled in it. She wondered why, and somehow this made her uncomfortable, just as she found the intimacy of his presence inside her home mildly embarrassing. He always seemed relaxed and to be enjoying the company of her parents, but she wondered what he really thought of them. This was not the real India, she told herself, this mass of unthinking, regressive, collective life form. She found the stench, the dirt unbearable and something deep inside her recoiled.

They were back on the river, drifting along at a slower pace. The boatman had had his fill of food, and with the sun overhead his oars moved lethargically. His skin gleamed with sweat, and his hands, callused from years of holding the oar, moved to a rhythmic pattern. Other boats crossed their paths, some teeming with tourists, others carrying cargo from one ghat to the other. At last Abha spoke. "The Ganges is inordinately dirty. Think of all the half-burnt dead bodies that float in the waters. The government should do something about it."

"I agree," Vandana joined in. "All this talk about Ganga's purity is hogwash. The entire filth and litter of this city is thrown into the river with impunity. I find all this quite disgusting."

"That was the first thought I had after coming to Varanasi," said David, "and I put the question to the Professor. I found his reply fascinating. Your Vedas have an answer to that as well. To all sceptics they say the river is pure and cleansing in a symbolic sense. Thus the etymology of the word Ganga is from the root word *gam*, which is 'to go'. The Ganges is the 'Swift Goer', always moving, displaying the energy of life itself. There is nothing stagnant about the Ganges, therefore she can never pollute."

"Convenient explanation," said Abha raising her eyebrows. "Purity as a cultural construct. Therefore the inverse of all that is impure and dirty."

'Exactly!" David said. "As an agent of purification the Ganga absorbs pollution and carries it away. A single drop of her water is sufficient to wash away many lifetimes of sin!" He scooped up the water in his hands and sprayed it playfully on Vandana. He opened his notepad and began scribbling furiously. When he had finished he handed Vandana the pad. She read, "*Here is the powerful eulogy to the river Ganges, the Ganga Lahari, 'The Waves of the Ganga'. Its author Jagannatha, the poet in the court of the Mughal King Shah Jahan. The poet expelled from court for his love affair with a Muslim woman. Finds shelter in Banaras. Calls upon the Ganga to restore his purity as a Brahmin. Sits on the stairs of the Panchganga Ghat with his beloved and sings the fifty-two verses of his hymn. At the completion of each verse, the river rises one step until it touches the feet of the lovers. Thus they are purified and finally carried away by the river.*"

Vandana felt her skin crawl. The boat had reached the
end of its journey. It was time to change course and return
home. From where she sat, home seemed far away. They
were here together, her English lover and herself, locked in
midstream, unmindful of the future and the past. This boat
ride was to remain in her consciousness for many years, long
after David returned to England and, whenever she thought
of it, she saw herself floating anchorless through the gigan-
tic stream. The river was there, everywhere, ready to
embrace her – the mother, the benefactor, ready to forgive
her love for this stranger.

And now, twenty years later, in another city, the words of
the *Ganga Lahari* floated back to her. She remembered
David's rendering of the verse, passionate, intense, carrying
across the waves, touching her body with the searing pain of
a reckless, unfathomed desire.

> *I come to you as a child to his mother*
> *I come as an orphan to you, moist with love*
> *I come without refuge to you, giver of sacred rest*
> *I come a fallen man to you, uplifter of all*
> *I come undone by disease to you, the perfect physician*
> *I come, my heart dry with thirst, to you,*
> *   ocean of sweet wine*
> *Do with me whatever you will.*

CHAPTER THREE

The Awakening

Sameer was home for the summer rather unexpectedly, or so his family thought. What had brought him home was a letter from his cousin Uma. She wrote jovial, newsy letters that made him happy in his own way, brightening up the weekends in a hostel, far away from home. But this one was particularly tense. "I need your help," it read. "I do not know whom else to turn to."

Sameer was at that time doing his senior residency from one of India's premier medical institutes in Delhi, and it gave him little time off for vacations. His duties were round the clock and rigorous. Besides, Sameer was aware of the fact that he had chosen a demanding career option, though it had seemed easy enough to slip into the family line. His grandfather had been one of Varanasi's leading doctors, whose private practice was well known throughout the old part of the city. Revered amongst his own community, Dr. K. G. Sengupta was remembered many years later as the "doctor with an amazing instinct". It was said that he could diagnose an ailment by simply touching the patient's pulse.

Of his two sons, it was the elder, Sameer's father, who chose to be a doctor and was later sent to England to do his FRCS. When he returned, the family clinic had grown to a sizeable proportion and did require an additional hand.

Father and son carried on with the family business with immense success. At the time Sameer's mother entered the household as a young bride, there was harmony all around, though the first seeds of dissension had already been sown.

Sameer remembered his grandfather as a man of few words. But when Sameer decided to enter the profession, he recalled the immense joy with which the news was greeted by the old man. Grandpa was then in the evening of his life, retired into his shell, his eyesight failing, his memory weakening. And yet he made it a point to visit the clinic everyday, as he had done even on the night the news of Bela's death reached him.

Whenever Sameer recounted that day to Vandana he felt the same sense of shock, as though he was reliving the incident all over again. He had no memory of Belapishi. In fact, the womenfolk of the family rarely spoke about her. Belapishi was his father's first cousin, Grandpa's sister's daughter. What made her distant was the fact that she was considered taboo, though Sameer knew that she had spent a few months of her life in their house. It was a matter that was never discussed. All that Sameer heard was that the decision to take her into the household was entirely Grandpa's. It met with murmurs of disapproval, especially from Grandma. She never spoke to the girl directly, and all references to her had to be oblique.

One day, Sameer's aunt, the irrepressible Chotoma, his father's brother's wife, had shown him a photograph of Belapishi. It was all done in a hush-hush manner after the curtains in her room had been drawn, and Chotoma had made sure that Grandma was in her prayer room, and was not likely to come out in a hurry.

Sameer looked at the picture with a tight constriction in his heart. He had heard accounts of Belapishi's beauty, usu-

ally said with a degree of envy, but nothing had quite prepared him for what he was about to see. It was an old, black
and white sepia print, taken in a studio against the quaint
background of a Victorian chair with velvet cushions, and
thick curtains at the back, but Belapishi seemed to fill the
picture frame with a strange, luminous radiance. She was
very young then, possibly in her late teens, but the first flush
of womanhood was apparent in the curves of her body. She
looked demure, and yet one sensed an all-consuming passion
in her that was both dangerous and alluring.

Sameer knew that she had disgraced the family by marrying a man old enough to be her father. When Belapishi's
mother had cried and begged her to reconsider, the girl had
turned a deaf ear to her pleas. "I can do nothing to change my
destiny," she had said stubbornly. A year later more shocking
news was to follow. Bela had precious little to do with her
husband, the old man; she was actually living under the same
roof with her stepson, a married man with two children of
his own. When her lover's lawfully-wedded wife had turned
up at Bela's home and pleaded with her parents to get their
daughter to return her rights, Bela's mother felt the world
was ending for her. Sameer recalled how she spoke about the
day with a shudder, tears of utmost grief coursing down her
leathery cheeks. "That day, my daughter died for me. I am
grateful to my brother for taking her into his home, but for
me she was dead."

A few years later Bela returned home, apparently deprived
of hearth and husband. The nature of the circumstances was
never made public. She turned up at her parent's doorstep,
only to be driven out without so much as a chance to plead her
case. Not that she seemed repentant; only a sullen silence permeated her being, as though she found life's burden too big to

bear. Grandpa had always loved his niece, a little recklessly Grandma thought. She reminded him of the daughter who had been born to them but had died in her infancy. He brought Bela home, and thus began her sojourn in a house that was to give her refuge for a few vital months of her life.

"It was a period in our lives that is best forgotten," Sameer's mother often said with a sigh. "She was trouble, this girl, right from the start. She kept your Grandpa tied around her little finger. He neglected both your father and your Kaku. Your Chotoma and myself, we suffered a great deal on that account. Who likes to see their husbands neglected because of a chit of a girl? But do you think Bela cared? No way. In fact, she was always wrapped up in her own self. There was something otherworldly about the girl, as though her mind was elsewhere, as though she never quite cared for what people were telling her. You see that corner room? She kept herself indoors and only sometimes emerged to take her bath or sometimes her meals."

That room, for many years to come, carried an aura of mystery for Sameer, as though its walls were witness to a passion that was never uttered or revealed. Then the truth started spilling out like a ghastly wound. Bela was carrying in her womb a child who was born eight months later. The birth was kept a secret, confined to an inner chamber that was transformed into a delivery room, where a midwife was ushered in to bring the hapless baby girl into the world. The child was miraculously healthy, and cried lustily into the dead of night.

Two months later Bela did something unexpected again. "It was all planned," Sameer's mother said in disgust, "but who was to tell your Grandpa that? He believed that it was good fortune that brought a message from Bela's in-laws.

Her husband was dying and wanted her at his bedside. She went back to her lover and never returned. The child remained with us; not even a name had been found for her. Grandpa picked her up and gave her to your Chotoma. After all, she was childless then, and what sin had the child done anyway?"

A year later Chotoma was to give birth to her son Vikram, but Uma remained hers in an inevitable way. Uma. That was the name given to Bela's daughter by Chotoma, and she became part of the family. Uma was an amazing girl. She was so plain that she threatened no one. She was born with a fund of laughter, so much so that nobody quite noticed when she cried. She was as unlike her mother as it was possible to be, and this made her Grandma's favourite. She also caught from Chotoma, almost like an infectious disease, a certain resilience to life's ups and downs. She lived through illnesses, the usual rounds of measles and chicken pox, without bothering anyone; nobody noticed when she stepped into adolescence, when her schooling was over and she was ready to enter college.

But the year she turned twenty brought a crisis in her life. That was the reason why she dashed off the frantic letter to Sameer.

"I think all of you underestimated Uma," Vandana often told Sameer.

"Yes, I think we did," Sameer replied a little sadly. "It is amazing how much a woman can be neglected in a traditional Indian set-up. We took Uma's loveliness of spirit for granted. She was such a plain Jane, we could so easily afford to ignore her."

"Plain? I find it amazing that all of you thought so. I found her so attractive, quite exotic, like a rare variety of orchid. None of you noticed that far-away look in her eyes, and that fund of indifference. That is why all of you were so shocked when she left home."

"At least Grandma was," Sameer said. "She took it almost as a betrayal. 'Her mother's genes run in her veins,' she said. Chotoma was inconsolable. I think she felt the parting of ways the most. She had always been closer to Uma than she was to Vikram."

"I think Grandma was right," Vandana added. "Uma was much closer to Belapishi than people realised. Did you realise it that summer after you came home?"

Sameer was unusually quiet, as though he was reluctant to talk about it. He simply said, "I met you that summer, that is all that really matters, isn't it, Vandana?"

≋≋≋

Uma had come to the station to receive Sameer. He noticed with a slight sense of shock that she had changed. He was seeing her after a gap of three years, and she had in the meantime grown from a child into a girl in the first springs of her youth. The laughter was still there in her eyes, but it was in a more muted form.

He tried to remember her face as he had known it, but it kept eluding him. She was wearing a salwar kameez instead of the usual skirt and blouse. Her face had become oval, and the eyes were narrower and the pupils grey. She had pushed back her hair and tied it in a heap near the nape of her neck. Her lips were fuller, and he could see that her smile was more fleeting. She hugged him generously, quick tears springing up in her eyes. "Dearest, Dadabhai, so wonderful to see you!" she exclaimed.

In the car he kept watching her, a little cautiously, as

though he was afraid of what she might have to say. Actually he had not given much thought to her letter. Uma was never one for having secrets. He had come home because he was homesick. He wanted a change from the killing routine of his curriculum. Besides, he had more or less decided that he would not join the family clinic. Varanasi had never been the city of his choice. He preferred Delhi, the capital of India; it offered him greater opportunities, particularly in the area of his specialization. He felt the time had come to talk such matters over with his parents.

Uma, too, was a little shy, as though what she was about to say was quite momentous. Besides the journey from the station to the house was too short to get beyond the initial inquiries about the rest of the family. Uma had lively accounts to give about everybody, especially Grandma. Grandma it seems was growing increasingly senile with old age. It was now over nine years since Grandpa had died, and soon after the initial period of grieving was over Grandma had become almost merry. Her face, puckered-up and wrinkled into a hundred folds, carried a constant smile. Her only indulgence was the hours she spent in the prayer room. "She rings that prayer bell all the time," Uma said with a grimace, "loud enough to wake the dead. I keep asking her whether her god is deaf!"

Sameer laughed. The sweet resonance of the bell was something he carried deep in his consciousness, like a slice of his childhood that he could summon any time, anywhere. It merged with other sounds: for instance, the ceaseless babble of pigeons on the rafter. Once, he had heard the same low gurgle on a hot afternoon in a friend's house in Delhi, and it had made him scramble out of the room into the empty streets. The sight of the vacant parking lot, the stretch of sky emptied of all colour, and the gusts of hot spiralling wind rising from the street curbs had filled his mind with a nameless terror.

As the car cruised into the lane in front of their rambling, three-storeyed house, which harboured three generations of the family, including Uma who belonged but only accidentally, Sameer felt a strange nostalgia sweep over him.

The family, near and dear ones, tumbled out to greet him. He asked them to pose for a photograph. It was a picture that remained captured in his mind's eye forever, fluid yet indelible, the frayed edges ever shifting, the outlines growing dimmer like the silent talkies of yesteryears. Uma was just behind him, picking up his luggage, something she had always done. She was therefore missing from the frame. Many years later he was to remember this with a shudder. She had vanished from the family fold; and that day, somehow, Sameer had a premonition of what was about to happen.

~~~

Though Grandma would never have acknowledged it to herself, it was she who was responsible for nurturing Uma's otherworldliness, and giving it the particular shape it acquired. She took the child under her wings and kept her as her own special treasure. Whether she did it to challenge Grandpa, who was indifferent to the child ever since Bela had left the house, was never quite known. But Uma spent a major part of her childhood days in the prayer room with Grandma, listening to the recital of the *Gita*. She had learned to lisp some of the sacred verses, though her attention was much more occupied by the cut slices of melons and papayas that were kept as offerings for the deities. At the end of the day she would be given some as reward. "The *Gita* says you must do your duty without expectation. Keep your heart pure from all material desires," Grandma would tell her solemnly, and Uma would listen with quaking heart.

Bela's absence hung over the house like a curse. It permeated every nook and corner like the silence that descended on Grandpa's lips. It was the nature of the silence that was so disconcerting. It seemed to grow with every passing year, and the seasons went by without making any difference to its intensity. Meanwhile, Uma grew into a lovely girl, enmeshed within the intricate folds of that all-consuming silence, and yet strangely unmindful of it. No one seemed to notice that she was Bela's flesh and blood, so that nobody quite pitied her motherless condition.

Besides, there was Chotoma to take care of her, a woman who was initially compelled to divide her attention between her infant son and this infant girl who was given to her as an added responsibility. In a sense Uma belonged to no one in particular, her easygoing temperament seemed to fit her anywhere. She had the amazing capacity to be happy without being possessed. And yet, after Uma left, Chotoma was disconsolate and so was Grandma.

It was late in the evening. Sameer was lounging in Grandpa's relaxing chair that had found a permanent place in one corner of the large verandah on the first floor. It was one of those mild evenings when the day's heat had evaporated, and a quick, moisture-laden breeze had sprung from the river and was floating aimlessly through the maze of the city. It made the trees that nestled close to the houses shimmer and tremble in tiny movements that spilled over as liquid green, melting in the half-light of a translucent sky. It was mystery time, and Sameer felt happy and sad in the same breath.

Uma was with him, leaning against the railing, strands of her unruly hair fluttering in the breeze. But her eyes were melancholy, and her mouth was strangely still, as though she was withholding a secret that mattered so long as she kept it. It was the extreme privacy of the moment that was to remain etched in Sameer's mind forever. He knew then, as he was to know many years later, that he had been granted the enormous responsibility of sharing somebody's secret. And the privilege of gaining that confidence was given to him at a price. Sameer was a patient listener, capable of empathy, perhaps one of the reasons why he had chosen to become a psychiatrist. But what Uma had to say, took him so much by surprise that, however hard he tried, Sameer could not practise the art of objectivity that belonged to him as a doctor.

Uma had decided beyond a shadow of a doubt that she wanted to leave home and enter an ashram as a devotee. She had met a girl named Abha who was spending time there as part of her research work. "I have found a direction in my life," Uma said. "I am ready to enter the ashram. Chotoma is trying to fix a match for me. But Dadabhai, I don't want to get married, not today, not ever. I am happy as I am."

Happy? Strange, how that single phrase hurt Sameer enormously. He looked at Uma. Why is it that the question of her happiness never quite crossed his mind and, now that she was talking about it so emphatically, that it seemed such a bewilderingly selfish decision? It was as though she was doing something deliberately for the first time in her life, and it hurt him personally.

"Do you know what you are about to do?" Sameer exploded. "What do you think would be the effect of all this on the family? It would kill us all!" He realised that he was exaggerating, being over-dramatic. Entering an ashram as a sevika was something many people did in Varanasi, often as a matter of choice.

"Don't say that," Uma began to weep. "I cannot hurt you or anyone else."

"Do you know what these ashrams are like?" he continued. "They are traps to capture your soul. They will take you in and wean you away from all your loved ones. They will teach you to forget your desires. They will take you away from us . . . just like Belapishi."

The errant breeze had stopped. The evening had descended quieter, the light almost fading. The streetlights were on, and the city had acquired an artificial glow. Sameer could hear Uma's sobs breaking against her chest. They had a peculiar animal-like quality about them, as though no amount of rational persuasion on his part could make her stop. There was pain, a seamless, amorphous pain that he could not distinguish as his or hers.

He was listening to her explanations but the reasons eluded him. "The realisation has come to me gradually. I have discovered something inside me that was not there. I will take you to the ashram, and you will see for yourself. There is so much peace all around."

He felt trapped, as if they were caught in a time warp, and he could not rescue her from her fate. He realised then that she belonged elsewhere: a long line of history tied her like an umbilical cord to a past that was not of her making.

Uma's face, with its austere plainness carried the same contours as Belapishi's detached beauty. That same sense of not belonging, of eyes ingrown with pain and longing for something not here, not now; of going through the mechanics of a daily routine like a creeper indifferent to the host tree that gives it sustenance; of someone utterly incapable of gratitude or of returning love. It was this feeling of absolute bereavement that consumed Grandpa and destroyed his soul.

"She was a selfish woman, your mother . . . utterly without morals . . . and she destroyed lives . . ." Even as Sameer spoke these words he was struck by their appalling untruth, and yet he could hardly stop himself. He felt as though he was looking into a crystal ball at a misshapen future, yet to take form; the links between past, present and future were unfurling themselves before his very eyes. Uma was Bela's progeny, and the midwife who had severed them could not do so without leaving behind traces of a primordial association.

Bela had died pitifully young, the news of her death reaching them a few months after the actual event. It arrived in the form of a telegram, terse, simply worded, almost indifferent. That was the year Sameer was getting ready to join his medical college in Delhi, and Uma had barely stepped into her eleventh year. Sameer's father had taken Grandpa to the clinic as usual; on the way back the old man had a stroke. When he died, Sameer was appearing for his final year exam, and could not come home for the funeral.

And now, almost ten years later, Sameer felt a sharp sense of loss that he could not isolate or define. It seemed to stretch endlessly across time, absorbing within its sweeping range the given and what was to be. And though Uma was only a small part of it, she became its living embodiment, and his heart reached out in empathy to her.

~~~

A meeting was fixed with Abha for the weekend. "You must meet her, Dadabhai," Uma said. "She will explain things to you. You will like her. She is unpretentious, not the university type. She has been such a big help to me."

"Well, I am meeting her for your sake," Sameer said sternly, "and I don't think I like people who go around influencing young girls to enter ashrams." But Uma looked happy, almost excited about the impending meeting. With the matter in Sameer's hands, she felt safe. "I am not going to take a single decision without your advice," she promised.

Strangely enough the first meeting between Sameer and Abha was quite a disaster. She arrived an hour late, keeping them waiting in front of the University Medical College. There had been an emergency: one of the young girls at the ashram had tried to commit suicide. Abha had been detained at the casualty, waiting for the girl to be shifted to a room in the ward. When she finally came down to meet them she looked tired and harassed. Sameer too was tense, and carried himself with an air of unfriendliness that was not his usual demeanour. Only Uma's face lit up at the sight of her friend and mentor.

"I am sorry to have kept you waiting," Abha said brusquely, "but what to do? A woman's life has so little worth, it can be weighed against cotton wool and found wanting."

"If that is your opinion," Sameer said bitterly, "why pretend to help others. Maybe they are better off left alone. Uma never thought like this before, I can see your influence working."

Abha was angry, really angry, and Sameer was to remember her speech with ironic amusement. Whenever he recalled her face it was the peculiar intensity of the eyes that struck him, and the thought that crossed his mind: "I love this face; it is so attractive." It was an amazing thought, laughably absurd to him, for he hated everything that she was saying. "I influence her? Well, Dr. Sameer, let me tell you something (it was the first time anyone had addressed him so). Young women are not receptacles, empty of substance, who can simply be influenced to take major decisions in their lives. If you care to listen to Uma you will discover a calling in her. Who am I to give directions to her life? In fact I am worried about her, very worried. Does she have the maturity to make such an important decision in her life?"

"That's just it . . ." Sameer began. "Stop," Abha said imperiously, thrusting her hand forward, making Sameer recoil in surprise. "Do not mistake her indecision for thoughtlessness. It is just that Uma needs time, and she needs to go through the experience, so that she can make up her mind for herself. I have asked her not to join the ashram instantly. Anyway they never take a novitiate without a preliminary process of initiation. The entire process takes anything between three to six months. What she can do until then is join me in my fieldwork. I am working with the widows of Varanasi, a tribe that you are totally ignorant of. You are a shrink, aren't you?" (This was a term that Sameer hated – it smacked of opinions picked up from reading pulp fiction.) "You should understand their plight."

Sameer was livid by then. How dare this girl presume so many things about him? And yet there was something compulsively attractive about her. He wanted to hear her through, to get his own opinion across to her and get her to change her mind. "I have been standing here and waiting for you for the last hour. Can't we sit down somewhere?" he said.

Abha gave a short, nervous laugh. "Oh, sorry," she said, and then turning to Uma she continued, "Sorry, sorry, Uma. My head is in such a whirl since morning. Let's sit down in the coffee-house. I am famished."

"So, Dr. Sameer," Abha said, more relaxed now, taking in this man, noticing his pleasant face for the first time. The successful son of a successful family, she thought ruefully to herself. "Have you come on behalf of your family? Are you Uma's ally or her guardian? Have you come to snatch her back into the family fold?"

She was being sarcastic, but there was an element of jollity in her tone that Sameer did not fail to notice. "I love Uma very much and I am concerned for her," he said with a simple seriousness that seemed to hang in the air for the rest of the evening. Abha felt chastened, her eyes muddled now with a faint touch of shame. She talked about the ashram at great length. Time sped by. Uma felt her life was being held in balance. They drank coffee and munched some snacks, but nothing seemed to mitigate the solemnity of the moment.

Abha was later to recount the incident in great detail to Vandana. "Despite myself, I liked the doc, you know," she said. "Why don't you fall in love with somebody like him, instead of your wretched David?"

"Stop it, Abha," Vandana retorted sternly. "Don't go around arranging people's lives. Leave that girl alone, it is too big a decision for you to be playing any rôle in it."

"I am not," Abha replied. "Something is compelling that girl. She is moving in a direction that is not of her own volition. I think Dr. Sameer senses that, there is a curious sadness in the man that I cannot place. It troubles me a lot, you know, Vandana. As though I am peering into a secret space in their lives."

"Well, don't meddle unnecessarily," Vandana added. "You have this habit."

~~~

Just before Sameer returned to Delhi, Vandana met him through Abha. She found him likable in a nondescript way. Besides, she was too preoccupied. David had asked her to meet him to discuss 'certain matters'. Vandana waited restlessly all the night. She felt her life was really at a turning point. Decisions so momentous had to be made. She thought of

David's philosophical ramblings with a touch of fear. "We need to explore the art of possibilities . . ." she heard him say.

~~~

They met. It was dark, a boundless stretch of whirling black. They moved through it unfalteringly, as though something in their bodies illuminated the narrow gravelled path they walked along. They held hands for the first time. The breeze buffeted them closer, bringing their bodies to a proximity that startled them. They spoke in a whisper. David had to go back to England. He would write every day. Would she reply? Promises hung like rich, exotic decor meant to keep the banality of life at bay. Without promises there was no scope for suffering, or the terminations that brought pain in their wake. They felt the need to bring a certain intensity to their relationship so that they would not waft apart casually like two strangers whose paths happened to cross. They had to commit themselves to understanding what parting without loss of hope entailed.

Were they afraid?

"No," said Vandana, "I believe you."

"I believe you, too," said David.

"We create our own possibilities, don't we?" Vandana asked, borrowing David's phrase. David was silent, a trifle afraid. But he laughed a fleeting, naïve laughter that almost broke Vandana's heart. He drew her close to his chest, and held her through the night.

CHAPTER FOUR

The Journey

Vandana paused briefly in front of the children's bedroom before entering it. She had always avoided using the computer to send letters. The computer belonged to Abhishek, the new generation. "I find emails too impersonal. There is something still intimate about writing a letter," she had said.

"Come on, mom, your letter writing may be an intimate art but the postal system that carries it is still impersonal! And if you add the element of inefficiency to it, it is a dead system!" Abhishek retorted.

"Well, can you convey your anguish and joy in a mail?" Vandana continued doggedly.

"Why not? After all anguish lies in the content not in the system!"

But today of all days Vandana wanted to send an email, for she wanted a system that would keep her anguish under abeyance. She had to get her message across with maximum efficiency and the least amount of pain. "Dearest David," she typed, and then, as she paused to delete the last three letters from the word "dearest", the pain came in waves, permeating her body, making her fingers tremble. She sat up astonished, as though the wildness of her feelings staggered her. She had not bargained for this, not after twenty years. Do not come back to India or my home, she wanted to write but the words sounded false.

"Dear David, Sameer and I would be very happy to have you over, if you come to Delhi." She allowed the chilling impersonality of the words to act as a balm. Perhaps it was better this way, a sort of tryst with destiny that would put every morsel of the past in place. As she pressed 'Send' and watched the arrow confirm the command that would carry her message through, she felt a strange sense of bitterness. No doubt she lived in a world infinitely different from the summers and winters spent at her parental home in Varanasi, but nothing seemed to mitigate the anxiety of waiting for a response from David. She felt humiliated, as though the years had slipped by without making any difference.

She stared at the computer, resenting its infallibility, and her inability to get back the message if she so desired. A sense of fatalism rose like bile in her throat, making her want to throw up.

Quickly she re-entered her own bedroom and sat down heavily on the armchair. I must take control of my life, she repeated to herself for the umpteenth time. Questions, so many of them, pressed against her head like a persistent ache that she could not get rid off. When had Sameer met David? Was it through Abha? Why had he never mentioned this to her? And why had he kept up his contact with David and for how long? Since when had they been in touch by email, and that, too, without giving her an inkling of what was happening? Was Avinash's arrival a part of a larger game plan? Did she understand her husband properly? Vandana felt something close to panic lurch at the pit of her stomach, a feeling that she had not experienced for many years now, at least not since she had finished her post-graduation and shifted to Delhi. It had not been an easy transition then, but she had made it with the kind of smooth finality with which brides in India make their move from their maternal homes.

≋≋≋

It was a year after her marriage, and relatives and friends commented on her luck at acquiring such an understanding husband. Sameer had continued to stay in his PG hostel room until his new wife joined him. By then he had fallen in love with her, and when she got off the train at the New Delhi station, he noticed the forlorn look in her eyes, and the stillness with which she stood in the midst of the milling crowd. She had removed the telltale signs of marriage from her forehead, and wore minimum ornaments. She was dressed simply in a sari, and inside the taxi he noticed a pair of tiny emerald earrings nestling on her earlobes and a thin gold chain hanging round her neck. It was a simplicity that remained with her for the many years that followed.

The elders in the family had arranged her marriage with Sameer, so that in many ways it had been steeped in conventions. But there was something reassuring about a man who was willing to listen to her side of the story. "Please, Abha," Vandana said to her friend, who was acting as go–between once again, "I need to explain everything to him. It is the only proper thing to do."

"Don't be sanctimonious," Abha replied. "There is nothing proper or improper about what you are doing. This is your choice, and I am not going to question it ever. One thing I know, you are going to be happy with the doctor."

≋≋≋

Happiness had indeed come easily for Vandana. She had spoken at length to Sameer about her relationship with David, and he had listened with the kind of forbearance that accompanies his profession. But he said very little, and if there was any sense of disappointment, then Vandana did not quite notice it. An unstated silence became a mutual arrangement that required little adjustment from her side.

Then a few years later a visit to Varanasi in order to complete the last rites for Grandma, brought Sameer and David face to face, and a friendship developed between the two men. The connecting factor was Uma, who was by then a full-time resident of the ashram. Sameer saw to it that Vandana was kept out of it all. It was a deal the two men made with each other. For Sameer it was part of the remedy he had worked out for himself.

And yet, why had David agreed to the arrangement, Vandana wondered, a dull anxiety replacing the feeling of resentment. What was bringing him back to India? Why was Avinash so important to David? Maybe he was coming back for her, simply for the sake of a renewal of contact. After all, so much had remained unsaid between them, like a bruise that was left untouched. The finality of parting – the time had come for a re-run of it – and surely with the years of maturity behind them, the process would be simple and matter of fact.

And David, had he changed? Was he still lean and angular with that lazy stoop, the brilliant green eyes that acquired shades of olive at moments when his face was averted from her; did he still amble as he walked or had age given him a different gait altogether? She stopped herself with some effort, allowing her mind to pause. She was afraid to cross the immeasurable gaps that lurked between the crevices of her consciousness; time and memory dawdled there, even as she hurried along, nimble-footed, skidding on thin ice. Then, slowly, bit-by-bit, she began to distil moments like dusting fine porcelain, precious and fragile and tender. She did something she had not done in many years. She leant her head against the bedpost and felt a rush of blood spread like a blush over her face. Dearest David . . .

≋≋≋

Grandma died in the month of July just after the rains came in. As Sameer got off the Kashi Vishwanath Express at the Varanasi Cantonment station, he felt the sleets of rain dampen his shoes and socks, making them squelch on the wet pavement. He was looking for a taxi, but the rain, falling in a thick unceasing downpour, had sent people scrambling for shelter. He waited just outside the platform in a covered area with corrugated tin awnings. The raindrops hit the metallic surface with a sound like that of truant boys playing a game of marbles.

He felt buoyant, even though he was returning to a house in mourning. The house seemed strange, its doors and windows wide open, and people moving in and out or sitting huddled in corners. The lounge and the adjoining drawing room, usually reserved for entertaining guests, had been transformed into an inner sanctum. White sheets were spread on the floor, giving the rooms an air of sanctity and, even from where Sameer stood, a swift permeating, gently evanescent smell of incense hung in the air. Flowers – not the usual marigold, hibiscus or jasmine that Grandma plucked from the front garden to give as offering to her gods, but bunches of white, demure rajanighanda – were arranged in clay pots and kept in the midst of the mourners. The flowers had a sweet, sultry scent that wrapped the morning in an unfathomed sense of life blossoming. It kept death in abeyance, and made everyone feel lighthearted. They spoke about the old lady, recounting her foibles with half-suppressed giggles. Grandma had died at the ripe old age of ninety. For her the transition from one world to another had already been made and, on the night before she died, as Sameer's mother told him, she sought in the midst of the living the faces of those who had died.

"Would you believe it," said Sameer's mother, "for the first time, she mentioned Bela in the same breath as she called out for your Grandpa! Spelt out her name clearly to your Chotoma, who was beside her till the very end. She even asked for Uma. 'Has the girl gone out to play with her friends,' she said! I think in her delirium Uma was still a child."

"Has Uma been informed?" Sameer inquired. He felt relaxed, now that he was away from the mourners in the bedroom upstairs. This room, with its heavy mahogany furniture and ochre upholstery, always gave him a sense of homecoming. He watched the rain falling in a slant against the windowpane. The torrid downpour of the early morning had settled to a gentle drizzle, giving the air a silvery haze. The thought of Uma made Sameer sad. He felt for the first time a heavy, brooding sense of loss that usually accompanies the death of a near one. But he was not thinking of Grandma. He simply remembered how closely Uma had belonged to Grandma. And now Grandma was dead, and a vital chapter of their family history had come to a close.

"When is the baby due?" his mother was asking him. She felt guilty about calling Sameer over at a time when Vandana was expecting, and needed him most. But Sameer looked happy, enjoying his mother's nitpicking worries as though she was dealing with children, not grown-ups. He realised with a slight sense of shock that he had not thought about Vandana at all, ever since he entered the house.

Memories of a different kind were flooding his consciousness. This was the room where he and Uma and Vikram used to play darkroom. They would exchange clothes, push the heavy furniture around to make everything seem unfamiliar, and then play hide and seek in the newly-created den. Uma was nimble-footed and clever, and she would crouch as stealthily as a cat, ferreting out the two brothers. He was the clumsy one, getting caught because he would fidget too much, making the corner of the chair slide at an awkward angle with a loud squeak. Vikram would giggle and the game would be up.

Sameer was looking into the past and the present simultaneously. The children were there everywhere, enticing him. Uma was sitting on the windowsill, doe-eyed, the jagged edges of her white teeth gleaming in the hazy, half-light of the room. The furniture threw huge shadows on the wall and ceiling. He moved forward as though he wanted to grab her, the awkward angularity of her thin body filling him with an unknown excitement. He loved her then as cousins often do with the intense, sensuous devotion of adolescence. She was full of mischief, dodging him behind the curtains, slipping in and out of sight. The rain fell steadily, monotonously, like the ceaseless pressure of pain that only memories can bring.

He stared at the familiar old chest of drawers, its edges slightly frayed but the polish still deep and dark. The photographs were ranged on top in time-worn frames. He could see each one of them, the familiar faces tinted and glossy, their vacant stare piercing the lens. Sameer thought of the unborn child stirring in Vandana's womb, and suddenly it occurred to him that the child too would find its pride of place next to these portraits. The family tree had branched out in different directions, the new nestling close to the old. And though the house was bustling with people Sameer could sense its emptiness, like a hollow bark peeling off at its skin. Suddenly the house seemed death-ridden, his memories bruised and hurting.

Vandana always insisted that Abhishek was a Varanasi child. It was after they had returned to Delhi from one of their annual trips to Varanasi that she had felt the first seeds of a new life inside her. Initially the news of his impending fatherhood had not made Sameer happy. The ghosts of Vandana's past had tormented him; the soft, droning passionate tone of her confessions had held them tentacle-like to the bed, the heat of the summer night wilting the mosquito net. Her eyes, tear-stained, were inviting, and he always wondered why he felt so little resentment. His face had the cold, stretched impersonality of understanding. Later her body was soft and yielding, but a tight knot of resistance grew like a canker in his soul. How strange that the union had resulted in their first-born!

But now, anticipating the birth, it seemed better this way. Once Vandana was reassured of Sameer's forgiveness she never mentioned David again. There was a curious doggedness in her nature with which she embraced her newfound happiness. The minor details of daily life seemed to fill her with joy, and soon Sameer discovered that the many nuances of routine kept her from falling apart. She was happy, he could sense that, and his own love for her, which had been tainted with anguish to begin with, had now settled into a comfortable habit.

That day sitting in the room in his old, ancestral home,

tied to the recollections of his childhood, Sameer felt happy and self-assured. It was as though he was connected to an invisible chain of existence, a family tree, the history of a house, a city. As his memories became intricate his soul began to expand, gathering in everything that lay outside its narrow confine. The rain, the moisture-laden air, the smell of death, the anticipation of birth, the thought of a young girl, the collective bereavement of her absence, a woman's passion, the silence of her betrayal, the myriad sounds, the feel, the touch, the movements – they filled his being with a yearning that was neither happiness nor grief, that neither belonged to him nor to the reality surrounding him. He was possessed by an elusive feeling that brought him a sense of deep peace.

Later he went downstairs to join in the funeral rites. It was the twelfth day of the ceremonials, and as the first-born in the third generation he had a definitive role to play. Vikram, who had strayed from the family fold to join the merchant navy, was unable to attend the funeral. When the news of Grandma's death had reached him, his ship had just coasted off the shores of Singapore. He sent a telegram conveying his regret. The burden of the family name was on Sameer, and he accepted its demands with an easy sense of compliance.

It was well past noon, and the large number of mourners had been spirited away to another part of the house where a huge feast had been organized. It was an essential part of the ceremonials, this feasting, a sort of farewell lunch meant to appease the soul of the departed. Sameer could hear the clanking of utensils, and the scraping of plates and spoons at a distance. Usually Grandma had been the presiding spirit of such occasions, but today her absence seemed incorporated into the many sounds that floated in the air. Sameer noticed his mother and Chotoma, gliding around in the background, bringing grace to the funeral rites.

In the room below, only the inner circle of the family sat around the priest, as he bellowed out the mantras in a loud and strident tone. He was the family priest, the one who graced many an occasion, and on seeing the boy his face broke into a wide smile. He beckoned to Sameer. "Come closer, my boy," he said, the spittle gathering in the corner of his pan-stained mouth, his teeth black from a lifetime of betel-nut chewing. It was a sight that used to make the children giggle. Sameer noticed his rotund, bare body gleaming with sweat, its nakedness of form combining the sensual and the ascetic. His eyes were shrewd and greedy, and his face was contorted with years of learning the mantras by rote. "You have to confer the gifts to the family deity in order to appease the departed soul," he spoke to the congregation. "Only then can she leave the confines of her putrefying body and swim across to the other world." The gifts were laden on the floor: stainless steel plates and utensils, mounds of rice, milk, fresh fruits, bedding, household cosmetics and yards of cloth. "I, the Mahabrahman, will transfer these material belongings to the departed soul in the netherworld. I can see the family in its generosity has given enough to appease the soul." Sameer smiled. Indeed there was enough to appease the priest, who would carry away the gifts as a token of his service. Death is big business in Varanasi, Sameer thought ruefully, a city that offers 'moksha' as final release from the cycle of rebirth!

The room felt confined. The flowers had begun to wilt, and the heavy incense had risen to the ceiling in a lurid haze, making it difficult to breathe. The verandah was strewn with discarded shoes and slippers, the muddy footprints leaving a trail on the white cloth. The rain had crept into the room, creating soggy puddles on the floor. Outside, the trees swayed in unison, and the wind and rain whistled against the windowpane, a soft pattering harmony like fingers pressing glass, making eddies of water spill out from the translucent surface.

The priest said, "This noble lady of noble lineage has earned a 'good' death. Her sons – pure of mind and body, now that the ganga jal has touched their lips, and the earthly priest [the barber] has tonsured their heads – have offered rice balls for the past eleven days, so that the 'ghost-body' can leave its material abode and merge with the bodies of its three immediate lineal forefathers. Thus the ghost becomes a benevolent and incorporated ancestor, a source of the future well-being of this family, its generations born and yet to be born, in eternal fecundity and prosperity." As he spoke, his voice rose and fell in a steady staccato note, its clear timbre ringing through the room like the sound of conch shells.

There was a large photograph of Grandma placed on a pedestal, with rose petals strewn at the base. It was a picture taken in her younger days when she was more solemn-eyed, and the formality of a photo session made her stiff and un-smiling, but she was looking straight at Sameer, and the dark pupils seemed to dance in the myriad reflected lights. Even from where he was sitting, Sameer could see the faces pressed against the window like friendly ghosts, beckoning him to come forward. He felt his entire being slip out from the confines of his body, as though death was a part and parcel of daily experience, as simple as breathing itself. He held his breath, allowing the feeling of constriction to press against his chest in a tight knot of pain that eased as he exhaled gently. He repeated the act once or twice like a yogic exercise, until his body floated free, a malleable and protean entity.

It was then that he saw her enter the house, disembarking from a waiting taxi. She was wearing a white, stiffly starched sari, its crispness defying the wetness of the atmosphere. She was carrying a black umbrella. As she folded it, she slipped out of a pair of black pumps. Even those were dry. He noticed with slight amazement that her face had mellowed, and that her body had acquired a strange sensuality, as though the flesh had ripened with the passing of years. She looked at him straight and smiled. As she took her position in the gathering and sat down, Sameer remembered the occasion when he had wanted to ask Abha to marry him, but had allowed the moment to go past without putting forward the proposition.

~~~

It was only after the last of the mourners had departed that the drawing room was rearranged to its original shape. The servants removed the white sheets, pulled in the sofas and center table and mopped the muddy puddles of rainwater from the floor. Only Abha remained behind, and after the family had gathered around her and made their customary inquiries Sameer had the opportunity to talk to her alone. It was dusk and the sky had cleared. They moved out of the house, walking along the pavement. The roadside had turned into little rivulets of rainwater, carrying wet leaves and scraps of paper and litter. The streetlights were dim and flickering as though their luminous quality had lost its original fervour. But the walkers' spirits were not dampened. A secret joy, like a tight knot of excitement, grew in their souls even as they spoke of mundane things.

"When is the baby due?" Abha asked, much like his mother had done earlier, but with a certain wry indifference, as though she was discussing politics. "Next month," he replied, happy for her dryness of tone. It was something that he had always liked about Abha, her non-sentimental inquiries about people.

"Is my friend happy, being married to you?" she asked again, a little jocularly, with just that slight tilt on the word friend that made him cringe. Though he did not turn his head he sensed that she was smiling, wistfully perhaps.

"I am happy," he answered crustily.

"I am asking about her, not you. It is not the same thing you know."

He moved ahead with long, angry strides, leaving her behind. She made no effort to catch up with him. He turned back, retracing his steps. She was laughing now. "You know something, you haven't changed at all. I thought the years would make a difference. They say when young boys leave their provincial homes and go to a big metropolis like Delhi, they change. But you are still gawky, you know, intrinsically timid. Afraid to speak out your mind. So proper. A bit of a bore, really." She was looking at him with eyes that pierced like gimlets through the rounded rims of her spectacles. The look was almost comic and suggested that her words were not meant to offend at all. He found himself relaxing in her presence. "I think Vandana is happy. Why not? She always wanted the stability of marriage."

He noticed that she had changed. The outline of her face was more flaccid, the eyes puffed up, and the skin a little wrinkled. But it was a robust face, a bit worldly-wise per-haps, with just that touch of candidness that he found so attractive. A gust of wind made the trees on the pavement shiver. A shower of raindrops slid off the branches and fell on her, drenching her hair. She folded her arms across her chest, bringing her shoulders closer. Her blouse had become damp and the starchness of her sari had gone. "I look a mess. I better go home," she said.

But they were reluctant to part. They walked on, as though a magic circle of intimacy girded them from the anonymity of the night. It was strange how Abha had always belonged to all of them, individually and collectively, without ever intruding into their privacy. No questions asked, no answers sought, she was just there for them. It surprised Sameer that he wanted her still, though he would do nothing in the world to get her.

"I think you must come and see Uma," she was telling him. "It is of the utmost importance."

"Why do you say so?" he asked urgently, drawing his attention away from her. A local bus rumbled past. They moved aside to avoid the splash of water. She was quick and agile, suddenly girlish, like a sparrow. Some of the water sprayed on his trousers, leaving behind turgid lines like tyre marks. He cursed loudly in the local dialect, startling her by the foreignness of the words.

"I hate the narrowness of the streets," he said. "Narrow streets, narrow minds. Like a labyrinth."

"I think Uma is dying," Abha said quietly.

"Let us go home," he said, suddenly afraid of the quiet-ness of her tone.

"I will find a taxi," she said, the lonely inflection of his voice rubbing against her skin. She began to walk away. He let her go; the dark, wet night stretching between them like a star-spangled sky lying wasted in the streets.

That night he saw the ghostly faces again. This time they invaded his room. Uma was sitting in the corner sobbing silently. She was wearing a white pinafore and white bloomers. She had hurt her little finger, and though there was very little blood she held it up for him to see. He blew on it, making her skin tingle. She was giggling now, in spurts of senseless mirth that made him sad.

He tiptoed downstairs to the lounge where the telephone was kept. He had not contacted Vandana since morning, though his mother must have spoken to her. She came on the line in a while, dragging her heavy body along. She was sleepy but sounded cheery enough.

"Not sleeping yet! Surrounded by family, eh?" she said in a good-natured way. She gave a little yelp. "The baby stirred inside me! You know something, Sameer? Just before the phone rang I had a little dream. It's going to be a boy!"

He smiled. "Take care, dear. Blow the baby a kiss." Outside, the rain began to fall again, one of those all-night affairs that would leave parts of the city flooded in the morning. In the burning ghats the funeral pyres would smoulder and fill the night air with the thick, putrefying odour of sandalwood and burning ashes. Even amongst the dead only the lucky few could get a clear night for the incarceration. Twelve days back when Grandma had died the sky was clear. The downpour began after her ashes had been gathered.

≋

"I got a letter today in the morning. It came by courier. It was from David, you know." Vandana uttered his name as naturally as she could. But it surprised her that she had begun talking on the matter, at the dining table, in front of the children.

"I see," Sameer answered in a nonplussed voice. "Has he come to Varanasi already?"

The children turned to look at their mother. She paused before she spoke, making her sentence hang midway. And then almost inexplicably she stretched out her hand to pass the salad to Mira. "You haven't touched the green vegetables, Mira," she muttered hurriedly. "It's not good for your eyesight." Her eyes met Avinash's. There was something intent and pleading about them.

"You have invited him to come to Varanasi. His letter says so. He wants to come to Delhi and meet us. He says . . ." she stopped, the words lost in a kind of infinite riddle that seemed to intrude into her consciousness, making her want to weep. She felt suddenly helpless, as though she was in the midst of a situation that was slowly getting out of hand.

"Who is David, mother?" Abhishek asked with the brutal clarity of youth. He noticed that his parents were showing signs of age. His father, who usually sat upright, had developed a slight stoop. His mother was not her usual self. Normally she ruled over table manners with a fastidiousness that annoyed him. But today she was eating sloppily, pushing the dishes around in random directions.

'He is an old friend of ours, son," Sameer spoke. "An Englishman whom your mother knew when she was in Medical College."

"An Englishman!" Mira cried in a hushed tone, suddenly excited. "Will he come and stay with us?"

"I don't know," Vandana answered. She was looking at Sameer, waiting for his reply. When he did not say anything, she lowered her face with a slight grimace. Abhishek watched the two with an unblinking gaze. There was something ridiculous in the way adults behaved. He could sense the tension, and yet the very fact that its source remained unknown, annoyed him immeasurably. "Is something bothering you, Ma?" he asked relentlessly. "No," she replied shortly, but there was a curious tremble in her voice that made him return to his plate silently. There was no point in flustering her anymore.

Avinash was staring at Vandana with a fixed, mesmerised look, his hand moving from mouth to plate, plate to mouth like a primitive ritual.

It was only when they were alone in their room that Sameer spoke, "What's the matter, Vandana? What makes you so upset? You upset the children as well." She began to cry softly, the tears streaking down her face in a helpless, continuous flow. He pulled her close to his chest and held her, a deep sense of pity overwhelming him. He had wanted her never to know. Never.

"I met David when I went to Varanasi for Grandma's funeral. I met Uma as well." He omitted any reference to Abha. "It was a strange meeting. I wanted to tell you about it, but Abhi was born soon after, and in all that excitement it seemed so irrelevant. We were so happy then. You were so happy. I did not want to take away any of that happiness. We can send the boy back if you want. I will talk it out with David. I will ask him not to come here if that is what you want."

"It does not matter now," Vandana said, moving away from him. "So many years have passed. Is David married with children? Where does he live in England? Has he kept in touch with Abha?"

"Married? No. Living close to that ashram turned him into a bit of an ascetic. I did not believe him in the beginning, but I saw the way he lived. He told me once, 'You have opted for the life of a "householder" but I prefer the mendicant.' Strange! You know, Vandana, he stayed on in India till the late eighties. In fact, I was surprised when he told me he was returning to England."

Vandana was watching her husband's face in wonder. Yet a tight knot of pain grew at the base of her skull, making her head throb. David had been in India for so many years. He had met Sameer regularly but not once did he try to contact her. Was this what forgetting was all about? She too had quite forgotten him. Busy with husband, children and an extended family of in-laws, friends and old parents, she had erased him from her mind. Why did a single letter make such a difference then?

She got up and wiped the tears from her face. "Ask him to come and stay with us, Sameer. I want him to see the children."

"I sent him their photographs," Sameer said, smiling. "He thought Mira looked a lot like you. 'She has got her smile,' he told me.'"

It seemed strange that David thought so, Vandana thought. People usually said Mira had a strong resemblance to her father. It was only she who noticed how much of Mira was like her inner self, how mother and daughter reflected each other in an intrinsic way.

But Vandana was not a possessive mother. She allowed the children to grow independent of her. She felt little of the anxiety of motherhood until recent time, until Avinash entered her life. He clung to her with an intensity that took her by surprise. She found herself responding to it with a kind of duty-bound vigilance. She kept an eye on what the boy ate, whether he was well or ill, whether he was happy or sad. She tucked him up in bed every night and said a little prayer on his behalf. He was happy and contented in her company, obeying her like a pet dog. When the children from the neighbourhood came to play with Mira, she was alert to how the boy was being treated. It made her happy to see the same kind of conscientiousness in Mira. Like her, Mira had always been a loner. They sought in the boy a type of attention that carried the pain of loving. It never struck Vandana that Avinash saw Mira as a bit of a rival. For the first time in her life an insidious demand was being made on her motherhood, and she found the pressure mildly pleasurable.

~~~

"I better go and check on the boy," Vandana said to Sameer, extricating herself from her reveries. Sameer noticed how quickly she regained her composure, settling her face to its usual expression of amiability. She straightened her hair, folding its waviness into a loose bun that rested at the base of her neck. It made her forehead stretch out just below the hairline, where fell tiny curls like delicate tendrils. She had arching eyebrows that met at midpoint; it gave her eyes a strange, luminous depth. She had never been conscious of her looks, but there was something finely etched about her face. In a sense she was plain, but with an unstated beauty of form that caught the attention of the onlooker.

Sameer remembered the first time he had seen her. She was standing in the central portico of the Medical College, next to the tall pillars, wearing a grubby white intern's coat and carrying a stethoscope in her hand. When Abha had introduced her, she had thrown a casual smile at him, as she would often do to Abha's myriad acquaintances. Abha was trying to goad a conversation between them, for she was very keen that Vandana got to know the doctor. It seemed a good proposition to work out a match between them. Who could trust an affair with a foreigner, an Englishman to boot! David was sincere no doubt, but his sincerity carried the vast ambiguity of someone who was enamoured of alien culture. Much of it was book-read, a quality of perception that Abha did not quite trust. "You are not a heroine in a novel, remember," she often told Vandana, "but David loves you the way he loves the Ganga . . ." She mimicked his accent, pronouncing the name with an absurd, mocking inflection that made Vandana shudder. The doctor was her kind, familiar and ordinary in his appeal, carrying depths that only a lifetime of habit-forming companionship can bring to the fore.

Sameer was both amused and annoyed by Abha's efforts, but he had learnt the art of dissimulation. He met Vandana with little interest, but with a vague sense that he needed to keep in touch with the girl for Abha's sake. Abha attracted him with a pull that was almost magnetic. Sameer had little knowledge of love, except for the kind that was whispered about Belapishi. That was part of a mysterious room in the corner of their large house and, on sultry afternoons when the curtains were drawn to keep out the glare of the sun, it engendered in him a vague, disembodied sense of loneliness. He remembered the photograph of a young girl, her slim body, her eyes inviting. Could this body have carried a child of passion? And why did she die without ever claiming that child as her own? Sameer thought of love with a curious sense of misgiving, as though its power would ultimately consume and destroy him.

He liked the way Abha treated love, with a kind of philosophical disdain. "I can never understand this need that people have to be loved all the time. I like it when someone is indifferent to me. It is more comfortable. I can relax in their company then. To be loved is to ask for something in return. But Vandana is different. She has the immense capacity to love another, without being mindful of what she is getting in return. But she must give, give, and give till she empties herself. It is a scary quality to have."

It frustrated him to find how little she spoke about herself. "It's you who empties herself in others," Sameer felt, but rarely uttered such thoughts to her. Somehow he had a feeling that Abha paid little attention to what he was saying. She was so fixed in her role as matchmaker for Vandana that she never noticed the desire in his eyes. And then one day, he decided to tell her the truth. He rehearsed every single line that he would speak. He thought of a venue and a time. He would talk and she would listen. He felt it was the first major decision that he had taken, far more momentous than deciding to leave home and the family clinic.

It turned out to be a perfect day. The river had a translucent grace as though it reposed in some grand benevolence. Hardly a ripple moved on its surface. The steps of the ghat were cleaner than usual. A few stray beggars slept under the open sky, their begging bowls clanking with the sound of coins flung by the passer-by, quite unmindful of the prone bodies. A few devotees faced the brilliant sun, muttering a prayer. It seemed such an unlikely place to declare one's love, but then Abha had to go somewhere soon after, and it was from the road adjacent to the Kedara Ghat that she had to take the turn into a narrow alley. She was always indifferent to her surroundings. Neither squalor nor beauty moved her much. She could stand in the middle of a crowded street and discuss with animated excitement a matter of great pressing importance for her. When Sameer asked her if they could go down to the ghat, she agreed with a slight nod. She followed him until they walked down to the last step, where the river water lapped continuously against the stone, with a brisk, undulating movement. He felt the presence of the river then. It stretched before them living and palpable, yet abstract, mystical, and unreal.

She looked tired, with dark streaks under her eyes. Her

clothes were crumpled, as though she had gone to sleep in them and not bothered to change in the morning.

"I was at the airport, seeing off David," she said. "It was well past three in the morning when we returned. Vandana asked me to come along. There was no way her mother was going to let her go alone. She was saying goodbye to David." She said all this with detachment, not in any way an explanation. It was always a little disconcerting the way Abha addressed herself to the person in front of her, without really being conscious of their presence. Her long speeches carried the air of an interior monologue. But today she was looking intently at Sameer as though his reaction to what she was saying was important to her. It moved him deeply.

"I was scared. I hate scenes that lovers make. So distressingly commonplace, like quarrelling shopkeepers. But you know, the two of them parted without so much as a goodbye. They simply laughed and discussed mundane things about airports and luggage and the security check. I stood there with an intense sense of doom. These two were parting forever – I could feel that. I envied them a bit. If I am ever to fall in love, that is, in the true sense of the term, I know that this is how I would want things to be. I do not know what made their relationship so impossible within the given conditions. I don't believe it has anything to do with the cultural differences between them. I think it is just the way they are, different people, made of different substances, knowing only a certain possible way of loving. Any commitment to marriage would have pushed them into a loveless state of being. I wonder if Vandana knew what she was doing at that point. She was making a choice. A difficult one, no doubt, but she was making it. They were saying goodbye to each other in a way that meant a commitment for life. You know in that very paradoxical way when you are free to pledge yourself to a life-time of loving, but there are no promises made, no wedding oaths to be taken." Abha paused briefly, her eyes taking in the wide expanse of the river. She turned to face Sameer, and then she did something quite unexpected. She reached out and held his hand.

"I am asking something of you that on the face of it sounds absurdly selfish. It is a proposal of marriage. Marry Vandana. She needs to settle down into something. She is quite unlike me. I have lived alone in this city for so many years. I rarely need the kind of cushioning that Indian girls want as a rule. I like being alone. But she will feel the emptiness in a way that will destroy her. She needs a husband, children." Abha looked at Sameer with sudden consternation on her face. Then she began to laugh a little, "Look at me, here I am asking you to make a solemn pledge on something as vital as marriage, with-out really finding out whether you are a free man! I hope you don't have a true love tucked away somewhere, or maybe your family has already found you a bride!" She waited for him to respond, but Sameer maintained a dogged silence as though he had lost his power of speech. The strangeness of the situation appalled him. Was Abha asking him to enter into a marriage of convenience? Did she believe that this is all that he deserved, a loveless union with a woman who had just dumped her lover? Or was this one of her many social con-science projects, her bid to change the world? By now he knew her opinion on such matters and the seriousness with which she pursued them. He tried to make out whether she was being non-serious for a change, but she spoke with an earnest-ness that confused him.

"Thank heavens!" she continued, smiling at him affec-tionately. "Oh, I like men like you! So eligible and still up for grabs! I book you straight away for my friend. You will find that what I offer you is best for your unattached heart. If you are planning for some grand love, remove it from your mind. Give her up at the altar of sacrifice! Remember that you will make the renunciation only once of that single great passion of your life! There is too much drama in real love and too much tragedy! Marriage asks for something quite simple: a bid for happiness in small measures, much like a habit one cannot give up." Abha was saying all this with the usual cutting edge in her tone, but something about her was different. He wondered whether it was the aura of the place, a certain weighing down of the spirit that comes with a setting that is unduly solemn. This was the place where hundreds of devotees flocked in the morning to pray, to absolve themselves of all their earthly ties. The river Ganges always takes away a part of the self, and man, hapless and overwhelmed, goes back home, small and naked. Sameer felt the presence of the river with a renewed sense of awe and bewilderment. It stretched before him, reeking of the washed sins of men and women.

Her bit of raillery over, she spoke seriously again. "Do not worry about infidelity. I know Vandana, she is too innocent and good, too committed to loving. She will grow to love you in a way that is different. Her own set-up has taught her the virtues of family life. She has always longed for its stability, and you can give it to her. I believe that about you. You are a good man, doctor, and you too hanker for a life of commitment and constancy. I admire these virtues in both of you and I know that you are made for each other." She smiled, a little tremulously. "What do they say about marriages? Ah yes, they are made in heaven! And here we stand in front of the holiest of rivers in India, and I ask you to pledge yourself to my friend." She was laughing again, loudly, spontaneously, overcome by an irrepressible mirth. He looked at her and smiled, the words and the laughter moving him with an intensity that felt like pain. When they moved out of the magic circle and walked up the stairs, they were still holding hands.

After a few days, Sameer returned to Delhi. It was the loneliest journey he had ever made.

~~~

Six months later, a marriage proposal was carried to and fro between the two families. Sameer came down to Varanasi to "see" Vandana in the formal sense of the term. The agreement came quickly. Sameer wondered whether Vandana was happy, but it was a question that went unasked in the midst of all the accompanying rituals. The two met briefly once or twice, and then they carried on writing to each other across the two cities. Every time Abha asked Vandana whether she was happy she answered in the affirmative, a fact that was conveyed to Sameer.

Vandana was finishing her residency and it seemed imperative that the actual wedding should be postponed for at least a year. But somehow the discussions veered towards an early marriage. Sameer felt that he had no problem with Vandana staying back in Varanasi until she completed her course. So the marriage took place with a great deal of fanfare. Soon after, the bride and groom bid farewell to each other. Sameer wondered whether the feeling that was coursing through his veins was really love. Vandana loved David and he loved Abha; that was the real thing. Then what did they feel for each other?

He found Vandana enchanting. She was encased in fine, gossamer-like, intricate bridal wear with jewelry that gleamed on her neck, forehead and slim arms. It made her look like a still-life painting with the colours bursting through the canvas. It gave her a vibrancy that took his breath away. Abha was quite right – Vandana had a spontaneous and natural ability to be happy and loyal, she was not given to brooding or sulking. Whenever they met on holidays, their youthful bodies sought solace in lovemaking. The nights were filled with a heady desire that wiped out memories of places and things. Her body, warm, pulsating, naked, responded to his delicate touch with a mysterious, nebulous yearning. His feelings for her had no name, but he felt it as a kind of love that carried an exquisite delicacy of form. He wondered whether she thought of David. He did think of Abha, not in a way that was intimate, but like the unseen depths of the river, dangerous, sensual, and mystical.

CHAPTER FIVE

The Abode of God

"You must be careful when you talk to him," Abha said anxiously, "his vocabulary lacks terms like cynicism and doubt. He is a dear old man, really, and he is revered in the ashram."

"Well, Swami Parm— What did you say his name was?" Sameer asked irritably, though his mood had begun to change imperceptibly. Abha's involvement with the ashram never ceased to surprise him. It was so much at variance with her general demeanour and the quick common sense that she brought to her thinking. There was nothing remotely mystical about her, and yet that morning they were embarking on a journey that was to take them into a world that seemed so mysteriously inexplicable. "The Abode of God," she whispered, peering from under the black umbrella that she held over her head. Its dark canopy shaded her eyes, allowing the sunlight to filter through, forming pinpoints of flickering, dancing light on her spectacles.

Soon thick rain clouds gathered in the sky and hid the sun from view. Sameer felt lighthearted and began to hum a tune. She looked up at his face, a trifle warily. Such moods came once in a while, and when they did she found it impossible to gauge the thoughts that were running in his head. He was far more predictable when he was sombre, or when he ruminated on matters that were weighing on him. But his lighter moments gave him an air of artistry, as though he carried a secret source of happiness that he kept concealed from others.

"Swami Parmananda, or Swamiji as he is generally called, is a wandering ascetic," Abha explained. "He travels extensively through the country from coast to coast. He spends the winter in the far reaches of the Himalayas, but during the warm, rainy season the ashram becomes his home. Nobody quite knows when he comes and goes."

"Ah, the utter irresponsibility of the ascetic life!" Sameer retorted with a short, snappy laugh. They were travelling in a cycle rickshaw and, as it clanked and swayed through the narrow streets, Sameer felt the fleeting images of the city press on him from both sides.

"Oh, no, you are quite mistaken!" Abha replied. "He is the second in command at the ashram. When he returns from his travels he has to take up the enormous responsibility of running the place. It is just that he lives life unencumbered. He has no attachment for place or people."

The rickshaw stopped at the point where the street was too narrow for any kind of vehicle to move through. They began to walk slowly, with a kind of measured deliberation, suddenly quiet. The slow thud of their footfalls seemed to echo in the air. Sameer felt a strange rush of feeling slap against his chest. He recoiled, as though he was uncertain of what he had to face in the immediate future.

The street had no pavement, its rough surface uneven, hurting their feet. Abha was wearing thin-soled sandals, which she removed dextrously and put aside on a cement platform specially built for the purpose, so they were barefooted when they entered the portals of the ashram. They moved up a flight of steep, winding stairs with whitewashed walls on both sides. It seemed to stretch endlessly, as though whatever lay beyond was not within easy grasp. The sedentary life that Sameer led, back home in Delhi, was evident from the way he panted. She was more nimble, the folds of her sari flapping against her bare calves, which were revealed as she mounted the stairs. He noticed her arms swinging to a rhythmic movement, the skin firm and supple. Her waist was narrow, the curves held firmly by the coil of the fabric draped around her. The loose end of the sari fell gracefully over her shoulder, swaying gently across her back.

The stairs opened suddenly into a large courtyard suffused with the brilliant sunlight. Rooms led out from buildings on all sides. Sameer paused for a second, trying to get back his breath. She was laughing at him, he could sense that, a gentle, affectionate laugher without malice. She spoke in a light whisper as though the place merited reverence.

The open courtyard, the sudden sense of infinite space merging with an azure-blue sky loaded with heavy, lumbering clouds, made Sameer stop in his track. He realized that the ashram had been built by cutting through a rocky hillock on the Rajghat Plateau, so that it virtually leaned against its lofty surface. He remembered the narrow, cobbled street and marvelled at the close proximity of that confined space and the open vista that met his eyes. At the level of the street were rows of tiny shops with concealed stairs leading upwards. Beneath the ashram was an old shop for repairing watches, owned by a Bengali Brahmin. He lived in a dingy room behind the shop that he had taken on rent from the ashram authorities. Way back in the thirties he paid them a princely sum of five rupees a month, which had been increased now to fifty after much haggling. But he never quite minded: this was a busy street with a cheap guesthouse almost next door, and the customers came to his shop because he boasted the finest collection of religious books they could pick up at a very reasonable price. For the past few years he had also started keeping charms, amulets and beads that pilgrims often sought out. A talkative, friendly man with a repertoire of anecdotes, many a customer returned to his shop to chat with him. Some of them even left their watches behind for repair.

It is said that centuries ago, when Varanasi was Anandavana or the Forest of Bliss, this place was a thick jungle, a garden of paradise so breathtakingly beautiful that it made the gods envious. In the forties, railroad contractors, while digging for landfill to rebuild the railway station, came upon the remains of an ancient city at this very spot. By the 1960s the place was taken over by archaeologists. They discovered old city walls, pottery and artefacts dating back to the ninth century BC. Until recent times the place was nothing more than a grassy plateau outside the confines of the city. But habitation had spread since then, with its ugly buildings leaning into narrow streets.

Many of the trees had survived, primeval, gnarled, growing on the edge of the ashram courtyard, their branches looming over the rooms. It gave the place an air of decadence. One such tree, so short and bulbous that it looked deformed, was growing inside the courtyard itself. Its surface was splattered with thick, red sindoor, and it was only when Abha moved close and touched her index finger on the bark and applied it to her forehead, that Sameer realized that it cradled within its craggy depths a shiva linga. He stood there awkwardly, not quite knowing what to do. Sameer was an agnostic by instinct, and places like the ashram filled him with a mild sense of dread. Varanasi was dotted with such sacred trees, sprouting on busy street corners in the midst of the endless flow of traffic. He always wondered how people paused to worship, making their usual offerings of flowers and incense. The trees were crusted with bright vermilion like fresh, foetal blood.

Abha led him to a central hall, large and roomy. "We have to sit here and wait for Swamiji," she said. It seemed an awkward statement to make, for there wasn't a single piece of furniture. Not even a mat on the floor. She squatted on the bare floor with immense ease. He noticed then how clean it was, and how cool it felt to the touch. A middle-aged woman appeared at the doorway, the first sight of people residing in the place. She glided past without a word, though her eyes acknowledged their presence. She smiled at Abha.

The severe austerity of the room, the silence that seemed to bounce off the walls, and the oddity of his own presence there, filled Sameer with an overwhelming sense of apprehension. He felt his arrival as a sort of intrusion, and he kept his eyes lowered so that no one would notice the lack of piety in them. Once in a while he glanced at Abha, surprised to see how quietly she sat, an intrinsic docility in her posture. She looked up at him, her eyes radiant but pleading. Wordlessly, without so much as moving her lips, she was asking him to join her in the spirit of the place. He thought of Uma and how much Abha had done for her, and he felt gratitude in response to her plea.

The rain clouds dimmed the sky, and somewhere at a distance a peahen let out a wailing, raucous shriek. The trees began to shiver, as though the memory of the forest danced in their veins and filled them with untold ecstasy. A constant hissing murmur seemed to rise from the bowel of the earth like primeval energy being unleashed. The rains were about to descend, and Sameer wondered whether the dwarf tree would let its colour run down the crevices like perennial unhealing wounds.

When Swamiji walked in through the door the rain had come down in white, blinding sheets. He was a tiny, almost diminutive man, with wiry muscular limbs like tight knots on a rope. He was bare-chested, and wore a dhoti that barely reached his knees. The sacred thread rested on his belly button, and three prominent lines of deep, flaming orange marked his forehead. His eyes were set in cavernous sockets with thick, busy eyebrows hanging over them. There was something remote and fierce about his face as though he had come into the room against his will. He asked the two to follow him with a quick, jerky move of the hand. He did not smile or speak in greeting.

They passed along a lengthy corridor with portraits of saints hanging on the wall. The ceiling was low, and the place smelt of acrid firewood and varnish. The floor had been swept clean with a mop soaked in water, and it felt wet and slippery as they moved barefoot on it. There were open rooms on both sides but a strange all-pervasive silence filled the place as though it was devoid of human habitation.

At long last they were ushered into a room with a mattress on one side, covered by a white sheet. Swamiji lowered himself on it, folding his legs into a lotus position. He held his back erect, and Sameer noticed the fine texture of his skin. It seemed to glow in the radiance of the room. On the wall was a map of India, an object that seemed so out of place that Sameer stared at it in amazement. There was something comfortable about the room, and though it was sparse like the rest of the building it was less severe and forbidding. A carpet had been spread on the floor. Sameer noticed that it was hand-woven and of intricate texture and design. Swamiji asked the two of them to sit down, and then he spoke in a voice that was surprisingly rich and resonant. "I want you to close your eyes and join me in my prayers."

He prayed in a slow, lilting cadence. There was something sensuous about the man as though his ascetic garb was only a costume that he wore for occasions. Sameer felt uneasy. But when he glanced at Abha she was praying with her eyes closed. The room started filling with people. They filed in, in ones and twos, and took their places on the floor. It was discourse time, and Sameer realised with a sense of inevitability that nothing happened in this place outside the routine. His private meeting with Swamiji had to wait.

"We have a special guest today," Swamiji began, addressing himself directly to Sameer. "He has come all the way from Delhi. I welcome him with open arms. But I can see that he has little faith. Like most of us, who are willing to accept nothing but worldly reality, he is restless and unhappy. He wants instant remedies. But science has failed to cure the maladies of the world. Tell me, all of you who are gathered here, what simple cure for heartache and disappointment?"

Swamiji was posing a challenge to him. Sameer could see the glint in the man's eyes, and he caught a smile streaking across his face. It was a shrewd, worldly face without compassion. The room did not feel comfortable any more. There was something garish and opulent about the carpet. Sameer spotted a large wooden chest in a corner with "donate generously" scrawled on it in white paint. Brand new fans were hanging from the ceiling. There was nothing spiritual about the atmosphere, and Sameer noticed that in this part of the building there was no sign of a deity or an inner sanctum. Only this man presided over the prayers, encouraging in his followers a kind of vulgar obeisance.

Sameer's eyes strayed outside the window to take in parts of the building visible from where he was sitting. He realised that this part of the frontage was only a façade. The ashram stretched for a distance across the low hillocks and undulating landscape that was part of the plateau region. There was symmetry to the rooms and the way in which they were ordered, like remnants of an obscure, sacred cosmography. The windows revealed slices of the sky, and the greenery outside merged with the woods in the background. This was an ideal location for an ashram traditionally associated with a forest hermitage. In the distance was the spiralling top of a temple, holding aloft its pennant, fluttering in the breeze. The rain fell at a slant, making the flag droop heavily. Sameer thought of the leaf-choked well in the courtyard, its mossy stone surface gleaming treacherously. Nothing was as it appeared to the eyes, aeons of silence encrusted in tiny voices speaking a mumbo-jumbo that he could hardly understand. The meaning was folded in codes and signs, and all around were prone and supplicant figures, offering themselves to distorted and fiery images.

Years later he was to remember what Abha told him then. "That map you saw in the central hall, it contained all the tirtha sthans of India. Varanasi is the center of the cosmic universe. When you touch the path of the panch koshi in Kashi you have seen all the holy places of India. Sitting in that one place you are in touch with the magnitude of the whole. Your body and your consciousness is broken into a million parts and scattered everywhere, and yet you feel integrated. How is that possible?"

"I was thinking only of Uma," he told her simply and starkly. "She was sick in mind and body. She needed me."

~~~

The meeting with Uma was organized in the hour following noon. The day had softened, and the wetness of the rain clung to the leaves and the brown bark of the trees. They had moved to another part of the building, a cluster of houses far away from the street, hidden so entirely from the eye that Sameer was intrigued. "As you can see we protect our women from stray glances," Swamiji said in a matter-of-fact way. The ashram was spread over a vast area, with connecting pathways. Huge fallow lands, and many stretches cultivated with homegrown vegetables and other crops, created the differentiated area over which the entire ashram was laid out. Sameer noticed young boys working in the fields; women too, with children tied on their backs like rucksacks. They worked in the drizzle with scarves knotted around their heads. The infants slept soundly, and Sameer noticed that the women sang lullabies in hushed, sing-song tones.

"They are all inhabitants of the ashram," Swamiji told him.

There were open-air shrines with cement platforms all around. Sameer was later to learn that these shrines were opened to the public during particular festivals. A pathway lead from the Adi Keshava Ghat to the ashram, and the crowd would move in, pausing briefly at the Varana Ganges confluence and the ancient Adi Keshava temple on its bank. There was never a sense of hurry; each step was taken with the consciousness of the timeless quality of life in this city.

Later, when he recounted the day to Vandana, he said, "I felt as though my feet had turned to lead. Here I was going to meet Uma because she was dying, and my professional instinct told me there was not a moment to lose, but we walked through the maze of the ashram's interior as though we had all the time in the world. Swamiji would pause at every step to explain something or the other to me."

Swamiji said, "The ashram is not a way of life that is mentioned with reverence in the Vedas. In fact, the ascetic order became an acceptable religious form of life after the influence of Buddhism and it is closely modelled on the Buddhist monastic order. Prior to that, the ashrama was only part of the rites of passage. You see these people, they carry on with the tasks of a householder, and they fall in love, marry, have children, renounce worldly desire, and then take on the garb of an ascetic. This is a prototype of the world outside, no different from the world you come from."

"Then why keep them here?" Sameer asked belligerently.

"When you say keep them, do you think they are here against their will?" Swamiji responded quickly. "They come of their own accord. They come because we have something to offer them. They come from all ranks, castes and different parts of the country. This is mini-India."

"Does the ashram really break the barriers of caste?" Sameer butted in, increasingly drawn by the direction of the argument. "I mean, are you able to establish an egalitarian order without any caste prejudice? Do shudras and brahmins sleep and eat in the same quarters?"

"Well, it depends on what you mean by casteless," said Swamiji, but there was a false note in his voice, as though he was hesitant to go into such matters. Sameer felt triumphant; years of practice as a psychiatrist made him sensitive to inflections in people's tone. To him, listening to others was the only way of arriving at the truth. "We are all one in the eyes of

God, but you earn your rightful position inside the ashram in terms of your conduct. Who can break universal laws? Only the brahmin can oversee the worship of the deity."

"Ah, I see!" Sameer nodded his head shrewdly. The Swamiji was taking in the scene with an air of deliberation, as though all this was part of an intellectual debate that challenged him. He was not ready to give in. Despite the tension in the atmosphere he liked the doctor. He preferred this kind of battling of minds to the vapid obeisance that he had to face day after day. To tell the truth he was a little bored of it.

They sat down on a bench under a jacaranda tree. It was seeping rainwater, cool and heavy with moisture. Abha sat at a distance, silent and deferential, as she was wont to be inside the ashram. She came into her own outside, in other forums. Sameer wondered why she was so quiet, listening, taking in the argument without interfering or posing her usual doubts. Little did he know that on that day Abha fell in love with him, in a hopeless, unhappy sort of a way. The realization was confirmed to her in the days to come, but today, the scenario took shape in her mind like a little tableau of infinite pain and forgiveness, like time's slow healing of wounds. She was looking ahead at incidents that were to follow, and if there was any clarity of perception then, she felt it was the ashram that contributed to her understanding of things. The debate going on between the two men skimmed over her consciousness like bird's wings whirring in the air before settling down.

Sameer too felt something akin to peace of mind, as though the place worked itself on him in a slow, all-pervading way. And yet he did not feel threatened by it; he knew that an entire world awaited him outside its door – a world to which he would return happily, without complaint. It was just the way he felt about Varanasi, the city of his birth and childhood. He left it behind with a sense of freedom, and he returned to it without any anxiety. There were two secret Varanasis in his mind: the one that belonged to his workaday life, prosaic, ugly, crowded, garish in its blatant display of things; and the other that belonged to Grandma and, now, to Uma. It was the unseen order of sacred things, fleeting, invisible, but palpably there; the turgid depths of a city's religiosity.

A few days from now he would meet David for the first time. In the course of their friendship he would lend Sameer a copy of Calvino's *Invisible Cities* and Sameer would think that the passages on 'mirror cities' reflecting 'what seemed not' described how he felt about Varanasi. Calvino said cities are dreamlike locations, revealing themselves as the expression of some desire or fear, or a combination of both.

The secret lure of the ashram was just this. It portrayed a diagram or mandala that contained within its circle everything that is holy – a miniature Kashi, the City of Light, encompassing darkness or the lack of light. It contained the ordinary and the mundane, the sick and the destitute, and the dying. But the invisible sacredness of the place was available for the eyes to see. Much of this seeing happened because of a certain consensus; the profane or sceptical eye can destroy meaning. And yet Sameer knew that he had come here only because he loved Uma, and wanted to understand the world she had exchanged for home, a place where she had been essentially abandoned. Was she happy here? The question mattered in a way that made Sameer shudder with terrifying foreknowledge.

They crossed the threshold into the interior space of the women's residence in the ashram. Swamiji made it very clear that Sameer was permitted to step inside only because he was a doctor. It was a homely place with a family shrine. They were made to offer prayers before they could enter the living quarters. Sameer saw the sacred object, circular in shape, made of five metals, containing the form of Goddess Shakti, the female incarnation of Shiva. Low walls with four gates surrounded the shrine. The pattern suggested inter-locking planes, and he noticed the bare simplicity of the room, the single oil lamp throwing a dim shadow, and the stone floor with a narrow seat for meditation. Here inside this room was the symbolic center of the world: the self in touch with the universal; and God, combining male and female energy.

Swamiji offered the two some prasad and, taking a hand-ful of flowers from the feet of the shrine, he touched their foreheads. They cupped their palms to take the offerings. There was a strange glimmer in his face, a look of pity. "Bless you, my children," he said in a sad undertone. "If you sit here at any time of the day and meditate, you will under-stand a simple truth of life. That life, birth, death are all one, part of the same infinite throbbing of this universe. We see it in isolation and therefore we are afraid."

~~~

"When I first saw Uma," Sameer would later tell Vandana, "I was shocked. Her hair was closely cropped, making her look like a wizened old witch from our childhood fairy tales."

Sameer had not quite prepared himself for the passage of time. Uma was no longer his younger cousin-sister. She was a sevika devoted to her calling. Why did she look so tiny and shrivelled was the first thought that came to his mind. Or was it because she sat huddled on the floor, pounding a thick saffron paste with a mortar and pestle? Her face lit up with an incredible smile when she saw him. Her eyes were instantly flooded with tears, but she brushed them aside and laughed with a spontaneity that was infectious. Then seeing Swamiji she moved forward and touched his feet. He held up his hand and blessed her with a light touch.

It was against the rules of the ashram to touch a sevika. Sameer tested her pulse and kept the stethoscope poised on her chest, while Abha did much of the physical handling. Only his eyes probed hers, asking a million questions, not able to utter them on his lips. Uma responded with her body, coiling and recoiling, her eyes clouded, the variations in mood touching her upturned face as swift, fleeting movements. She never spoke. As Sameer looked closely at her, he realised that his first impression of her as an old, crumpled woman was wrong. There was something young and untouched about her face, like a delicate creeper clinging to an old tree. Traces of childhood were locked inside her, and they peered out at him as from a window without shutters. At the same time, Sameer understood in an instant that Uma had gone beyond the pale of his memories of her. There was nothing familiar about her, and he relived the sense of her going away with renewed pain.

This part of the ashram had the air of lived-in quarters, more squalid and crowded. He could hear the sound of voices just outside his door, and the traces of women's belongings were hanging awkwardly from clotheslines strung across the verandah. The room smelt of strongly-scented hair oil and carbolic soap. Later, he was to associate Uma with this odour, and that clean, scrubbed look of a body that had undergone rites of penance. Her skin had grown pale and fair, protected from the sunlight. It was as though she was a creature confined to an interior world, rarely glimpsed by anyone from outside. An exotic, delicate pearl curled up in an oyster, waiting at the bottom of the sea amidst coral and seaweed. Sameer was aware of the fact that there was no point of transition into her enclosed world. But he clung on to the fleeting possibility of discovering some kind of contact that eluded him at the moment. There was no door or point of transition into this world, and he felt at a total loss for words.

He was to know later that Uma's own involvement with her world was like the routine of a child, a matter of familiarity and repetition. She had learnt to assimilate her experiences at a given level of understanding, like crowds of worshippers moving on the riverfront in synchrony, repeating what generations of devotees had done. This was not religious frenzy, but more a kind of conformity. Sameer had felt humbled in Uma's presence. He had come face to face with the endless flow of confluence, the meeting of worlds, the inward and outward drift of crosscurrents. Indeed Uma was dying, as Abha had suggested, but not in the strictly medical sense of the term. She had begun to recede into her own inner world, as though she was seeking a return to some pristine, undifferentiated source of life energy. She was slipping away, and to Abha this was the closest she had come to understanding what dying meant. Long before Sameer had immersed himself in medical science, his geography books in school had taught him how the Ganges in its eastward flow to the Indian Ocean took a backward loop at Varanasi, changing its course to return briefly to the Himalayas. This holy spot, where the Ganges turns its face, is considered very auspicious. Here all meanings cease to be, and the outward, flowing current of life moves inward to seek unity with its origin.

"She has not spoken a word for the last six months. She

sits on samadhi and has to be force-fed. She is making this concoction day and night," Abha whispered.

Sameer bent low and touched Uma's face. "Talk to me," he said. "Do you want to meet anyone with whom you would like to talk? Somebody in the ashram? Somebody at home?"

"She cannot be permitted to go home," Swamiji intervened, "not now while she is still undergoing stages of her training. Please hear this out, doctor."

Sameer paused and looked at Swamiji with great attention. He understood the rules of protocol, and the need to circumvent them with patience and tact. But he was not willing to give in either. Sameer had a certain persistence in his character that Abha had learnt to respect. It was a stubborn rectitude, born of empathy and a great capacity for compassion.

"To allow her to return home now is to nurture in her a certain individuality that we at the ashram are not willing to permit. When she comes here she loses her individual identity, and leaves behind her previous ties with family and friends. She becomes part of our family. We are her brothers and sisters. You see, doctor, if we permit individuality then it corrodes the effective working of the order. That has been the bane of ashrams India over; too many cult figures have risen and formed breakaway groups. It is nothing but the clash of powerful individuals."

Sameer watched the man speak with passionate conviction. Had Swamiji come into the fold of ashram life to give up his individuality, he wondered. Was he speaking of real threats or of something that was only a possibility? Was this peaceful abode of god no longer as tranquil as its propagators would like it to be?

Uma brought her face very close to Sameer's and, touching his ears with her finger, said in a barely audible voice, so distant that he wondered whether he had heard it in his dreams, "She lives." Her face was impassive.

"Who lives?" Sameer asked, his own voice lost to him.

"Mother," Uma replied, but not to him. She had cradled her face on her knees as she used to do as a child inside Grandma's prayer room, ready to trick the old woman into a mood of compliance. Grandma would promptly work herself up into a flurry and ask the girl what was ailing her. Uma would refuse to divulge, keeping her face hidden from view. This was their game of hide and seek, and Uma knew she could score on the old woman's frailties.

"What do I do with this girl," Grandma wailed, "send her away with her good-for-nothing mother?"

"Do, do, Granny," Uma giggled, "straight to the other shore with Mother." Grandma clicked her tongue in horror, sending her false teeth clattering in her mouth.

"Mother. Mother. Mother," Uma repeated the name thrice, and then she lapsed into silence. Sameer tried cajoling her, but no more words came to her lips. She rested her face on her knees and waited, as she had done on the day Bela's death was announced to her.

CHAPTER SIX

Penance

"Belapishi was alive?" Vandana asked.

"No. Of course not," Sameer replied, "How could she be alive? We had buried her years back. But she was alive in Uma's mind, and that is what mattered."

Vandana was sitting on her cane chair, her head resting against the back. She had a look of deep forbearance on her face, as though life was taking strange twists and turns and she had to prepare herself to face the consequences. Once in a while she reached out to touch Sameer's hand. The present moment mattered to her far more than what was being narrated about the past.

She had this nervous feeling that the way she negotiated the past, especially her thoughts about David, had a great deal to do with factors that belonged to her life now. She wondered whether Sameer felt the same. But his face was inscrutable as always. His hair had was greying in light salt and pepper shades around his temples and forehead, and the skin beneath his eyes, chin and mouth was sagging just a little. But there was something brittle and youthful about his face, like arrested time, and a touch of deferred emotions, as if he had much to say to others but was keeping quiet out of choice.

Today he spoke at great length, yet Vandana felt there was

much that he was not saying. It made her feel lonely in a way that she could not describe. Wedged between them were his memories of Uma and a lifetime of contending with her delusions.

"Uma believed her mother was alive, and for a long time I was mystified. She was barely eleven when Belapishi died, and in all that time she had rarely expressed any feelings for her mother. What had triggered off this particular kind of delusion? Was it something to do with the place? Was the fact that her life was given over to devotion responsible for her mental state?" Sameer sounded puzzled.

"And then the realisation came to me like a sudden revelation," Sameer continued. "It came to me one night when I was sitting with David in his room." Sameer looked intently at Vandana, as though he was about to present a fact so obvious she would immediately recognise it as true. Neither wanted to hurt the other, and it was their mutual concern that made things difficult rather than simple for them. But Sameer felt impatient: his primary concern was Uma, and he felt the need to move on with his narrative.

He understood Vandana's anxiety to know more about his meeting with David, but he was not quite willing to provide the details just yet. She would have to wait, and he noticed with a sense of relief that she revealed nothing of her impatience. She seemed immersed in his account of Uma. "There was only one way of making Uma get over her mother's demise. The last rites had not been performed here in Varanasi, the city of the dying. They say the dying flock to Kashi, and wait for the soul to slip away. It is the most merciful form of coming to terms with death. At the Manikarnika Ghat the fire smoulders and the ashes are readied in earthen containers to be immersed in the waters of the Ganges. I felt

then a sense of mission to have Belapishi laid to rest here in
our own city. At home opinions were sharply divided. Why
rake up a morbid past about which father felt strongly?
Mother was appalled at the idea of having funeral rites after
so many years. It is a travesty of the memory of the dead, she
told me. Chotoma was agreeable but uneasy at the idea. When
I told her it was mere tokenism she was shocked at the profanity of it all."

Sameer's meeting with David was incidental to the entire
sequence of events. But he had liked it this way. He was not
very sure what he was expecting. Perhaps he was looking for
some clue that would enable him to understand Vandana
better. She seemed so happily married. Was there some
other expectation that she had from men in general and
lovers more specifically? He wanted to seek out the single
most important quality that Vandana had loved in David.

He found a man indolent and abstruse, with just a touch
of sensuality that was foreign and intriguing. David spoke
very often about Vandana, but without the slightest trace of
longing, as though she was a mere acquaintance who sur-
faced in their conversations. Sameer relaxed in David's company, though there was a formality between them that
operated along the lines of an exquisite type of etiquette.
But there was something else that worried Sameer. David
was staying in a rented room outside the university, and it
became the regular venue where they met Abha as well. She
hung around his room with great familiarity, and often
stayed on late into the night. He noticed how she pottered
around the kitchen and helped David prepare his meals.
One day she excused herself and took a quick shower. She
stood on the balcony and dried herself, allowing the fine
spray of water to dissolve around her like dewdrops dissi-

pating in a million pinpoints of light. As she dried out the towel in the sun, he noticed the thin contours of her body silhouetted against the bland sky, and the fact that she had draped herself in David's dressing gown. Are they lovers, he wondered? Are they having sex? The thought left traces of resentment, as though David was intruding into areas of experience that were rightfully his. The feeling left him muddled.

He marvelled at the fact that an Englishman had chosen to stay behind in an alien country. What impelled him other than an obscure need to do research? Could it be his love for the two women? Unlikely, Sameer felt. If anything, David spoke of Varanasi as an eternal love affair. "People have asked me why Varanasi? I tell them Varanasi is my temporary home, and yet my sojourn here has more value than pleasant days spent in a familiar landscape. I take in everything this city has to offer and, believe me, the only place that feels like home is this tiny room. Not because it has any resemblance to home in England, far from it, but because it is the only spot I return to every night and sleep off the day's weariness. I have grown accustomed to its nook and corner. Otherwise, things are frighteningly different. All around me I see differences so basic, so deep-rooted that sometimes I wonder whether there is anything called universal. Then my mind balks, and I want to catch the next flight home. But I return. Varanasi is to me the ultimate alien city. Yet its very alienness is my obsession."

Sameer had stretched himself on David's wooden bed, the bare planks hurting his back. But he could feel his limbs relaxing, and the thin mattress held his spine ramrod straight. As a doctor he knew it was the best possible posture. The room was devoid of almost any furniture except

for a study table and chair. On the wall was a large reproduc-
tion of Botticelli's *Birth of Venus*. In one spot David had
fixed with Sellotape photographs that he had taken of his
Kailash Yatra. The Lake Mansarover was pristine blue with
clods of snow in the background. There was a picture of an
ice cave and a near-naked sanyasi sitting in a yogic posture in
the foreground. Sameer turned his face away with a mild
sense of annoyance. The typical face of India captured by
the lens of a camera.

Abha noticed his mood and came forward to join Sameer.
"So typically touristy," she said. "I keep telling David that."

"I know . . ." said David, shamefacedly, "couldn't help
myself. But the lack of privacy in India and especially the
erotic images of Hindu religion never cease to fascinate me.
In England this man would be confined in a loony bin, but
in your country he is revered. By the time I had finished
photographing him a small crowd had gathered. They
offered him food and small change as alms. He even pissed
in full view."

"Pretty disgusting," Sameer smiled, "but that's it! What
to do except ignore it totally. I never meddle with this part
of religious experience. The unreasonableness of the human
mind depresses me at times."

"But that's the nature of your job," Abha intervened.
"How can you allow it to depress you?"

"As long as I am sitting in my medical chamber things
seem part of a routine. Few people know that hyper-religios-
ity is an ailment that is very much curable with medicines. I
have treated a number of patients. For instance, there was
this man who willed away all his assets to religious institu-
tions, leaving his family on the brink of penury. His wife
came to me and begged me to do something. You should

have met this man. Charity was all that he could think of. Charity and salvation. But six months of medicines and he was completely cured. But how many actually come for treatment?"

"I like the way our friend describes religiosity as an ailment," David carped good-naturedly. He rolled a bidi in his fingers and lighted it. He moved out to the verandah. A strong smell of raw tobacco carried into the room. He flicked off the ashes with a light shake of his hand into a broken saucer that was kept on the ledge. He offered his friends some milk cakes, soft and spongy. Sameer noticed the frugality of David's life. The room was strewn with books, standing in piles on the floor and the wide windowsill. There was an indulgence here that fascinated him, frugality and plenitude mixing in a rimless, amorphous way. David was wearing a sarong tied around his waist, his body strong and burgeoning, his skin white and gleaming, and his eyes a brilliant green.

Over the years he had become well-versed in Hindi and Bengali and used local words with great ease. He spoke to the landlady in correct Hindi making her splutter and blush. But in Sameer's company a certain formality entered his bearing. He held himself erect, and used a clipped, formal language that highlighted his foreignness. It made the distance between them and their cultures more prominent. The ice was never really broken between them, but there was mutual respect. Vandana did not matter. She bridged their friendship in a way that a shared bonding can often do.

David asked Sameer about Vandana only once, in a manner that was strangely intimate. They were sitting in the coffee-house at the university. A sense of nostalgia tied them to the place and it was one of those 'weighing over matters' hours when the mind is languid and preoccupied. It was a few days before his departure, and Sameer felt sad in a way that he could not describe. He thought continuously of Uma, Abha and David and the new circumstances that tied him to all three of them.

The canteen was filled to the brim with young men and women, nondescript and anonymous in their variety, shuffling in and out, and settling down to a quick bite at tables strewn across the entire length of a large hall. One corner was the counter with an ancient coffee machine hissing out espresso coffee, the pungent smell of cocoa beans floating in the air. David signalled to the boy who was serving, to take their order. There was little to choose from, but the boy rattled off his list. They settled for bread and omelette and some coffee.

"My usual lunch," said David.

"Nothing English about your digestive system, I can see that," Sameer said jocularly.

"Mercifully no," David replied. "Boy, that took a long time though! At one stage I felt I had to go back. Water I avoid meticulously."

"Delhi is no better. But my life now is more streamlined."

"Lucky man," David ruminated half-seriously, "loved by two such lovely women."

"Two women?" Sameer puzzled. "I don't understand you."

"Abha loves you. You know that surely?"

"Oh no, you have got it wrong. Abha does not love me. Sometimes I think Abha is incapable of loving anyone. She is too absorbed in her own self for such things. See how wrapped up she is in her work. That's how it is with her." He was keeping David off her, Sameer realised ruefully. Somehow the thought of Abha choosing domesticity with some other man seemed painfully commonplace and not becoming of her. It snatched away the significance of his sacrifice.

"Ah then! She has not spoken to you." David looked serious. "Quite unusual of her. Truth is something that Abha never flinches from. It's an obsession with her, this truth-telling. She spoke to me only the other day about how much she cared for you. Loved you, that's the word she used. Normally she is objective, and speaks as though reporting a news item. But this was different, there was a catch to her voice, and her eyes kept filling up all the time. I have made a big mistake David, she said."

Sameer was to remember this moment for many years, and it never failed to make him shiver with a sense of irony.

The two men were silent for a while. Then David spoke. "It's amazing how love demands a proper context. The trouble with our love, Vandana's and mine, was that it had no viable context. We did think of marrying, though. You know that, don't you?" Sameer nodded in assent. These narratives were getting repetitive, like fingering old wounds, making them bleed. It had been a strange homecoming for Sameer, full of dark reminiscences and fateful crossovers. Yet listening to others was what he did all the time, and his nerves were fine-tuned to the meaning behind the words. He listened without turning a hair, and in the background a transistor baled out a soulful tune. The boy who had served them earlier shuffled from table to table humming the same tune. His adolescent face was intense, as though he was seeking, in the midst of a life of extreme drudgery, some sort of reprieve. Sameer felt sorry for him, and decided on an instant to give him a handsome tip.

"Right from the beginning I was aware of what I could

not give Vandana. She wanted marriage, children, and all the usual things. I went back to England to test my feelings. I made promises to her, too many and too complex. I was nervous and at a loss for words. But Abha assured me that Vandana would make a good marriage with you that you would give her all the things that she wants. I am so happy the two of you are having a baby. What I like about your society is the unstated quality of its denial. Your women take my breath away. Vandana and Abha, they live simple lives of compromise, as soulfully and easily as you and I breathe."

The word compromise hurt Sameer immensely, but he said nothing, wanting to hear more from David.

"I left Vandana. Do I have any regrets? Honestly, I can't say. But I find it increasingly difficult to leave your country. The beauty of this region is one of desolation. Varanasi fills you with the sense of things that can never be the same again. You have seen Uma, how she mourns for a woman who deserted her in her childhood. Do you think she really understands the meaning of death and dissolution? I think not. What we witness is surrender to the rhythm of things asserting itself, a way of coping with the disengagement that her life at the ashram has taught her. Your therapy cannot cure her. There is no cure for the void or absence that parting from loved ones can bring. You simply learn to fill it up with something else. She too will do so, and go on living out her life. I will be returning to England next year and be away for a few years. I am getting a teaching assignment. It will enable me to save enough money to see me through my days here. It is very important for me to remain foot-loose, to make these journeys to and fro. You understand, don't you?"

"What do I tell Vandana? Do I tell her about our meeting?" Sameer asked.

"I should think not. It is better this way," David said emphatically, and left it at that. He continued his musings in an aimless sort of a way, for they had a few hours to kill before Abha would join them. "At the foot of Mount Kailasa is the lake Manasarovar, 'lake of the mind', isn't that what it means? It is 15,000 ft above sea level, covering an area of 200 square miles. Amongst the pilgrims it is known as the 'blue lotus cup', and folklore has it, though rather erroneously, that the rivers Ganges, Yamuna, Indus and Brahmaputra have their sources there. But I think I can understand the meaning of this popular folklore. There, at the very source of the mind, 'mun' as they would say in Hindustani, is creation's yearning for human habitation. Thus the rivers branch out and flow through the valley in the thick of human civilization. Standing at that spot in utter isolation, taking in the electrifying blue of the lake, I understood why in the Indian tradition water as substance is considered the beginning or potentiality of all things. From this obscure beginning, undefined, unformed, comes the world of tangibilities and iron habits – the infinite desire to be fixed in time, place and language. In the beginning there is the yearning, and I come back to your country because I want to understand a philosophy that captures the desolation of such yearning."

Sameer listened, his mind in a whirl. As a student of science he was ready to dismiss all this philosophy as hogwash. Yet something held him back, making him take in the words like music straining from a distance. Later, in his attempt to recollect the time spent with David, he remembered the words but not the mood in which they were spoken. He wondered what had spurred on that moment of intimacy. The next time they spoke like that matters had progressed and nothing was quite the same again.

≋

The funeral rites of Uma's mother had to be a solemn affair, carried through with utmost secrecy. Sameer felt that nothing of it was possible without David and Abha's help. "Is there anything in our shastras that permits a death to be relived after so many years," he said ruefully, with a tiny laugh at the irony of his words.

Abha looked worried. "Why not? We do have death anniversaries, don't we?"

"I need something more elaborate," Sameer interjected. "Something vaguely ritualistic with a burial and ashes to be immersed in the river. I have no idea how we will make Uma participate, what with the strict rules of the ashram. I cannot take Swamiji into confidence. Where will I get a priest willing to go through this entire charade?" He was sounding more and more doubtful, until David asked him to consider an idea.

"Give it a hearing please, even though it will sound preposterous, especially to you, Abha. A number of people are brought into Varanasi to die, and then for one reason or the other they are abandoned. Maybe we can find such a person, act the good Samaritan for the few remaining days of his or her life. When the hour comes we can give the poor soul a decent burial. See, we have the occasion for a funeral, and for Uma this can be the experience of mourning that you think will cure her of her delusions."

"Stop it, stop it, both of you," Abha shrieked, suddenly angry. "Just hear yourself, you sound obscene." Sameer felt contrite. Yes indeed, it was a far-fetched idea. He felt alienated from the occasion, the city, from all these people. He missed Delhi, Vandana and the baby that was growing in her womb. He ought to be by her side. What was he doing in this place that bred such irrationalities, such wild conjurations? He looked at Abha and said quietly, "I need some time to think things over." Increasingly he found himself spending time in David's room, attracted by the bare, minimal life-style. Abha seemed at ease here in a way that she could never be in his house. Surely, Vandana did not fit here, not since her marriage and her shift to Delhi.

He felt a sudden pang of guilt at the thought that his sep-aration from Vandana was not simply a matter of getting involved in unforeseen circumstances, though that is the explanation he had given her. "I have to extend my leave for a while," he told her. "Uma needs long-term treatment, and I have to work out her course of medicines." Many ghosts from the past need to be laid to rest, he thought to himself. He said nothing about his long meetings with David and Abha.

He was permitted to visit Uma once a day, along with Abha. The meetings were conducted in Uma's room. For the first time he was able to take in the details of the room. It was tiny, with a large bay window that overlooked a stretch of greenery. The room was bare except for a tiny cot and a straw mat. A few clothes were hanging from a clothes-line that was strung horizontally across the breadth of the room. It gave the space a touch of warmth, breaking loose from the austerity of the surroundings. They were not permitted to bring in anything from the world outside.

Uma sat on the floor, her body stooping forward as though her spinal cord had contorted itself into a supine position. Her eyes were restless, wandering. When Abha came forward and held her close to her body, she began to groan softly. After the first visit she hardly noticed Sameer's presence in the room. It was strange, this deflected communication between them, with Abha as the medium. It made Sameer's job doubly difficult. The enforced proximity to Abha, the piquancy of the situation that had brought them together made him self-conscious and mildly anxious. Outside the room they could hear the dulcet chant of prayers and the faint rumblings of a distant thunderstorm. The rainy season kept the air moist and cool, and despite the sparseness of the room everything around them seemed loaded with the richness of nature's bounty. The birds chirped continuously, a joyous cadence that floated in through the window, making inroads into their consciousness.

"Good morning, Uma! See, I am here again to meet you, but I don't have much time. I have to return to Delhi soon. You have to cooperate with me, otherwise how can I help you." He spoke in a chiding, singsong voice that made Abha smile.

"You sound so pedantic, like a schoolteacher scolding a reluctant fifth-grader," she said. "I can see from her face that Uma does not believe you."

He sounded false even to himself. He was here because the events of the past few days had broken the thread of reality that strung his life together. Uma's delusions were only the tip of the iceberg; the dangerous currents lay beneath. Was Abha aware of what was going on in his mind? Why did he want to give a second burial to Belapishi? Why did he want to prove to Uma that her mother was dead? And why was it that all this – Uma's illness, his meeting with David, his feelings for Abha – was tied up inextricably with an awakened sense of rootlessness, accompanied by a knowledge that he would eventually return home? At this moment he felt the need to be here more than anywhere else in the world. And he wanted to linger on, savouring the minutes, hours, days.

Right through his growing years Belapishi had been a myth, part of adult discourse about family secrets that were best kept hidden. She had never really existed for any of them, except perhaps Grandpa and, in a way, Grandma. Her death had been a non-event in the family, and no one had quite worried for Uma. A mock burial for her seemed strangely in place, except that Uma was refusing to make it easy. "Mother lives," she repeated again and again, like a truth learnt by rote.

"No, Uma, no," Sameer said emphatically. "Your mother is not alive. She died . . . we got the telegram, don't you remember?"

"Chotoma . . ." Uma said, staring at Abha with unblinking gaze.

"Yes, yes, what about Chotoma? She gave you the news, remember?" Sameer interjected.

"Chotoma is crying . . ." Uma was responding to his voice, but her face was turned away from him.

"Yes, yes, Chotoma is crying. It is because she has heard the news. Belapishi has died. Your mother has died. Chotoma takes you to her room. She gives you the news. You remember, don't you?" He had shifted Uma to the cot, and was sitting close to her. Though he was looking directly at Uma, Sameer was acutely aware of Abha's presence. Abha was sitting on the straw mat, her face upturned, her mouth slightly open, her breath coming rapidly. He had noticed a change in her. She was more hesitant, tentative, a melancholic expression fleetingly clouding her face. He was to come to know its meaning, but somehow he had the sense of it even then.

"Chotoma is crying . . ." Uma repeated herself.

"She has started stringing words together. It is the effect of the medicines," Sameer explained to Abha. "Once the dosage can be stabilized the process of healing will be quicker."

"You notice one thing, Sameer," Abha whispered. "In Uma's memory her foster mother is continuously crying . . ."

Sameer looked startled. Foster mother had been a taboo word in the family. Grandpa never wanted Uma to feel that Chotoma was not her mother. And Chotoma had lived up to her task of bringing up the girl as her own, despite the fact that she was burdened with the knowledge that in her womb she was carrying the seeds of life. Vikram was born soon after, and it was a common sight to see Chotoma tending both her infants. If there was any sense of distinction it was never displayed. Only Grandpa shunned the girl so completely that it became a matter of concern for the rest of the household. "Why does he take out his sorrow on the child? How is she to blame?" Chotoma complained bitterly.

"The roots of Uma's denial lie somewhere else," Sameer said to Abha. "I think part of her mind knows that Belapishi is dead, that is why she says 'Chotoma is crying'. But it is her own refusal to mourn that she conveys in her next statement, 'Mother is alive.' It is the typical syndrome of a mind in conflict."

"How does the conflict resolve itself, I wonder? Is there a resolution?" Abha sounded fearful. "Do you think she is absorbing what we are saying?" Abha was suddenly quiet. The thought that Uma was listening to their conversation and registering the pain made her stop in her tracks. But Uma seemed oblivious of their presence. As the sky darkened with the approaching rain her face broke into a wide smile. She pointed to the wind whistling against the windowpane, and then she began to hum a song, "The raindrops fall, tip top, tip top, the raindrops fall . . ."

"She is trying to cope with her memories, distinguishing the ones that are painful from those that are happy," Sameer explained. "It is the twin process of acceptance and rejection. We do it so easily all the time, we hardly realise how difficult it can be."

"Does the resolution lie in rejecting the painful memories?' Abha queried.

"No, I think it is in accepting the happy ones," Sameer replied quietly. Abha averted her eyes for she did not want Sameer to see the rush of tears that was in danger of spilling over her cheeks. "We make our choices whether we like it or not. Sometimes choices are thrust upon us. I think Uma's denial is her refusal to be constricted by choices."

"Then why cure her?" Abha asked forcefully.

Sameer did not answer. He moved towards the window and pushed it open. A fine spray of raindrops fell on his hand and trickled down his elbow like a rivulet. A gust of wind swamped them. He turned to Uma and he said in a voice that was slightly high-pitched, "I think you remember how the rains came on the day your mother's death was announced. Chotoma was crying because she found it difficult to convey the news to a poor, motherless child. Grandma was muttering something about the unfairness of fate. We were only worried for you, Uma. But you took in the news without a whimper. Next day you went to school, you ate your meals and you played as usual. Chotoma stopped crying then. She said, 'How can the death of an absent mother matter to a child? It is better this way. What has Bela done for the child anyway?' I think she feared the worst – that all her pains of showering you with love would come to naught. Why did you choose to leave us, Uma, why did you? Chotoma has never stopped crying since then. I think you know that as well.

'Mother lives,' you keep saying. Is that what you really believe? You remember the blinding rain, and Baba's car inching through the driveway carrying Grandpa's inert body; and the vegetable-like existence of the remaining days of his life; his wasted, shrunken limbs that one could cradle in one arm by the time he died. He knew for sure that your mother was dead. You know that so well, Uma. You do . . . You know too much, more than you can bear."

By the time Sameer had finished speaking, his voice was muffled by the tearing rain. Both Sameer and Abha knew that Uma was listening, for a shadow crept across her smile like a wayward cloud covering the path of the sun. A knock on the door broke Abha's reverie. It was one of the inmates of the ashram announcing that time was up. "There is a phone call for you, Abhadidi. I have kept the call waiting."

When Abha came back after attending to the call she sounded distracted. "It is David. He wants to meet us urgently at his place. He has some positive news about arrangements for the funeral rites."

~~~

They reached David's house by wading their way through a half-flooded city. The streets were stinking with piled-up garbage floating freely in the swirling water. The rickshaw pullers were standing idly on the pavements, puffing at their bidis. They had hiked their rates so much that irate customers were turning away in disgust. The bus was crowded, spilling over with people. Normally Sameer felt impatient with the city's lack of civic amenities. But today he was in no mood to grumble. Everything seemed strangely inconsequential. Ever since Abha had received David's phone call she was preoccupied and distant. They had not exchanged a single sentence since they left the ashram.

"Why did you ask me to marry Vandana?" Sameer spoke at last.

"Why?" she shot back, the spark of fire igniting in her eyes. "So you feel it was a choice thrust upon you, is that it? No, man, it was a choice you would have made anyway."

"What do you know about me?" He was sounding bitter despite himself. These quick outbursts were becoming too frequent between them. "Anyway, you have not answered my question."

"I am not obliged to answer you, not now, not here in the middle of the road," she retorted, but he could sense the confusion in her. "Why are we discussing all this? It is not fair to Vandana or to—"

"Yes, it is not fair, but we are accountable for all that we do. It is only places like the ashram which permit you to make choices without the necessary obligations. It encourages denial of the kind that Uma is suffering from. Its walls cocoon you from the outside world and keep you safe from its pressures."

"No, don't say that, Sameer. Uma is torn apart by pressures. She is not safe inside the four walls, though I think she chose to enter the ashram because she needed a refuge."

"A refuge from what?" Sameer almost shouted, and then, suddenly conscious of the people around them, he lowered his voice to a tight whisper. "Was there anything that we did not give her? Grandma and Chotoma doted on her to the point of distraction. If anyone was neglected it was Vikram, and as for me I was the eldest, called upon to give up everything at the drop of a hat. Yes, that is me!"

"You don't give that impression," Abha spoke more gently. "If anything you are the one who chose to stay away from the family business. You have always made your own decisions. In fact, I get the sense that it is your absence that corrodes every brick of that big, rambling house in which you were born."

"I have been away physically, but I carry the burden of the family on my shoulders. I am tired, Abha, tired." He sounded spent, dejected.

Abha was afraid. She wondered why the conversation had taken this direction. She did not want to touch the core of his life where his commitment to Vandana was preserved. Nothing should dislodge that, she felt.

"You are tired because you are worrying for Uma," she said cheerily. "It will pass soon. Besides, you have nothing to complain about. Your life is poised for good things to happen. Maybe this tiredness is the effect of the city. You know how its crumbling exterior gets at you, but there is solace deep in its core. David says he can bring to the ghats of Varanasi his darkest musings and feel the spirit getting lighter and lighter. David often tells me that he discovered mirth in this city. What an odd thing to say, Sameer? Sorry, never realised that shrinks needed counselling as well."

He was watching her closely, and he noticed how the mention of David's name brightened her face and made her strides more purposeful. He felt a twinge of envy, a passing irrational mood. Once inside the house she slipped into the kitchen and began chopping onions. David was making lunch for them. "Sambar and rice," he said, stirring the ladle vigorously. Sameer thought of the elaborate meals being prepared at home and remembered his mother grumbling, "Three days in a row and you have not eaten at home, why bother to cook at all?"

They sat on the floor in a semicircle with the food laid out in the middle. David broached the subject. "In the course of my research I have made many friends, informants really, who provide me with access to places. And, you know, Varanasi is crowded with places that are out of bounds for foreigners. I know a fellow, a ghatiya at the Kedara Ghat who has promised to help me. He brought in some interesting news today. He has met a family looking for cheap lodging in the city. The old man is dying, and he has been brought into the precincts of the sacred zone so that he can breathe his last in peace. Seeking a way out of this deadly circle of rebirth! At this moment he is lying under the open sky at the Manikarnika Ghat. The stray dogs keep him company."

Abha shuddered. "There should be some law preventing the living from being left behind in the cremation ground. What an awful thought!"

"Well, Varanasi prides itself on being the only city in the world that has the traditionally polluting spots, the cremation grounds, in the very centre of the city. Polluted and sacred nestle together. Your eyes must seek out what they want. I know how you feel, Abha. But who do you blame? This family has left a dying member at the shamshan ghat without a twinge of conscience. As far as they are concerned they are fulfilling a pious duty," David said.

"This lack of accountability gets my goat," Sameer said angrily. "An entire city can shift the blame for all that is going wrong onto something vague like . . . what did you say? 'Polluted and sacred nestling together.' Humbug! This dying man should be in hospital!"

"Hospital? Prolong the misery of his life? What for?" Abha intervened.

"I am tired of these discussions," Sameer snapped back. "Let's get down to brass tacks. What did you say about this man needing help? Where do we come in?"

"The family is eager to embark on the Avimukta yatra.

They need a sponsor; in return we have the freedom to take over the body once the man dies. They will make no claims on his ashes or his bones. His body will undergo the last rites of someone abandoned. You see, once they deposit him in the sacred zone their own presence or participation becomes redundant. He is outside the threshold so to speak: the same way in which corpses are kept on the floor in a corner of the room. It literally means the dead man no longer belongs to the house and is ready to commence his last journey. I spoke to the other family members, the old man's younger brother, and his two sisters. I could not meet the old man's wife. She is eager for the family to perform the yatra, for these were her husband's last wishes. I gather the couple have no children."

"Can't be his last wishes if he is still alive. What prevents him from changing his mind?" Sameer sounded sceptical.

"He is in a comatose state," David explained.

"Oh, I see! It actually means he is in no position to make a last wish. How long has he been ill? What about his widow . . . well . . . almost. Did you get her opinion, directly I mean?"

"She is speaking to no one. Her husband's brother is doing all the negotiating," said David. "All they are looking for is financial assistance. You know the Avimukta yatra, it is the less popular pilgrimage that begins at Avimuktesvara and crosses seventy-two shrines. Avimukta is the sacred area that preserves Shiva's consciousness. It is said that Shiva did not leave this spot even at the time of dissolution. This is not the best time of the year to undergo this yatra, yet the one who carries it through is liberated from transmigration. Awesome, isn't it?"

Both Abha and Sameer paid little attention to David's

long-winded explanations. They saw Varanasi with jaded eyes, and only rarely found this kind of abstract view fascinating. "But how do we use all this to cure Uma?" asked Abha in a concerned way.

"It is like this," Sameer explained. "I am doing this on an experimental basis but I think it could have a proper long-term effect. What Uma needs to do is relive the entire experience of hearing about Belapishi's death. When I say 'relive', I mean the news has to be broken to her in such a way that she understands it as a reality. You see, when the actual news was given to her many years back, she was a child who had to be protected from the grim reality of the situation. Everything about Belapishi has been so hush-hush in our family that we had kept her mother away from her. Now the time has come to bring Belapishi back, even though it means snatching her away once again."

"I hope you are doing right, Sameer," Abha said fearfully. "What if she cannot bear the thought of her mother dying? What if reality is too much for her?"

"That is precisely the reason why we need to recreate the rituals that accompany a funeral. Sometimes, rituals act as buffer for the human mind. The return from the cremation ground, the carrying into the house of the ashes, the final consecration into the holy river: these are all means of coping. If Uma witnesses the entire family participating in the rituals, it would give her a sense of being part of something that involves everyone else. Simply telling her that her mother is dead is to isolate her and make her bear the cross of grief all alone. Funerals are collective occasions, when the individual feels at one with the community."

"Ah, the meaning of 'Avimukta' is Never-Forsaken," David mused. "They say the one who completes the yatra

can commune with Shiva's consciousness, his love for life
and matter. There is no forsaking of love that accompanies
the liberation from the thrall of re-birth. Strange paradox, is
it not?"

"I tried convincing Ma and Baba that since we did have
one funeral in the house and some peripheral ceremonies
were still left for Grandma, we could pretend that the rites
were meant for Belapishi," Sameer continued, "but they
refused to comply. It would harm Grandma's soul, they said.
I don't agree. Grandma would do anything for Uma, even
jeopardise her soul. But you know how some matters are
closed for any further discussion. So I thought we would
need to recreate Belapishi's funeral."

"I can bring Uma here on some pretext," David suggested.
"Maybe some tests to be done at the hospital. They allow the
family to take out the ashramite for a few hours in such cases."

"I will tell you when," Sameer added. "You and Abha
will have to bring her home. Maybe I can take her to the
cremation ghat and get her to see the pyre burning."

"In an orthodox set-up a woman is not permitted to visit
the cremation ground," Abha retorted. "The priest would
take it amiss."

"We can keep her at a distance, "Sameer said. "Who
would know anyway? Remember the whole thing is like an
elaborate pretence. She witnesses the burning of a stranger.
To me this is a medical ruse like getting children to swallow
bitter pills with sugar coatings. It is well within our work
ethics, so no guilt feelings. Religious feelings? At this
moment I find it difficult to muster up any feelings at all!"

He smiled wanly but something close to hysteria was
building up inside him. He felt it as mirth rising like bile on
an empty stomach. Abha was sitting in front of him, her face

solemn and funereal. David scooped up a spoonful of sambar and twirled it in his mouth.

"So what do we do next?" Abha asked.

"Wait for the corpse, I guess," David replied.

Sameer felt the laughter spluttering inside him, ready to burst like a volcano. Abha choked, the food spilling out from her mouth, spraying Sameer's shirt. She dashed into the bathroom. He followed her. They were laughing helplessly. She scooped up water in her palm and began scrubbing his shirt. "I am so sorry," she said hooting with laughter. He could feel her breath on his face. He held her upturned arm and pinned her against the wall, using the weight of his body. His face, shining with mirth, inched forward until his lips brushed against her cheek. Then he deflected it slightly and brought it close to her ears. "Thank you for helping me see through this ridiculous plot," he whispered. He could not see her face for the upper part of his body was pressed against hers, flattening her chest until it ached, making her heart thud painfully.

~~~

The old man obliged the Sengupta family by dying quickly in the early hours of the morning. As soon as David got the news he rang up Sameer. "We will have to wait a while before we can take Uma out of the ashram. They are strict about timing. Will you be sending the car, Sameer?"

"Yes," Sameer replied. "It is important that Uma is in touch with things she is familiar with. Our old Fiat is one of them. We used to travel in it for all our family outings. It's in perfect running condition thanks to my father."

Abha came to the phone. "Hello, Sameer, good morning. I am getting ready right away and going over to the ashram. What about you? Will you be coming over?"

"Later," he said sharply. "I need to take care of things at

this end. The family will have to be mentally prepared to meet Uma. You see, it is the first time that she will be returning home since she joined the ashram as a full-time inmate. They know about her ailment, but they do not understand it fully. Chotoma particularly, her heart would be crushed."

"I understand," Abha said softly. "I thought you might need us early in the morning, so I stayed the night over at David's."

As he put down the phone he noticed that his hands were shaking slightly. Calm down man, he told himself firmly. He thought of Abha with an overwhelming sense of loneliness. He moved out to the verandah and sat down heavily on Grandpa's reclining chair. Soon his mother would arrive with the morning cup of tea. Nothing changes in this house, thought Sameer. Its rituals remain intact though people come and go. His eyes wandered across the length of the corridor and the outline of the rooms behind. He had heard from his mother how Grandpa had built this house after sinking in almost all his savings. The piece of land was inherited, including a small built-up portion where he brought Grandma soon after their marriage. Grandma spoke of this house with a great deal of pride. "You should have seen it then," she would say, her eyes twinkling. "It looked like a jungle with weeds growing right up to your knees. 'Is this what your father has left you?' I used to chide your grandfather? But he built it brick by brick. 'Why so many rooms?' I asked him. But he felt a house must harbour generations."

Sameer could sense the emptiness of the house. He understood why Chotoma and his mother often grumbled about its vastness, the numerous rooms, the long stretch of verandah, the majestic columns and the reverberating silence of its walls. "Who will be there to look after all this once we die?" his mother said ruefully. "It will crumble to pieces from sheer disuse." Sameer remembered Abha's earlier remark, 'It is your absence that corrodes every brick of this house.' Is it really true, he wondered? Do houses mourn the dead and the gone? He stared at the room in the corner, the one that had been taboo for so long, the one that contained deadly secrets in its bosom.

His mother came out of her room and sat next to him. He could sense her tension, and he knew that much of it centred round him. He had been elusive this time, staying away from home most days. Though she understood the seriousness of the task he was handling, she felt uneasy about his regular association with David. Abha she did not worry about. "Vandana rang up yesterday. She was asking me when you were likely to return to Delhi. I was not able to give her a clear answer."

His mother had this strange way of voicing her complaints in a reasonable tone. It felt oppressive. "You know, Ma, as much as I do, that I cannot give a clear answer myself. So much of it depends on what happens today. I am not expecting any miracles, but if she can absorb today's events then the recovery will come sooner or later. I can then modify the course of medicines. I need your help, yours and Chotoma's."

"But who looks after her once you have left?" his mother asked.

"Abha and David," Sameer answered promptly. "Uma trusts them, and they have access to the ashram."

"Can't we bring her home, however temporarily?"

"No, Ma, Uma has renounced the world. Her life begins and ends in the ashram."

He made it sound normal but he sensed the agitation in his mother's voice, "Don't say that. It doesn't bring luck."

And then pausing a little, she added meaningfully, "I have not mentioned anything about David to Vandana. It is best for both of you that the past remains buried." He felt grateful then for her intuitive understanding, though he did not miss the gentle disapproval in her tone. He sipped his cup of tea and wondered whether Abha had left for the ashram. He thought of her in David's one-roomed apartment, in that tiny bathroom, her body plastered against the wall, her breath coming unevenly. The image had haunted him through the night, and now, in the bland daylight, it jarred his thoughts like fingernails being drawn down a wall. He shivered.

David's phone call came soon after. "I will go to the ghat and oversee the cremation. They burn the abandoned body quickly, without much fanfare. The ashes are only ready the next day, but I will see what I can muster up. What else do you need?"

"I am not in such a hurry," Sameer replied. "These things can take their time. The important thing is Uma's return home, how she reacts to the familiar environment, does it trigger off any memories?"

"I understand," said David. "That is why I think it is better you go to fetch Uma from the ashram. You can explain matters to Swamiji, and get at least a few hours permission for Uma. Abha has already left. She said she would pick up some breakfast on the way."

"I cannot thank you enough, David," Sameer said, a flood of gratitude sweeping through his body. He was up in a shot and getting ready.

They were not able to get Uma's release until well past

noon. Too many formalities had to be completed, and Uma herself seemed very quiet and withdrawn. "She has slept fitfully," Abha said to Sameer. "I think it is better this way. It will make her rested."

"Let us not hurry her up," Sameer agreed, "otherwise she will sense something is wrong." Soon another inmate from the ashram came to take Uma away. "She has to go for her meditation classes," the girl announced. Sameer noticed how young she was. "Abhadidi, can both of you leave the room. I need to get Uma ready. Swamiji says once her meditation is over, Uma can leave with you."

They went down the stairs into the undulating stretch of open fields. The rains had made the ground soggy, and clumps of red mud crumbled under their bare feet. At a distance they saw a raised platform made of brick and mortar. They moved towards it. Sameer realised that it was a cement water tank dug into the ground.

"A kund," said Abha. "Have you ever bathed in one of the larger kunds? The water is deliciously warm and soothing. If David were here he would tell you the significance of these kunds, how Varanasi used to be our very own Venice with waterways criss-crossing through the city. Most of them have dried up or flow underground; these kunds are natural and some have been here forever."

They sat on its edge, Sameer wriggling his toes to dislodge the clods of mud. The sky had cleared up, and the sharp rays of the sun made his skin tingle and burn. The trees were heavy with the moisture of last night's rain and thunderstorm. Leaves were strewn on the ground, and branches lay where they had fallen, like a woman's clothes after a night of passion.

"It is strange how Belapishi revisits our family again and

again. The more we have tried to brush her under the carpet, the more difficult it has been to forget her. I can see my family suffering greatly today. For them every step of the remembering is painful."

"Uma is her living link," Abha interrupted him, "and as long as Uma is there you can hardly wish away Belapishi."

"You know, Abha," Sameer continued, "when I was younger I had no sense of blood relations. To me Uma was the closest thing that belonged to me. I first greeted her with as much curiosity as children welcome a pet in the family. She was pink, alive and crying. Later she never cried, only laughed a great deal. I never experienced sibling rivalry with her. Neither did Vikram. We loved her unconditionally. Belapishi did not matter to us; she was as remote as the myriad characters in Grandma's religious texts. I must admit, though, that through my growing years Belapishi fascinated me. Her moral turpitude and its impact on Grandpa had cast such a shadow on our family that I always thought of her with resentment."

"And today, what do you feel?

"Only a great, yawning empty space, as though morality is a blank category. I feel neither anger nor resentment nor fascination for Belapishi. She is just a link in the chain of loving and losing that has to be restored for Uma. Once that happens, normalcy will return to Uma."

"We better go back," Abha said.

Uma had changed into her outdoor clothes, a white sari with a pale blue border. Inside the car she reached out and held Sameer's hand. He squeezed it lightly. It felt soft and cold. He noticed that she was not looking out of the window at the passing scenery. Her attention was turned inwards as though she was still meditating. But her face glowed, the skin luminous and white. 'She looks like a precious commodity that has just been unwrapped from its outer cover, something unexposed to the lightest of touch,' Sameer thought. 'Can I bear to see the pain of understanding dawn on her face?'

The family was there on the front portal, Uma behind him as usual. The tears flowed uninterrupted from Chotoma's face. "Tush," said Sameer's mother, "help me get the girl inside." Abha moved away and sat in the drawing room. She felt nervous. The servants joined her, peering in from the room outside. They were weeping openly like children.

"Dadabhai, where is Grandma?" Uma asked, her first complete sentence in many months. The elders looked at each other with a fearful glance. Sameer drew Uma into the inner room and pointed at grandma's large photograph with the marigold garland strung around it, and the thick incense floating like wisps of cloud in front of it. "Uma, Grandma died a few weeks back. She died in her sleep, peacefully."

"Grandma died?" Uma's face began to buckle in under the pressure of her emotions. She staggered a bit, sending the elders swooping forward. Sameer held out his hand to keep them away. "Come, I will take you to Grandma's room," he said leading her by the hand. As she mounted the stairs she began disengaging herself from his grasp. Sameer moved away, signalling the family to remain at a distance.

For the next half an hour Uma moved from room to room like an animal frisking aimlessly in its natural habitat. She picked up things lying strewn in her path, held them briefly in her hand, and then restored them gently back in their places. It was only in Grandma's room that she began to croon so inaudibly that Sameer thought he was imagining the sound. He held his breath, not quite knowing what to do next. Chotoma began to sniffle loudly, the storm breaking in her heart. It was the saddest sound that Sameer had heard, and it filled the room like the unendurable wail that accompanies the knowledge of pain.

Uma turned to Chotoma, her eyes lucid. "No, Chotoma, don't cry," she said. "It is all right. I knew all along that Grandma was lying. After the telegram came, I asked Grandma if mother would ever come home again. Grandma said, 'Over my dead body.' When I asked her whether mother's soul would haunt us then, she said, 'It will rot in hell along with her body. We will throw her body into the river and leave it for water rats and vermins to chew.' I knew she was lying, Chotoma."

Sameer came forward and held Uma's hand. When he spoke his voice was loud and firm, "Do not worry, Uma, we will bring Belapishi's ashes home. Then we will consecrate them in the river. Your mother's soul will rest in peace now."

~~~

After the ashes were strewn in the river, David and Sameer made their way home. "Strange isn't it, David," Sameer said in a sad voice, "how ashes are devoid of all individuality? How does it matter whose ashes we have thrown into the river today? For Uma her memories have been cleansed. Now she can talk of Belapishi in the past tense." Sameer wanted to tell him that he was experiencing the miracle of give and take between perfect strangers. Suddenly the abandoned corpse acquired an identity, and he felt a curious gratitude towards everyone, especially David.

Late at night the phone rang again. He moved quickly towards it, knowing it would be Vandana. He had to give her the news that he was starting for Delhi the very next day. It was Abha. The secret knowledge of her love seared his breast, making him pant. "I have some strange news to give you,' she said, a little breathlessly. "When is your train tomorrow? Can you come and meet David in the morning?"

Abha made him wait outside David's door. "Please Sameer, you need to hear this before you go in. There is a woman sitting inside. She is the old man's wife . . . the widow. The rest of the family has disappeared, abandoning her in Varanasi. She refuses to go out and search for them. She says it will kill her. She does not want to have anything to do with them or her past life. Please listen: I can talk to Swamiji and get her a room in the ashram. They do have a wing for destitute and abandoned women."

"You better do it quickly." Sameer looked blank. "You cannot keep her here. Have the police been informed? An old lady, abandoned . . ."

"She is not old, maybe not a day older than twenty five or so. . . . I do not know under what circumstances she was married off to a man old enough to be her father. . . . She has been a school teacher . . ."

Sameer was to remember his first glimpse of Romola as vividly as though it was coloured in his mind with a painter's brush. Her eyes were large and eloquent, her forehead narrow with lustrous eyebrows. Her hair, raven black, was dusty with grime and soot from the burning ghats. But her face, her clear skin and the well-etched contours of her nose and mouth suggested the fullness of youth. She radiated an intelligence of spirit that took his breath away. But she looked so ephemeral and unreal that Sameer felt as though she would rise any minute and take her leave, and walk out through the door never to be seen again.

Looking back on that day, Sameer felt he knew then what the future held for them. He knew that Romola and Uma would become inseparable, that Uma's recovery would hinge upon this stranger's presence, and that Romola would give birth to Avinash just around the time Vandana was going into labour and bringing forth his daughter into the world. And he knew that David would choose to leave India, and that Romola would carry a plate full of offerings and disappear into the lap of the river. He knew, then, that not everyone chooses a life of compromise as David would have liked him to believe.

"Please understand why I had to keep this terrible knowledge from you,' Sameer begged Vandana. "I did not want its shadow to cross your path or come in the way of your happiness. I was thinking of the children."

"Whose son is Avinash, Sameer?" Vandana asked, her hands moving rapidly across her face, as though she was chasing away traces of a bad dream. Outside, the night was dark and, as usual, the Delhi skyline did not show a single star. A truck rumbled its way through the quiet colony, breaking its equanimity.

Anandavana,
the Garden of Bliss

CHAPTER SEVEN

A Visitor

"Psssst . . . are you awake? It's me."

It was becoming a sort of routine for Mira to wake up early in the morning and make her way downstairs, pausing at the landing to check whether her parents were still in bed. Once she slipped into Avinash's room she felt at ease. She knew she would find him curled on his stomach on the floor, his chin tucked under the crook of his arm, his eyes shut, and the mouth slightly parted as though he was breathing laboriously. She knew that he was waiting for her.

That day when she did not find him on the floor she let out a little yelp. She felt a sharp blow at the pit of her stomach making her breath come out in spasms. It was part of her recurring nightmare that she would get up one morning and discover that Avinash was gone. Then she caught sight of him under the bed. He had obviously rolled over. She knelt down, peering into the cave with tears of relief streaking down her face. She crawled in under the bed holding him tight. His face was wet with the sweat of a hot summer night. She noticed that he had not switched on the fan, and as usual his austerity moved her deeply, as though he was denying himself the basic needs of life. She always wanted to replace it with her infinite caring. The oppressive heat made her nightclothes damp and clammy. In one swift move she took off her pyjamas and lay there in her shirt and panties. He watched her intently, his eyes solemn. She was laughing now, a soft laughter that echoed inside the hollow of the bed.

"Did you have your bad dreams again?" she asked gently.

He was learning Bengali and spoke it with a quaint lisp that held in its folds a string of mismatched words. It made Mira alert. She helped him get the nuances of words like a tutor chiding a slow learner, and he half listened with his attention wandering here and there.

But today he sounded tense when he said, "yes" in a small voice.

"You can tell me your dreams if you want, Avinash," Mira muttered gravely, using the tact that she noticed her father used increasingly with her mother.

"I don't know," said Avinash in a small voice, but he turned to face her and put his arms around her. Mira felt safe under the bed away from prying eyes. She noticed how Vandana too sought her own safe corners and sat there all alone, deep in thoughts. She tried asking Abhishek about it, but he was too involved with his approaching exams to really care. Sameer too seemed preoccupied, talking non-stop on the phone or busy tapping away on the computer. Mira felt reckless, floating on a thin cloud of unmediated emotions that kept her nervous, yet excited.

"Are you thinking about your mother again?" Mira asked.

She knew that this question would elicit an instant response from Avinash. "No, I was not thinking about her." But today he said something different that startled her.

Avinash had spent the night thinking about his mother. But his memory of her was hazy as though she existed in a dream. In his dreams she was dressed in the mandatory white sari with blue border, which was the uniform worn in the ashram. But inside the room she often removed her blouse and wrapped the sari tightly around her small breasts. Her skin was firm and smooth and white, without blemishes, and he had memories of her feet, small and compact and bare on the hard, cold floor. He remembered her hair, cut closely near the nape of her neck. He could hear her voice like the metallic timbre of brass utensils clanging inside the temple. And sometimes, only sometimes, he heard her sobbing, like a forlorn animal mewling in the night.

The memory of the sound frightened him. At such times he felt the urge to run upstairs to Vandana's bedroom and enter its secluded space, and stand next to her armchair with his legs pressed against its side. He knew that she would look at him and smile and say in her usual inquiring tone, "What is it, Avinash?" Then she would run her fingers on the frayed edges of his shirtsleeves making his skin crawl. "Have you brushed your teeth and washed your face, son?" Avinash wanted to climb into bed by her side as Mira often did, but a certain shyness kept him waiting at a distance. Later, he would return to his room, measuring the distance with the fast receding echo of his own footsteps on the stairs. The only other sound that he could hear was the music system playing inside Abhishek and Mira's room. He rarely went in there.

That night the images were indistinct, fading into a kind of never-ending spiral. Even the sound of his mother's voice was muffled, as if it was coming to him from a great distance. And yet he felt a strange urgency to make sense of the images that were floating in front of his eyes. He stirred in his sleep in a state of half-wakefulness. But soon he was sitting up for he had heard another sound, soft and stealthy, coming from the direction of the drawing room. He stared at the darkness around him, thick and speckled with the fine dust-haze of light filtering through the open skylight in his room. The light flickered, merging with the darkness, and he felt he could stretch out his hand and touch its bottomless pit. Fear gnawed at him, making him shiver slightly, though the night was hot and oppressive.

He was not aware of when he had left the room, or the direction in which he was moving. His feet were hurting, for the hot sun on the terrace had bleached them until they felt sore. In his dreams he often dragged his feet, particularly at the point when he was going to uncover something startling. He would wake up then and pull in his feet until they curled up near the pit of his stomach. The sound was becoming more and more distinct, and there was something familiar about it that distressed him.

He was inside the drawing room, and though the thick curtains were drawn across the entire stretch of the tall bay windows, the room was suffused in a glow of warm, translucent light. It glistened on the floor like a mirage in which he could see clumps of dark shadows. He sensed a presence, and then his eyes caught something that made him draw in his breath sharply. His mother was there, and she seemed to be floating gently, like a bright, shimmering object that skimmed over the surface of things. The tight knot of fear uncurled from his chest, and he felt his heart beat becoming slower and gentler, until a wave of happiness swept through his limbs. Her face was still hidden from view, but a jab of light fell across his feet, holding his attention.

"Maji," he called out, using the formal etiquette that he was taught at the ashram, "you have come back." Relationships were always formal there; there was a code of conduct that nobody was permitted to break. Because Avinash was born inside the four walls of the ashram he was its natural inmate. Everyone was taken to be his elder and guardian and no one could claim extra affection for him.

"Yes, beta." she whispered. He knew she was smiling, but it was not something that he could detect or touch or feel.

The object was moving away from him, swaying gently like shimmering, disintegrating light. He stood rooted to the ground, not knowing whether he should move forward or continue to stand still. There was something ethereal about the figure, and he felt the room dissolving around him. Something touched him, like vapours rising out of mist. It fell in a spray on his face, shoulders and neck, tickling him. The faint rumble of water pressed against his eardrums, making them ache. He wanted to cry out then and reach for her, but she was sliding away, the bright flash of light streaking away rapidly from the range of vision.

The room was back in focus. It was dark but familiar. He sank heavily on the floor, drained of all emotion, except for the niggling sense that a happy moment had eluded him. He realised then that the memory of his mother contained this ever-increasing sense of emptiness, of something vital and nourishing abandoning him. He shut his eyes tight and tried to concentrate. Breathe in, breathe out, he recited lines from the exercise regime that he was taught at the ashram, getting himself into a yogic posture. He felt the undulating rhythm of his heartbeat falling into a regular pattern, his mind going blank and the sound of the river receding into the background.

He opened his eyes, not aware of how much time had gone by. He allowed his mind to adjust to the setting of the room. He had left the images behind, and with almost a sense of relief he found himself back in the familiar surroundings. He could see the sofas and the center table, the wooden bookstand with its array of old and new books, curios and expensive electrical gadgets. In one corner of the room was a writing bureau with photographs laid out in a row on top, and a crystal vase in which Vandana arranged her favourite flowers. The walls were decorated with paintings and mounted wall hangings. It gave the place a muted feel of ceremonies that were over and done with. There were indoor plants with large, green, looping branches and hanging leaves in delicate, ornate patterns. A Persian carpet was laid on the floor, and next to it were terracotta figurines of Ganesh and his divine consorts. They looked ghoulish in the half-light, like menacing life energy arrested in stone and metal form.

Avinash's eyes were wandering elsewhere to detect the source of the sound that he had heard earlier. And then he saw her. She was sitting at the writing bureau. She held some papers in front of her eyes, but her body was stretched rigidly against the back of the chair, as though her attention was fixed on a vacant spot in the far corner of the ceiling. The concentrated light of the reading lamp threw a large, jagged shadow against the wall, enveloping her face, neck and hair in its fold. She was so still that Avinash wondered whether she had transformed herself into one of the stone idols standing on the floor next to the carpet. But then he heard a low moaning, and a wave of shock sent its signal through his body. He felt his bones rattle, and the harsh, grating squeak hit the walls and resounded across every bare surface of the room.

Vandana turned and stared at him. Her face was wet with

tears. And then, as in his dreams, she averted her glance and looked away, as though she was willing his non-existence.

He was sitting upright on the floor, his face close to Mira's, his pupils dilated and burning like melting fire. A feeling of deprivation weighed him down. It was a burden that he had to bear all by himself, and could not share with her. For once Mira looked withdrawn, as though she was trying to make sense of his narrative. She looked stricken.

"What was Ma doing downstairs in the middle of the night?" Mira asked incredulously. "Maybe you were dreaming. And you saw her crying? I have never seen Ma cry!"

Avinash's account of his dreams stopped there. He did not have the words to explore it further. Mira too felt the need to be discreet. Somehow the recent turn of events was beyond her grasp. "Guess what," she said, changing the topic quickly, "one of Ma's old friends is coming to visit us next week. He is an Englishman. His name is David. He lived in Varanasi many years back, when Ma was still a student."

Avinash looked intently at the girl, as though he was trying to make sense of what she was saying. He shook his head in disbelief. He tried to recollect bit by bit the vision that he had had, but it seemed totally out of place in the pale daylight that enveloped the room. He noticed how keenly Mira was watching him. And that intent, anxious look reminded him of Vandana. In a rush of feeling he stretched out his hand and touched her mouth and chin. She smiled mysteriously, and suddenly for Avinash the elusive smile that had deserted him the night before, seemed to emerge from nowhere and brush lightly against the edges of his conscious, waking self.

~~~

David's plane arrived at the international airport soon after midnight, but by the time the formalities were over and he and Sameer found themselves outside the terminal getting into the car, the first streaks of a new day had begun to light up the city. The arching streetlights were silhouetted against a dull, blue-black sky. The air was balmy and a quick breeze dispersed the slightly foggy, metallic smell that clung to David from the long hours he had spent cooped inside the aircraft. He stretched out his limbs and the two men embraced, the joy of reunion making them dispel any tiredness they might feel from the long wait.

"Boy, oh boy," David cried out energetically, "a fleeting time, and we are back together! I have dreamt of this moment, Sameer. I have really!"

Sameer was laughing, for this was David of yore – except that a decade spent in a British university had given him a different exterior. For instance, he noticed that David was wearing blue flannel trousers and a pinstriped shirt with long sleeves that were held by a pair of cuff links. He wore trendy sports shoes, and his luggage was large and heavy. Sameer remembered the dowdy brown and orange rucksack that used to be David's only bag, and smiled meaningfully.

"I know what you are thinking," David said heartily. "Has my friend settled down to gentility, to a life of routine? Has he discarded his Varanasi obsession? Given up the Ganga, given up his passions? The answer, Sameer, is yes and no. We will talk about it later. Tell me more about yourself."

"I must admit you surprise me." Sameer refused to change the topic and draw attention away from David. "You seem different in a way that I cannot pinpoint. You have not said a word about Avinash . . ."

"Or Vandana, or Romola or Uma or Abha . . . you have

noticed that as well. Honestly, Sameer, what are you expecting of me?" Sameer looked steadily at the traffic, which was surprisingly heavy near the airport. They were moving in a crawl and the occasional honk from a passing tempo and truck was making him jam on the brakes, throwing them forward. They slipped under the huge overhead hoarding announcing the city limits. Then they moved into the vortex of the city, the streets somnolent and friendly, the houses huddled together like spirits in the dark and the trees trapped on the pavements shaking in unison.

"I have spoken to Vandana, told her all that I could." Sameer spoke cautiously, the tension making him sweat under his armpit. He felt the heat rising from the tarred roads and the brick inlay of the city. Even the sky seemed to hang heavily outside the open window of the car, the luke-warm gusts of air whistling against his ears. David turned to look at Sameer for the first time. His green-mottled eyes were wide with surprise and, in the depths, something else, perhaps fear or pain. In an instant Sameer saw the past uncoiling, bringing into their lives vast reservoirs of all that had remained dormant. Nothing really changes, he thought hopelessly, despite our pathetic efforts to the contrary, nothing changes. As he manoeuvred the car into the garage he saw Mrs Chopra prise open her bedroom curtains, and he saw the house coming to life as the light came on in Vandana's room, and he heard the sound of doors creaking open.

"I asked Sameer not to wake any of you," David said in a whisper. "We could have met properly in the morning."

"I have made your room ready," Vandana whispered back. "You can go off to sleep and get rid of the jet lag. We will meet later."

Once in the guestroom David stripped off his clothes and wrapped himself in a soft, cotton dressing gown. The snugness of the room held him in tight embrace, melting away the sense of alienation in a new place. Sleep tugged at his eyelids but his mind felt as though it was bursting to the brim. He switched on the night lamp, allowing its bright, pointed light to throw the rest of the room into deep, dark shadows. He knit his eyebrows trying to concentrate. At one point Vandana knocked at the door and came in to leave a bottle of water and empty glass. "Goodnight," she said archly, a tiny laughter breaking out like a spasm in her chest. Her face was playful, tender. He noticed with a slight sense of wonder that she was naked under the thin fabric of her nightdress. Her breasts were taut and rounded and her stomach flat, though it moved gently, as though she were taking quick, deep breaths. She stood with her legs slightly apart, and he could see that they were shapely and strong. He opened the bottle of water and bringing the lid to his lips gulped the water down and allowed it to splay down his chest and torso.

~~~

When David awoke he was surprised to hear how quiet the house was. The children had left for school and Vandana had gone to the dispensary as usual. Only Sameer had taken the day off. The two men sat on the verandah adjacent to the master bedroom. A fibreglass awning kept the harsh glint of sunlight at bay and a low fan droned continuously. Vandana had decorated the place with her potted plants, and the little bit of greenery added to the charm of a space that was secluded and yet overlooked a busy neighbourhood. David felt rested and calmer than he had the night before.

Sitting at the Burmese table across from Sameer, sipping

his cup of coffee, David realized how little he had really been prepared for this visit to India. He was aware that Sameer was giving him keen looks, demanding an explanation if possible, and he knew equally well that his thoughts were in a muddle. He had to move with the tide, allowing the course of events to take shape. And then the question slipped out almost casually, though Sameer knew what had prompted it, "Do you and Vandana have any plans for Avinash?"

"Listen David, I have not discussed the future with Vandana," Sameer said in a low voice, "she is presently very distraught and tense. I have told her that this is only a temporary arrangement. I am waiting for further communication from Abha . . ." Sameer watched the Matador cruise into the lane and stop in front of their gate. The children were trooping out one by one. Avinash was holding his school bag and waving at the lady who was minding them. He had grown tall and lanky, and his close crop of hair fitted his head like a woolly cap. But there was something diffident about his posture, as though he was part of a jigsaw puzzle in which a vital clue was missing. He turned briefly to look at the men, and perhaps the novelty of their presence made him avert his eyes a little shyly. As usual Shantabai was there to see him into the house.

"Avinash," David murmured the name quietly, but it hung in the air like a question mark. He was rooted to the spot. The coffee cup was suspended in his hand, and he looked awkwardly inelegant. Sameer noticed for the first time that David had aged considerably in the interim years: his face had become puffy and tired-looking; his waistline bulged over the elastic of the checked shorts he was wearing, and his calf muscles were flaccid and untoned.

"Avinash," he spoke the name again. "Whose son is . . ."

Sameer stood up, his eyes moist with the intensity of the emotion that overpowered him. "Look David," he spoke bitterly, "do not complicate matters. Do not rake up the past that best lies buried. It is my sincere advice to you."

"I am sorry," David replied in a small voice, "it is just that Avinash is so much like her. I was unprepared for that. Forgive me if I am impetuous."

"He is like her, but how is that important?" Sameer said harshly, "The fact remains that he is unlike her in every possible way. His mind is a blank as far as she is concerned. He is as rudderless as a boat left in a storm without an oar or an anchor. I have no idea what we can do for him."

"You have a home, the stability of a good marriage, two lovely children and, more than anything else, you have what is needed for him."

"Really, what is that may I ask?

"You have Vandana's assurance, her maternal instincts that will never let her down when she knows the truth."

Sameer felt angry, a red-hot anger that rose from the depths of his being and reached his gut. He was ready to belch it out. He gulped in the hot air that poured out from the whirring fan. When he spoke, his voice was thick and heavy with pain. "You mean you are banking on my instincts. Why have you come back, David? You have not kept your pledge to take care of those you have loved. And what has been the end result? And now you leave it to me to decide what is going to happen to Avinash? Why? Give me a good reason why?"

David kept his eyes averted, and sucked in the last dregs of coffee lying at the bottom of the cup. Somewhere from the interior of the house he could hear the clamour of Shantabai divesting the boy of his uniform, school bag and tiffin box. In the midst of Shantabai's querulous monotone, he felt the boy's presence in a lucid, pool of silence. Avinash did not pay any attention to the two men who were suddenly home, least of all the guest from England. It was only after Mira returned from school and whispered something in his ears that he gave David a keen, slightly askance look. It was too fleeting to be noticed by anyone other than Mira, who held his hand and took him away to do his homework.

~~~

When David and Vandana met alone for the first time, days had already passed and David's impetus to move on to Varanasi was becoming weaker. "I would be happy if you can stay back and see this thing through," Sameer said to David in a rather impetuous way, but the two men had in reality worked out a code that made communication easy and direct. They talked about the past in a functional way, holding back a great deal behind sealed lips and breath drawn in sharply. David assured Sameer that he had taken an entire term off from the University to be here in India. What he never quite revealed were the long, vigilant hours spent behind drawn curtains, allowing his memories to settle in the space that this generous household offered him. He was not in a hurry to leave.

Compulsively he began shedding his western clothes, buying cool, cotton pyjamas and T-shirts made of hosiery material that could absorb the heat. He spent long hours into the night on the terrace with the children, the balmy night air making his skin wrinkle and shrink until he felt a part of him had become invisible. The family could only see what he offered to their eyes. The exchange was amicable and fun-filled, like a holiday that would soon come to an end. This was a barren month in Delhi and its harshness held David in thrall, as though the season posed a challenge he had to overcome.

When Abhishek asked the inevitable question, "How long will you stay in India?" David found himself responding rather glibly, "Who knows?" Once Abhishek had overcome his sense of misgiving he found himself relaxing in the company of this man.

"I know," Mira butted in, "He is going to stay here forever. Aren't you, David?"

"Forever?" David felt the sharp sting of memory, bittersweet rush against his palate. He smiled ruefully, taken aback by his own vulnerability.

"What a stupid thing to say," Abhishek retorted sharply. "There is nothing that is forever in this world!"

"I don't quite agree," David replied. "I think we all believe in forever. Forever and a day. Have you given thought to that phrase? We like to believe that we can stretch beyond forever even if it is for a day. Permanence and transience have always co-existed. These were some of the ideas that I learnt while doing research on the Ganga in Varanasi. And do you know who was my teacher? Your mother's father, your grandfather!"

"Grandpa was your teacher?" Mira said in wonder.

"Yes, he was my co-supervisor. But he was also my guru, philosopher and mentor," David responded eagerly. He was reliving the happy days of the past, and he realized with a slight sense of shock that the memories filled him with yearning. Vandana was part of the yearning, and he noticed how she emerged from the shadow of the night and took her seat besides Mira and Avinash. "Ask your mother about those days! How I was visiting them everyday. And do you know what I remember the most? The lovely fish curries that your grandmother cooked for me! Your grandfather gave me his nuggets of wisdom, and your grandmother filled my belly. Your mother . . ."

"I was busy studying in medical college," Vandana added simply.

"Were you and mother best friends?" Mira asked.

"We were great friends. I was going to say: your mother and Abha showed me so many of the fascinating aspects of India – the ghats, the temples, the river – it seemed to me then that I was going to stay on in Varanasi forever! Perhaps write a book based on the vast material that I gathered in the course of my research."

"Did you get to write your book?" Abhishek butted in pointedly.

"Never quite finished what I had begun . . ." David replied. He noticed that Vandana had averted her eyes, and that instinctively she placed her hand on Avinash's shoulder. The gesture moved David deeply. The boy had not spoken a word but he held his head high, in attention, like a student listening keenly to a teacher in a classroom. Once in a while Mira gave him an anxious glance. Suddenly David felt the need to disengage himself from the family and retire to the privacy of his room. Fleetingly his eyes met Vandana's. They were hooded and sullen, but they sought him out.

~~~

Back in his room he waited for her. When he heard the soft knock on the door, he moved towards it, his feet heavy and leaden. She came in swiftly, and as he held her in tight embrace he noticed that her face was wet with tears.

"I need to hear everything from you," she whispered.

"Yes, yes," he chanted, rocking her gently. The heat made them wilt; the soft, cotton fabric clung limply to her body. As he touched her hair it came loose and twined wetly

around his fingers. The skin on her forehead pulsated, her
eyebrows were arched and taut with tension that ran like
currents down her limbs. David felt as though the twenty
intervening years between them fell away. His green, mottled
eyes glimmered with excitement. How little she had changed!
If anything, the growing years highlighted the familiar contours of her face, like the slight movement of the hand to
reveal a familiar landscape behind drawn curtains. He
remembered the odour of her body, and the teasing nearness
of her thoughts.

His memory of Varanasi was layered in the manner in
which the city had arisen from the throes of destruction. In
the course of his studies the structures of the city had come
alive. His first vivid memories were of days spent in
Vandana's house, in her father's study, poring over the vol-
umes of the *Kashi Khand* and listening in rapt silence to the
many interpretations, like secret maps of the city being
redrawn for his convenience. He knew now that these memories were indelibly connected with Vandana, and his love
for her had been an extension of his intellectual cravings. He
had wanted someone with whom he could share the excitement and wonder of discovering a city. He had fallen in love
with Varanasi and with Vandana: for him they were the twin
souls to whom he had dedicated his thoughts, readings, writings, desires, physical craving for touch, smell, everything
that constituted sensuality. The university campus was a
world apart: its lush stretches of green; its mammoth trees;
the ornate, orange, rust-edged buildings; the gravel pathways; and the hallowed silence of the Vishwanath Temple in
the precincts. This was where he had allowed his feelings to
grow in strength. But outside the campus there was the
ancient city that beckoned him, like dark cravings that broke

his dreams into a million prisms. He could cling on to one, at the expense of the other. Only the Ganges straddled both the worlds, for the river existed in the many parchments that he consulted in the library and the book-laden room inside Vandana's home, and at the ghats, where the water had lapped against stones through aeons of time.

He said, "The dirt, the grime, the sheer alien-ness of the city fascinated me. But I know, after many years of staying away, that the reality of Varanasi was something that I grasped intellectually, through my readings. I loved her because she was for me an eternal enigma, and like the many travellers of yore who had come from distant lands to see this holy city, I was 'seeing' her in my mind's eye. At the same time, for me it was such a deep-rooted physical experience that I felt the need to translate the experience into something tangible, like a book for instance. But such a book never really got written because I wanted to study and live Varanasi at the same time. You were always so sceptical about my academic involvement, remember? Ah, you smile. That familiar know-ing smile! I was ill at ease and enchanted by the way you were, and Abha too for that matter. As though both of you were see-ing through some game I was playing. But believe me, Vandana, I was sincere in my love for you and the city. It is just that the viable context for our love was missing then. Marrying you, taking you back to England or settling down in the city within the folds of domesticity seemed so oddly out of tune. But coming back to India, and seeing this family that you have built with Sameer, I feel myself getting sucked into it. You have replicated that home of yours in which I had found my foothold in Varanasi. If I was ever to stay back in Delhi I would fall in love with you all over again."

She was laughing and so was he. They parted, but the

gentle pressure of her body remained on his skin, and he could feel the ripples of his blood course down to his fingertips.

"You are doing just that, you know," she said.

"Falling in love?" he asked.

"Writing out your life. Is that the only way you can experience it?"

He noticed that her mouth was smiling, but the hurt remained in her eyes. He had not forgotten this look in her eyes, he wanted to tell her. But he allowed the privacy of his thought to remain with him. Long after she had left the room he continued to lie in bed, staring at the darkness, feeling the undulating movement of his heartbeat like the rhythmic pounding of oars hitting the surface of water. There was much else that he had to tell her, but not tonight, not while her eyes were breathing life into his memories of days filled with love, and the passion of learning.

~~~

"I am going to take a few days off from hospital and show David around the city," Vandana said to Sameer.

'That's a good idea," he replied. "There is a lot of catching up that both of you need to do."

"There is so much he has to tell me," Vandana said quietly. "It is better said in instalments."

But once they were alone, they hardly left the house. They settled down in the children's room, soon after Shantabai had finished her sweeping and swabbing and left to do her daily chores in neighbouring households. That gave them a few hours to themselves, and Vandana grew to like that quiet time. In the beginning she pottered around the room putting Mira's clothes in the cupboard, but soon she felt no need to cover up the deep longing she had to hear his voice. He too spoke without pausing, as though this communication alone defined their relationship and set it part from the general bonhomie he shared with Sameer and the children. There was something intense and forbidden about their exchange, and though what he was telling her filled her with grief, she felt the need to know the truth. The pain was part of the waiting and the revelation.

"For a very long time the only emotion I felt in connection with Romola was a deep, unshakable guilt. It seemed as though I had brought her into being from the ashes at Manikarnika Ghat. She was as unreal as she was beautiful."

"Will you describe her for me?" Vandana said with immense curiosity. She remembered Sameer's words describing this strange woman. He too had been aware of her beauty.

"Have you seen the Manikarnika Ghat in the glare of the noon-day sun? Those slow, burning embers and stacks of logs waiting to be consumed by the fire. It is a sight that I have always found both horrific and compelling. I was told that the fire is never extinguished at the burning ghat, so one day I went there in the afternoon. Sure enough a corpse was burning, half stretched on the last steps of the ghat so that fire and water mingled in defiance of nature. But I was aware of only one thing: the ceaseless animal-like keening. It was near, far, everywhere, as continuous as the muddy eddying of the water and the bobbing of flowers and scraps of sandalwood on its surface. I could see a pair of gnarled feet jutting out from under the pile of logs, and for me it was the most painful reminder of our mortality.

You want me to describe her beauty? Let me see. Romola's face gave a human shape to that constant sound of mourning. Her beauty had nothing redeeming about it, as though she represented something that was forever hurting. I would wake up in the morning and feel a relentless urge to see her, like the way I used to crave to see the first break of sunrise on the ghats. My feet would carry me there day after day. But inside the ashram she was not available for me. I used to go to see her during visiting hours. She trusted me, and I guess I became her conduit, connecting her to the world outside. I was not permitted to bring anything for her, though I had this strange urge to pick up things I had seen in the market. I told her this. Little trinkets maybe, the kind that are ferried on carts in the Kashi Vishwanath gali. She had girlish hands and feet. Do you know what she used to tell me then? 'You bring fresh air from outside, that is enough. I can feel it in your breath.' But do you know what she wanted most from me? This would surprise you. She used to listen avidly to every word that I had written down in my research paper. She became the epitome of my Ganga. I fell in love with her."

"There you go again." Vandana shook her head in despair, but David noticed that she was smiling. "You live out life in the pages of a book. Was this the viable context for love that you were looking for?"

"Yes, it seemed so perfect! At long last I had a purpose in life. I told myself that I had found the reason why I had come to India, and why I chose to remain behind in this country. I was looking for that elusive something that defined India and, lo and behold, it stood before me in the guise of a woman. Like in any fairy tale, she was locked within a fortress, and I had to rescue her. Trapped in centuries of blind superstition and oppressive relationships, she too had been waiting for that single moment when she could hold somebody's hand and proclaim her freedom. I was wrong, of course, woefully, woefully wrong! Indeed Romola had found her freedom, but not in me. She had found it in Uma, and in the unlikeliest of places: inside the ashram that had imprisoned her in the first place. Once I knew this I should have packed my bags and left India forever. But I had the irresistible urge to see this relationship through to its very end. My quest had begun with Varanasi, and now it seemed destined to end with Romola. I must tell you about her relationship with Uma. It is for me the sweetest and saddest tale of human bonding."

CHAPTER EIGHT

Forbidden Fruits

That day Avinash woke up with slight fever. When Vandana came down to check whether the boy was ready for school, she was surprised to see him sitting on the bed, his hair uncombed and his school uniform lying in disarray in a corner. On seeing her, the tears welled up in his eyes. She felt guilty. She had been ignoring the household for the past few days. It was as though she was in the grip of a narrative that bound her, body and soul, to the stranger who had entered unbidden into her life. But she was well past her fascination for David. She had ceased to pay attention to him. It was the two women in the narrative that held her attention.

"No school for you today, son," she said amicably as she tucked him under the blanket. "You go to sleep now, and when you wake up you will find that the fever has gone." Once the boy was taken care of, she found herself waiting for David. Why was he taking so long? Was there something in the narrative that was difficult for him to reveal? She put the medicine down on the bedstead and noticed that Avinash's school bag was lying in a heap on the floor, the books strewn all around. On an impulse she bent low to pick it up. She saw the brown, rexene bag in which he had brought all his worldly possessions from the ashram. It was lying open.

She pulled it out and peered inside. It seemed empty,

except for a large white envelope. Again something more compulsive than curiosity made her open the packet. There were papers, official looking. One was a release order from the ashram. Others looked like affidavits and a copy of an FIR, filed at the police station. It said something about an inmate drowning in the river. She caught her breath. There were a few paper cuttings as well. Suicide, said the newspapers, cause unknown. There was a smudgy picture of a woman, and the caption underneath identified her as the victim who had died. Vandana stared at the photograph for a long time. The woman was beautiful indeed, in a distant sort of a way, like the fragrance of a flower that lingers in the memory. Vandana carried that thought back to the children's room.

At long last David sauntered into the room. His face looked pinched, as though he had spent a sleepless night. He came forward and held her hand.

"I do not know whether you will like to hear this part of the story," he said shakily.

"Please, David," she mumbled, "go on. Not knowing is far worse than knowing. You should understand that. Sometimes I wonder what my life has been. Blind man's bluff. Being taken by the hand to different corners and left to find my way, without being given any directions. If I am angry with anyone more than myself, it is Abha. She was my best friend. Surely she owed it to me to tell the truth."

"No, Vandana, do not blame Abha or yourself, or anyone for that matter. We were only trying to protect each other. We wanted to keep you out of the loop, for your life at that point seemed so untouched by all this, so fulfilled by your new role as a mother. I think Sameer, too, revelled in this newfound bliss. He had to keep his nest untouched. Also, he was pledged to secrecy by his profession. Remember, Uma was still under his treatment. He was doing a lot of it from Delhi, but once in a while he had to come to Varanasi."

"Strange, he did tell me about Uma, but not a word about you or Romola or even Abha," Vandana retorted.

"Uma's illusion about her mother was over, but it brought in a new kind of problem. Something that Sameer had warned us about. The clarity of realization that follows the hazy, half-light of dreams is often painful. She suffered the pain of loss and abandonment for the first time. An absent mother gripped her life and tore it to shreds. Romola became her confidante and, as Romola often said to me, she shared with Uma the rage of the betrayed." David paused and Vandana made her way to Avinash's bedroom to check on the boy. He was asleep, but she saw the dried tears on his cheek. His forehead felt moist and cold, suggesting that the temperature was in check. Her feet faltered as she climbed the stairs back to where David was waiting for her.

"I am puzzled by Bela's story," Vandana said honestly, "I think she cast a malicious shadow on the lives of the Sengupta family. First it was Grandpa and the way he died, or rather the way he lived the last few years of his life. Then it was Uma abandoning the household and joining an ashram, such an unlikely thing to happen in an educated, upper-middle-class home. I have felt the impact of all this on Sameer as well. Somewhere he is afraid of love. He has chosen a safe path, away from the muddle of emotions. I thought I knew him, though not anymore. He had a secret life that I was not aware of, and maybe what I mistook for equanimity was the seal that kept the lid on. But I never loved him any the less for it. It seemed so convenient then to be married to a man who was never probing or harsh or unreasonable."

"Look at him now," David said, shaking his head. "How easily he gives us this space to search our souls. Do you really think he feels comfortable? Don't you think this is trust?"

"Or is he just playing games," Vandana asked darkly, "waiting to catch us at a weak moment? I wonder at times. I know what you are going to say, 'How does it matter? You have everything.' Yes, I do have everything, things that I may once have sought from you. But so what? So you did abandon me for another woman! Abha used to go on and on about how Sameer and I were made for each other; that my relationship with you held no future. But did anyone really ask me what I wanted out of the future? A marriage was arranged, and I concentrated on building a home that would house the perfect, happy future. The Garden of Bliss, Anandavana. Who would want to sully its happiness? But like it or not, forbidden fruits did grow on the branches. Today you are here; so is Avinash. But go on . . . go on with your story, I am all ears."

~~~

"When I asked Romola to marry me, she refused. I felt that the ashram was a trap for her. I told her that although widow remarriage was unheard of in the annals of the ashram, it was not outside the law. I remember that day as vividly as though it is now. See, how my hair stands on end, how my hands tremble. It was Thursday, the only day that the inmates were allowed to take time off and be with their friends and families from the world outside. The large, open area was dotted with people, sitting huddled, some embracing, some quarrelling, and some sitting next to each other in silence. I spoke at great length about my plans. She listened, her brows knit tight, with just that slight quiver running down her chin. She did not speak a word in response, and

for a moment my heart was gladdened, for this was the shy
way of expression for Indian women, and I thought I did
recognize a certain willingness in the way she held her head,
bowed and demure. But the next minute she raised her
brows, and I saw something in her eyes that terrified me.
There was laughter, a searing, heady laughter that made her
eyes shine like dark pools. The night before, I had prepared
my dissertation chapter on Vishnu's toil at the Manikarnika
kund, and how the sweat had filled it up, and how Parvati's
earrings had dislodged themselves and fallen into the water.
Romola's ringlets of hair were dancing in the breeze, and I
could feel the madness descend on my soul. 'Take Uma and
me to the Kashi Vishwanath Temple at the Dashmavamedha
Ghat. We kept a mannat, and now my wishes have come
true.' I said yes, as though she had with her plea pledged her
life to me.

"I knew what 'mannat' meant from my study of the
Ganges. People flocked to this city in answer to the mannat
they had kept. It was their secret pledge to fulfill a promise
kept to God if he complied with their wishes. A trade-off
really, like so much else in your religion. I love this bit of give
and take that happens so often in the way you people pray, as
though God is a personal buddy who is there to grant wishes
at a price – as though he keeps a kind of ledger book and
marks down the debits and credits. The whole business of
salvation in Varanasi is such a mighty industry, with all the
paraphernalia available in package deals. Name the price and
you get it. Come to think of it Romola had entered our lives
as part of one such deal. I thought her mannat was granted
when I had asked her hand in marriage, and she wanted to
make her offerings to the deity in thanksgiving. I was drunk
with pleasure. That look in her eyes had been so alluring, and

it kept returning to me in my dreams. I passed the days in excitement. I mapped out the way to whisk them away from the ashram for a few hours and take them to the temple. I would take them for the sandhya arati, the most forbidden time for inmates to be away from the ashram.

"It was dusk. The streetlights had been turned on. We must have made a strange threesome. A foreigner and two young women in the familiar garb of ashramites. We walked briskly, as though the probing eyes would stall our pathways. Out in the streets, I noticed how Romola held Uma's hand in a firm grip. Uma's eyes were darting fearfully at the melee of strangers. Hawkers were peddling their wares in loud, nasal tones. They always found easy targets in foreigners and women. I swept them aside and moved ahead with long, bouncy strides. Once we entered the Vishwanath gali, the street was too narrow to hold more than two people. I let the women move ahead of me. The pujaris and their pimps stood in open doorways, stretching out their hands to catch customers. They carried little baskets laden with samagri. They called out their prices like at an auction. I had already made arrangements. Our man looked smug and happy with the bargain he had made with me. The blood darted in my brain.

"There is no concept of open space in Varanasi. The houses on both sides of the street were hundreds of years old, and they were hewn from solid rocks. They had narrow slits for doors and windows. A bull sauntered by, unmindful of our presence. There was a strange harmony here between rock, flesh and the smell of incense and flowers that we clutched in our hands. I could see the bare body of the pujari who led the way for us; once in a while he asked us to mind our heads as low archways led us deeper and deeper into

into narrow alleys. For a second something close to panic
lurched at the pit of my stomach. It struck me that I was
being led into the interior of a labyrinth, and I was at the
mercy of this man who showed us the way to the abode of
God. What if he was to stop at some point and ask for more
money? I dug into my pockets to check the cash; I always
carried some extra for unforeseen eventualities. I had a
penknife, an advice I was given in Venice. But, deep inside, I
felt the fear was unfounded. The man was mercenary no
doubt, but he belonged to a religious order, and he would
take money from me by more dexterous means. Sure enough,
at one point he led us into a small room and asked us to
remove our shoes. He spoke in a low voice to another priest,
dressed in the saffron garb of a mendicant. This man smiled,
revealing pan-stained teeth, and then he prepared three baskets for us, putting in, in some kind of an order, a pink and
white lotus, milk cakes, white puffed rice, blobs of sugar
ground into wispy white flakes, a small pack of vermilion,
yellow paste, and baked clay pots filled with milk. As he
handed us our wares he blessed us with his grubby hands. He
shoved the money I put in his hand under a cash counter, and
I knew that he had counted the amount with practised ease.
He seemed satisfied, but I could see the sly, greedy look in his
eyes as he noticed the youth of the two women accompanied
by a foreigner. It was only when I spoke to him in chaste
Hindi that the eyes hardened and the smile vanished.

"I noticed that the attitude of our pujari had changed. He
was more advanced in age than the priest, and he spoke a
smattering of English. My reply to him in Hindi went un-
heeded. He was encountering my foreignness with a kind of
deft reminder that I had encroached on his territory, and that
he was ill at ease in my presence. I knew the mantras by heart,

many of them taught by your father. But I waited for him to enunciate them first, in deference to his age and his profession. But I sensed that the clarity of my diction took him by surprise, for he gave me sharp looks over his shoulder. But at that point I was scarcely interested in him. My mind, every sinew of it, was watching Romola. I noticed how her feet were caked with the mud and grime of the floor that was awash with milk and the holy water of the Ganga. The precinct of the temple was so narrow that it filled me with surprise. People jostled in that narrow space and I could feel my body lurching forward and touching hers. The delicacy of her skin and the contours of her breast covered by the blue edge of her sari carried for me a pattern of perfection. She was like the hallowed body of some goddess who dwelt in those streets, pure, without blemish, and yet obscene in her erotic appeal. Hands were pushing me from behind. Some of the milk from my clay pot splashed on the back of her neck. She cringed, the skin curling slightly. I noticed that a river of milk descended over her shoulder and plunged deep into the crevice between her breasts. I felt shock waves spiral through my loins. The clashing of cymbals and the sound of the chanting was deafening. We were moving deeper and deeper into the inner fold of the temple. The linga stood in the middle: dark, bulbous and gorging the milk poured on its head with religious frenzy.

"A priest stood at the helm and sucked us into the front row. He pushed the others away. He asked me to donate generously to the temple, and for the welfare of mendicants like him who lived on the generosity of believers. When I took out a certain sum of money he pushed it aside almost angrily. I took out more. He grabbed it, and then in a soft, wheedling tone he said, "The child in her womb will grow into a bracing, young man." I was dumbfounded. My eyes took in her wet, heaving bosom, so richly ripe that I felt that the fecundity of the earth was rooted here in this tiniest of tiny spaces. My knees jerked forward and hit the base of the linga. The smooth stone spurted its thick, white liquid and my feet were wet with the flowing river of milk.

"It was only when we were in a small courtyard under a giant banyan tree, and our pujari was asking us to make wishes that would come true, that we first noticed that Uma had been lagging behind. But I was not worried. The path was too narrow and the area too small for anyone to get lost. The tree was colossal, the trunk massive, and from where we were standing we could see only one branch of the tree. "This tree exists from Shiva's time," the pujari was telling us, but I had ceased to listen to him. I was watching Romola. She closed her eyes and prayed deeply, and in that single posture I discovered the meaning of my quest. I felt at peace with myself. There is nothing in the Western civilization that can capture a moment of such pure vulnerability, beauty so fragile and so infinitely passive, as though the flesh transcended time. I felt I could never quite possess her, not in the physical sense of the term. I wondered what had brought her to Varanasi. What had made her marry a man old enough to be her father? Had she discarded this part of her life forever, or was she like the city, layered in infinite folds of meaning. Only in some miraculous conjoining could I even begin to possess her. She was dressed in white and her bare arms and neck and forehead had an ascetic purity. Who in that congregation would have taken her for a widow? I felt at that moment that she had turned herself into an ashramite for reasons of convenience, and that what I had just seen in her eyes was her true nature. She had wanted me to come to this ancient temple so that she could demonstrate what words could hardly explain."

~~~

"I am beginning to understand just a little bit of your narrative," Vandana said, "but it is time for me to return to see how the boy is doing."

David felt the beads of sweat running down his body. Why was he telling this woman things that he had buried deep? Ten years in England had cured him of his obsession with a country so frighteningly obscure. His thesis was gathering dust in some remote corner of the library back home. He had not heard of a single student who wanted to consult it.

"No," he said almost brusquely, "listen till I finish."

"Come down with me," Vandana replied. "I think your story has not reached its finishing touch yet. The chapters must go on unfolding."

~~~

"Once the prayers were over," David continued, "and I had finished haggling with the pujari over his final fee, I noticed that Uma was still missing. But Romola did not seem unduly worried. 'Let her be for once,' she said emphatically, 'this is a temple. Who can get lost in God's presence?' There was a strange gaiety in her, so unlike her usual demeanour that I felt pleased, as though I was somehow responsible for it. We moved outside the precincts of the temple and stood against a low arch that marked the entry point. I kept an eye out for Uma, hoping to spot her emerge from the temple. The crowd was surging forward in single file. I could sense the night growing, but here amidst the light and sound the darkness was held in abeyance. I felt I could wait a lifetime to realize my dreams.

"One of the things that fascinates me about your country is the way time stands still. None of you are ever in a hurry.

I like that. Look at it this way: I meet you after twenty years, and it seems as though there has been only a gentle passing of time – that I can simply pick up from where I left off."

"Oh, no, you are wrong. There are things that elude us by simply becoming the past. We cannot make up for time lost." Vandana spoke with seriousness. "I have begun to talk like you!" she giggled.

"Please no! I prefer the way you are. You bring to my story a sense of normality. You know, seriously, one of the reasons why I could never finish writing my book was because it all sounded so unreal, like a life lived in a dream. Who would believe someone like Romola or, for that matter, Uma or Bela? The river, too, how mystical it sounds in any narrative that tries to capture it. You are right: time lost is time irretrievable. Romola is dead, and if I speak about her today it is only in the way memory relives a person. I guess what I want to find out, even today, is why she chose to die. That alone is the reason why I am back here in India. Not Avinash, not you. It is important for you to understand that. Only then will this story make sense.

~~~

"We caught sight of Uma after many hours had gone past. Romola seemed unfazed by it, which strikes me now as inexplicable. And it is not that she had forgotten about Uma at that juncture, for in the few hours that we waited for her we spoke only about her. I felt Romola was seeking this space to let me know about herself and her life inside the ashram. She told me that Uma and she used to play this game that they referred to as 'make belief'. They used to pretend that they were long lost twins who had got separated at birth, both abandoned by a cruel mother. The ashram had reunited them, but not before they had lost contact with their mother.

They tried to learn mantras which make lost people come back to the fold: like grabbing a wandering soul and restoring its memory, so that the yearning to return then holds the soul in its vicious grasp. They practised the mantras night and day. Uma refused to take the medicines that Sameer would send over. They would dig deep holes in the garden and bury the medicines. They waited day and night for communications from those dead and gone. Romola felt little need for her own kith and kin. She was happy there in the midst of strangers, and there was Uma to fill up the void in her. But Uma was different. She relived every nook and corner of the large house that she had left behind when she entered the ashram. There was one particular room that fascinated her. She said it was the room that Bela had occupied in the few months that she had been there. Uma spoke of it as the 'womb'. It was their game to think of ways to find access into the womb – something like getting into the private recesses of somebody's mind. But Bela's mind was a closed door. Nobody spoke of it in the house. So both Uma and Romola would spend hours talking about it, as though this alone would make Bela return. It brought the two women together; their bond was woven with words. They became recluses in the ashram, the butt of many jokes. But they cared little; what they shared kept them happy together. Today was the first outing for the two women, and Romola was not afraid of Uma's absence. Their connection did not depend upon physical proximity; Romola could feel Uma's closeness on a different plane. Those narrow alleys were traps that imprisoned their bodies, while their souls rollicked and galloped elsewhere.

"She said all this without the slightest sense of its absurdity. I too believed every word that she said. Why else would a woman's eyes be so lucid and so forthright? I knew then that I had no place in Romola's life; that I had been only a conduit to help shape a moment. What was happening now was far beyond what I could grasp. I felt humble and sad in a way that I could not describe.

"When Uma did return, the two women held hands, and in the narrow streets of that religious city I saw the fusion of their bodies, like the river meeting its ultimate destination in the sea. But along the river's arduous journey, its water could be touched by the bodies of the believers; they could gather the water in the folds of their hands, dip their brass utensils into and carry the holy substance back to the narrowness of their homes; and they could pour it on the head of the shiva linga and touch the infinite, being and not-being all merged into one. I felt that these two women had achieved the pinnacle of creativity. What Sameer's medicines had failed to do, Romola had achieved. She brought sanity back into Uma's life. Uma did not need the physician any more than did these hordes of madmen that collected on the ghats and rocked to Shiva's cosmic dance. Varanasi was throbbing on my pulse, and I could feel the beat of the cymbals and the clanging of the bells rush through my brain. Though Romola had rejected me in so many words, I felt little resentment. I thought that I had earned her confidence that night. I had been witness to a miracle, and the fact that she had asked for my help was reason enough for me to feel wanted. But I was wrong, and I was to discover this soon enough."

~~~

For a while they were both silent, lost in thought. David continued: "It was Abha who brought me the news a few months later. She told me that Romola was with child, news that rocked my world. How was it possible inside the four walls of that fortress? I realized then that what I had seen in her eyes was wantonness; the outward austerity of form was only make-believe. She had cheated all of us, Sameer, Abha, Uma and me. She had made us bury her husband, and suddenly it seemed to me that she might have lied about her former life. Who was the old man? And why did her in-laws abandon her? Would you believe it? For a very long time after the initial numbness was replaced by anger, I spun all kinds of stories about her in my mind. I remembered her that day inside the temple. She had symbolized innocence and fertility. I had been overwhelmed by the love I felt for her, as though she had elicited from me the blind faith that divinity demands from man. She had sprung from a corner of this enticing city, but suddenly it seemed as though the narrow alleys of Varanasi had cunningly hidden her from my view. I wanted desperately to abandon this city, this country, everything that reminded me of her. I bought myself an air ticket and packed my belongings. For the last few days of my stay I kept myself indoors, as though I was scared to encounter life in the streets. Abha tried to contact me, but I did not return her phone calls. Sameer was in the city, and he, too, tried to draw me out of my cocoon of silence. And then one day there was a knock on my door. I recoiled from the very sound. When it persisted, I opened the door. She was standing there. It is my last memory of her."

"I will not try to recount the words we exchanged, though the memory is vivid. What I cannot bring into words is the look on her face when I chastised her, so cruelly that my heart trembles as I remember. She refused to answer every query that I threw at her face. 'How does it matter?' was her only reply. She looked neither defiant nor submissive, only detached, as though we were discussing a report in the newspaper involving people we did not know. But I sensed something else, a sort of deep commitment as inexplicable as a vocational calling. Nothing I said or could have done made the least difference. I cannot describe how it made me feel. I felt discarded in a way that only my foreignness could make me feel. For the first time, I felt I could not continue to live in a city whose ceremonies and ways I could not understand. Yet she was asking me to understand and participate in her experience. When she saw my obduracy she cried, bitter tears. 'Please, David, there is nothing more I can tell you except that my body must fulfill its task of carrying life for nine months.' To tell you the truth, I was horrified. How could she treat her body like a receptacle? Her body, encased in the white sari that marked a widow, seemed both pure and tainted at the same time, and I felt that I could not bear to witness this contradiction.'

~~~

"I sound like a man babbling, don't I? I am hardly able to understand what I am telling you, how can it make any sense to you? I see from the look on your face that you are shocked, Vandana. But please hear me out. I have made this long journey so that I can put things in perspective. I was bitterly disappointed then. I am trying to understand why.

The thought that Romola was going to have a baby seemed such a travesty of the image I had built of her. She and Uma, the sheer madness of the world they had created together. How deeply moved I had been by her story. I had believed her in the same way one indulges the imagination of children. Unlocking the womb, trying to gain entry into it. Suddenly, with almost sickening clarity, I remembered what the priest had said to me inside the Kashi Vishwanath Temple. Her womb will carry a child! I had exulted in the image then, as though the priest was describing a divine occurrence. I had interpreted everything metaphorically, and now the reality of the situation hit me like a ton of bricks. Did Romola actually mean that she and Uma were trying to have a baby? That in fact they intended to use a real womb. But how? Then I saw the ashram for what it really was: a closed world, governed by its own rules. How many delusions could flourish there? The prayer times, the communal eating, sleeping, waking and doing of household chores. Relationships that were undefined. How do you know your brother, father, mother, sister? The ascetic and the erotic co-existed. These ashramites were married to God and served his lust. I had seen pregnant women and suckling mothers inside the ashram. I felt sick to my soul.

"I know now that I should not have reacted the way I did. My moral outrage was nothing but selfishness. The only way I could possess Romola was to invoke the age-old precepts that constructed her image as a widow of India, of Varanasi. I had read about widows in the many tomes that your father had preserved in his library. The shorn head, the emaciated body, the hollow eyes and the sunken soul. She was meant to eat food left out of charity in her begging bowl. She was meant to give up the desires of her body. Her strictly vegetarian diet that was devoid of onions, garlic and spices was meant to control her body and mind, so that nothing could pollute her. I remember how severely critical I felt when I first read these tracts. I had endless arguments with your father who saw my agitation as a purely academic exercise. But my response to Varanasi was on one level emotional; the sight of the women at the widow's ghat would distress me terribly, as though I was witnessing something truly evil without registering social protest. Increasingly I had begun to 'see' Varanasi with the skewed eyes of a purist, who sees but not rationally. There was so much that was wrong here: the institution of beggars, the lepers, the vagrancy, the poverty, the naked display of religious jugglery and super-stition; but I found the plight of widows the most blatantly inhuman.

"I would spend hours discussing my thoughts with Abha. She had this no–nonsense air about her as though Varanasi was one of the many things that she had to school me in, and the sooner it was done the better it was for everyone. But about widowhood she was more emphatic. She said it was the basic malaise of relationships in India that they were institu-tionalized, and people had distinct roles to play. The minute a woman lost her husband she became disengaged like a piece of property; she had to be owned by somebody. In a family she became marginal, and the object of universal charity. In Varanasi she was owned by the religious estate. At the same time, she had to be de-sexualized so that no man would desire her. So she became a divine consort, her hours spent in prayers and abstinence. The purity of her body was marked by its emaciation. I was supposed to see the sign of God in her, Abha told me, and not flinch. I had to treat her with both indifference and reverence.

"One of the reasons why I fell in love with Romola was because she defied every letter of the book. She was sensuous and beautiful and compassionate. She spun relationships with the people around her. We all loved her dearly, Sameer, Abha, Uma and me, and she showered us with her love. She used to pick flowers in the garden inside the ashram and make garlands out of it. The scent of the flowers would drive me crazy with desire. She coined names for each one of us. I became Davie, Sameer was Meer and Uma she called her

angel. Abha, she said, was her other angel, but without wings!
Her daily chore was to serve food to the inmates. She had
little appetite and would eat off an aluminium plate. But her
feet, white and small and unblemished, would carry her from
one plate to another, and she would pause and delve into the
large pan she was carrying, and as she poured the food I felt
that the earth's abundance was unfurling from her hand. Her
eyes were moist and her lips would utter a little prayer. Soon
after she became pregnant a certain illness overtook her. Her
eyes had dark rims under them, and she shuffled as she
moved around. She was kept in confinement, and nobody
was permitted to meet her. After Avinash was born, she did
ask to see me but I did not go. That night I had a strange
vision. She was lying in her room, her body so wasted that I
could not help but cry out in pain. But I noticed something
else, too. Her hair had grown down to her waist, shimmering,
black and lustrous. The sight of a widow with long hair was
sacrilegious. But Romola wore it like a shroud. The vision
shifted. I thought Romola had drowned, and that they had
fished her body out of the river. I was a little shocked to see
the scraps of flowers and leaves entangled in her sari. Her lips
were blue and her body sodden and heavy with moisture.
Sometimes I wonder whether this vision was a premonition
of what was to come. When I got the news in England from
Abha, I spent the day quietly near the Thames. But my memories burned like the fire at Manikarnika Ghat, and it seemed
to me that I could not bear to think of the fire consuming her
body. I knew how bodies were readied for funerals in India. I
wondered whether her hair was shorn and her body encased
in the crisp white sari with blue border. In my thoughts her
arms were bare, and the flesh seemed white like alabaster.
Once the burning was over I wondered whether her ashes

were dispersed in the lap of the river, a silvery glimmer of life's luminous form. I found myself praying to the river to carry her to the edges of the sea, into the vastness of that empty space that denotes death. I forgave her then, in the cruel way that society's norms work. In death, she had recovered her purity. She had become as elemental as the river. But I felt a relentless, all-consuming grief. In losing her I had lost the direction of my life, my years of research seemed meaningless, and my sojourn in this country suddenly seemed futile. What options did I have now?'

"I picked up a new job in a new set-up and I changed home and friends and habits. I entered relationships that were as distant from my past as possible. I revelled in England's cold weather, the neatness of life, the orderliness of the tube train, and the blandness of the food. I discarded my eastern ways, and slipped into the anonymity of what I recognized were my roots. Did I miss Varanasi? I cannot say for sure. I felt a sense of relief at having got my life back in order. Romola ceased to haunt me. The women I now met had lives so different from hers that my sense of morality got back its balance. Why would I be so shocked to know that she had borne a child out of wedlock? Romola was dead, but she had left a son behind. I began to think of Avinash for the first time. I wrote to Abha and asked her about him. I got to know that the boy was now a young lad, and that he had been brought up strictly, according to the rules of the ashram. For a while Uma took up the task of nurturing him. She had grown forlorn after Romola's death but the child kept her occupied. I sensed that Abha was worried for the boy. Then one day she wrote and told me that Uma was taking up sanyasin. What would happen to the boy now? Abha did say she was consulting Sameer as well, but she felt my opinion was as important. I was confused. I asked Sameer for advice. That was the time we began to communicate regularly across continents. We were tied by our concern for the boy, and through him for Romola. Once again I felt that my past had caught up with me."

"Then one day I got a letter from Abha that stunned me. Here it is. I want you to read it." David held out an envelope, Vandana took it from him. He noticed that her hands were shaking slightly. She had been silent for so long that he had almost begun to feel he was imagining her presence. He was conscious of her now, and with it came the realization that she too had a role to play in the story. She was not an impartial witness, and her understanding mattered more than anything else.

Vandana opened the pages of the letter but before she began to read she asked in the quietest of tones, "Sameer told me Avinash is your son. Is he not?"

"No, not in the biological sense. Though I had been consumed by desire, I had never touched Romola's body."

"Then it is true . . ."

"Romola was correct when she said it did not matter. Life's inception is so mysterious. Who are we? What is our identity anyway? I should have listened to her reasoning then. But I was so enraged, so caught up in the selfish act of loving her that I saw all of it as betrayal. As though by loving her I had every right over her. Why did I want to marry her in the first place? Was it because I wanted to remove the brand of widowhood from her forehead and give her the status of a married woman? I understood that was the only way I could possess her. Now I see my reasoning for what it was: the singular brutality that makes us want to possess the commodity that we choose to cherish and love. By loving Romola I destroyed her."

"You could not have kept her in any other way in our society. It would have been interpreted as prostitution."

"Oh, the horror of it all! I did get to prostitute her. It must have been just a simple game for her and Uma, unlocking the womb, searching for a cruel mother who had deserted them. But why did Romola join in this make-believe? Was it her way of showing solidarity, by sharing the experience of pain? Or worse still, was it her way of sharing bodies like the collective prayers at the ghats? Don't you see? She asked me to take both of them to the Kashi Vishwanath Temple, and I witnessed the game they played. She took me into her confidence, so that I would know her. Perhaps this was Romola's way of pledging her love to me. But I was in no way prepared for what was going to follow."

"Do not fill your self with so much guilt. It never helps. I have realized that in so many ways," Vandana said impetuously, as though she wanted to silence David and let him retain some privacy. She felt more than anything else the need to maintain her sanity in order to grasp what was written in the letter.

Dear David,

I am writing this letter to you against my best judgment. I have made a discovery that has shocked me beyond belief. I cannot share it with you in a letter. But if you promise to come down to Varanasi I will disclose the truth to you. I have spoken to Sameer as well. It is time both of you take the responsibility that you owe to Avinash. The poor boy continues to languish inside the ashram. I have spoken to Swamiji. He too feels that the boy should be given the option to live within a family. When I mentioned the same to Sameer, he said he would have to wait for your arrival

*before he makes up his mind. He needs Vandana's consent
as well. I agreed with him that the entire situation is hard
on her. But I know Vandana, and her sharp sense of right
and wrong. She would not let Sameer down. I will make
arrangements once I hear from both of you. Until then I
wait in agony.*

Yours affectionately,
Abha

"This letter speaks in riddles." Vandana put down the letter
impatiently. Her eyes burned feverishly, like someone witnessing something horribly immoral.

"Yes," David replied, "but I am here now, and the truth
will be out once I go to Varanasi and meet Abha. She refuses
to say anything beforehand; she is adamant about that. I too
believe that there is a right time for everything. I am not in
a hurry. It was important for me to give you a clear picture
of all that has happened. I have promised both Abha and
Sameer that I would do so."

"So this is what it was all about! Truth-telling sessions so
that I could be brought up to date. How meticulously things
have been planned! This is a good way of dealing with truth.
It takes away much of the anguish, I can see. What more do
I have to hear, David, from you and from Sameer? Tell me
now, so that I can prepare myself."

"No, Vandana, there is nothing else to know. I do not have
the details of Uma's illness. Sameer can fill you in on those,
but my part of the deal has been more difficult than you can
ever understand. I have carried a heavy burden in my heart,
and my visit to India is part of a process of soul cleansing."

"Soul cleansing?" Vandana spoke with dread. "You

surprise me. Do you think we can really clean our souls and go back to living our lives as usual? Why is it that from the day Avinash entered this house I have been filled with a deep sense of misgiving? I knew his arrival was tied up with some kind of hidden secret, and that sooner or later I would be dragged into the process of discovering it.

"I have always trusted Sameer that he would never do anything to really hurt anyone. His profession, the fact that he takes care of people with sick minds, makes me respect him. You know, the way you respect priests, and think that they will mend hearts and souls. But I saw the way he cringed when he came near the boy. He was afraid. I thought he was withholding something that would break the peace of this house. Once in a while I observed how keenly he kept looking at me and the children. I got the sense that he wanted to say something to us. But Sameer often told me that being part of a large family had taught him to leave things unsaid. I learnt to respect that, and the reticence of the man. But the day he announced your arrival I knew that matters far more significant were about to unfold. Think, in all these years he never mentioned even once that he shared a friendship with you. Why, I ask you?"

"Maybe it was not important," David mumbled, pinned down by her frank gaze.

"For whom?" Vandana exploded. "For me it was! My attempt to forget you and go on with my life was honest, but there were moments of doubt. I wondered why I was doing this. Whether it was a condition laid down for the happiness that I was seeking. Forget David or else! Sometimes the best way to forget is to allow the person or the event to become commonplace. It removes the guilt and the pain. I think I understand now, all too clearly, what Sameer was doing. Obviously, he did not want to forget. And what better way to keep remembering than to nurture the deep, dark secret in one's heart, like a wound that keeps on festering? But don't you see? It was not you and I or our relationship that he was remembering! We were only a small part of the general back-drop . . ."

Just then the front bell began to jingle. Mira was back home from school. She looked impatient, for she had been kept waiting for a while. "Mom . . ." she complained, and then, seeing her mother's face, she stood still. "What is the matter, Ma?"

"Nothing, child," Vandana replied. "Avinash had a fever in the morning."

Mira skidded into the room, throwing her school bag hastily on the floor. But Avinash was sitting quietly with his homework, and looked quite all right. The flushed look on his face was replaced by something more intent. His eyes were bright and slightly sunken in the oval face, but it was the expression on his face that caught Vandana's attention: it was that slightly inward expression of someone who does not care about his immediate surroundings. She saw the way Mira had put her slim arms around his neck, and how Avinash remained impassive, like someone who took all the love for granted. Suddenly Vandana felt her breath squeezed out of her ribcage. She remembered the Sengupta ancestral home, the long, lonely corridors, the large rooms with the bay win-dows and drawn curtains. She saw the family portraits hang-ing on the walls, marking the lineage from one generation to another. Why had she not noticed the resemblance?

"Come away, Mira," she muttered. "You will catch an infection."

CHAPTER NINE

The File

"Will you do me a small favour, Ramakant," Sameer said to his man Friday, "will you take out file 24 and keep it on my desk." He spoke amicably but the tension was audible in his tone. For the past few days he had been worrying a great deal about Vandana. He knew that David's recounting was over. "Yes, I have heard everything. But where do we turn from here?" she had asked, and the pain in her voice hit him like the vortex of a storm. Something about the question puzzled him. As usual he kept his silence.

He noticed that her chest was heaving and that tears gathered around the dark pinpoints of her eyes. He sensed that she was holding something back, and the exercise causing her enormous stress. For once he felt he would have preferred the storm to break over their heads.

"Why do you ask?" he said.

"Maybe because I believe that I do have some rights over you. You need not have married me, whatever the circumstances. I have done my best to keep my part of the bargain. Yes Sameer, I know I am speaking a language that sounds crude. But was it only a bargain, and why was I not party to the truth?"

He looked at her, the amazement written large on his face. "What are you talking about?" he asked loudly. "Why should our marriage involve a bargain? I know you have done your best, but was that asking too much? Have I not too fulfilled the pledges we made? You speak in a riddle, Vandana! What has David been telling you about our past?"

"He has told me everything about Romola and her son," she replied in a hushed tone.

"Well, what about them?" he retorted sharply. "He told you that he wanted to marry her, but as usual he had his good reasons not to do so. He left that woman with child. It is a form of abandonment, you will agree. What reasons did he give for doing that?"

"He said he was not Avinash's biological father." She felt her heartbeat pummel against her ribcage. The truth was about to be disclosed. She wondered whether such moments arrive quietly or whether the skies open up in rage.

Sameer looked surprised. "He told you that? Do you really believe him? If he is not the father, then who is?"

"I do believe him," she said fiercely. "After so many years what can warrant such a lie? He said he never had sex with her, that neither Romola nor the rules of the ashram permitted it. Yes he did desire her, and from all accounts her beauty could have provoked any man."

"Vandana, this is the strangest bit of information you are giving me. If the rules of the ashram did not permit her to have physical intimacy with him, then how did she conceive? Which other man could have been responsible in those circumstances?"

A hollow laugh broke against her throat, and for the first time the tears spilled over and almost choked her. "I don't know," she spluttered. "I thought maybe . . . I don't know. He said she and Uma used to play some game which they called 'entering the womb'. It sounded bizarre. One of the reasons why David left her and India was because he too was puzzled by the turn of events. He feels guilty now, about judging her morally. He thinks it killed her."

"Say that again? What did they call the game? Entering the womb?" Sameer looked at Vandana with utter amazement. In a flash the expression on his face changed from bewilderment to that of someone possessed of terrible knowledge.

~~~

He picked up Uma's file and, before he summoned David and Vandana to his room, he reread it with the curiosity of the professional for a case that remains unsolved. He was willing now to disclose the truth about Uma, and though he felt he was crossing the line of medical prudence, the facts of the matter had to be brought out in the open. He owed it to Romola, Avinash and Uma.

He pondered over the case with a sense of misgiving. Where had he gone wrong in his diagnosis? Was it because he was viewing Uma less as a patient and more as a relative, whose family circumstances were part of his own? He had not asked himself the single most important question about Uma: why had she left home to enter the ashram? He realized now with the clarity of someone who could see the light at the end of the tunnel that he had dismissed the reasons as innocuous because the truth would hurt the family. As usual he had protected his own against the outsider. The use of the word made him shudder. No, no, his mind revolted. Uma had never been the outsider! Chotoma had flooded the child with her love; the mother who was responsible for the betrayal was scrupulously kept out of Uma's life. Then what had really gone wrong?

Were Uma's delusions about her mother manic? Did she

want to bring Bela back to life in stubborn opposition to what her family was doing? Suddenly Grandpa's silence rose like a spectre from the dim outlines of the past, and loomed before his eyes. He had never thought of his grandfather as tyrannical, but he understood now how the old man must have seemed to the child Uma. Grandpa had shunned the little girl as though she was a waif who had usurped the space that rightfully belonged to Bela. A strange tug of war had ensued in the family. Uma and Vikram with Chotoma's divided responsibilities towards them; grandmother pitted against grandfather; loving mother against child, and vice versa. Only the children had loved without invisible barriers, but not without the sense of whispered secrets behind closed doors. The subject of unequivocal love had been taboo in the household.

He had wanted to drag Uma out of her delusion. Your mother is dead, he had said to her in no uncertain terms. He saw the list of medication that he had prescribed for her. He remembered almost with a sense of shame the elaborate charade that all of them had enacted to make Uma realize that Bela had indeed died. But what had been the fall-out? Had Uma been cured? Romola had been resurrected out of their game-playing. No, he reminded himself, it had been part of the treatment protocol, and it was only looking into the hazy past from a distance that made it appear as heinous as it now seemed. It had made sense then, and it did turn out to be a successful experiment. Uma buried Bela, and replaced her with Romola.

Another thought, more niggling and terrifying, gripped him, making beads of sweat drench his forehead. Who was Romola? What had made her so enticing? He knew that Vandana had come close to believing that Avinash was his son. He and Abha had put the secret to rest after David left India. Abha had believed that David had gone back heart-broken because Romola had refused to marry him. She gave Uma as the reason. The two women had become blood sisters, and now the child in her womb had fused them together. Romola had chosen her life in the ashram over and above any other. This had been the story they had nursed all the time. But now another reality stared him in the face. If Avinash was not David's son, then a deeper secret lay buried somewhere. Had Romola carried the secret of paternity to her grave? But why had she chosen to die, leaving both Uma and the boy behind?

He wished fleetingly that he could have asked Romola the many questions that remained locked in his mind. When he had heard she was with child he had gone to meet her, with the sole purpose of knowing the truth. It was a Thursday, and the inmates of the ashram were coming out of the open portico to meet their family and loved ones. Romola did not appear for a very long time, and just when he was about to leave with a vague sense of dissatisfaction, he saw her emerge from behind the foliage. It was approaching winter and some of the plants were in full bloom. He noticed then the fulsome youth of her body, and the defiance with which she held herself against the world. He was not sure what he had been expecting. He had thought of her as the one betrayed, left to carry the burden of sin in her womb. He had come to meet her solely for the purpose of commiserating with her predicament and, perhaps, offering her a helping hand. He was thinking as much of Uma and the world she and Romola shared. When had Romola and David turned lovers, and what illicit passion had brought forth this child? He had wanted, then, to stand by her.

But when she came forward and held his hand and raised her head to look into his eyes, he had seen something that had made him recoil with shock. He could remember that feeling vividly, and now with the truth unveiled that she had not been carrying David's son, the shock was accompanied by a sense of outrage. How do you describe a woman who flaunts her condition with pride? Her eyes were daring and innocent like someone who was unaware of the implications of her acts. But there was something else as well: a whiff of freedom from convention, and the singular lack of complacency that usually accompanies knowledge and acceptance of norms. Sameer was minded of cavorting animals or the intense beauty of a lotus growing wild in a pond of weeds. Romola was unaware of the power she yielded over men. He understood why David had felt so bereft at her rejection.

"Why have you done this?" he asked her sternly, like someone admonishing a wayward child. She was carrying a basket of morning glories and hibiscus, the deep colours staining her white garb. "You understand what it means? You are denying a child its legitimacy and its home. David is willing to marry you."

"Who is he to offer me legitimacy or anything else?" she cried with pouting lips. "You men are so arrogant! I often tell Uma that. Even when you claim to take up responsibility, it is with a sense of possession. This child belongs to Uma and me, he has no role to play. We will bring the child up in this garden, the ashram, far from the metropolis and the market. Have you come to lecture me? Then please go away."

He had been moved by her words, but he pretended to be angry. "Hear yourself speak," he said. "The four walls of the ashram might protect you from the world, but it cannot give your child what he or she needs. The sanction of society. Why bring a child into this world if you had no desire to fit into the family mould? Stop, Romola, stop. Don't drag all of us into circumstances that can only cause a lot of pain!"

He had never seen her happier, and her body, ripe and burgeoning with life, seemed oblivious of the world outside. He understood then the reason why Uma and David were both enslaved by their love for her. He had this wild desire to pluck her out of this environment and take her home.

"In the ashram I am married to the Lord Krishna. There is pain and love in this marriage. The child will unlock my womb and, like Ma Yashodha, I will surrender it to the river. Homes are only temporary abodes. Swamiji says it is only our vanity that makes us believe our temporary homes are everlasting."

"Unlock the womb." The words returned to Sameer and made him shiver. This was the kind of delusion that he understood was Uma's mental condition. Why had Romola participated in it so avidly? What had the two women shared? He tried going over every word that they had exchanged, searching for some meaning that might have eluded him. David says Avinash is not his son. Had Romola given some indication he was? Had he misunderstood the meaning of her words? He realized now that she had dismissed paternity as irrelevant. She had hardly dwelt on David, and she had certainly dismissed the idea of marrying him.

Sameer felt bewildered by this case. Who was the patient here, Romola or Uma? And then another thought, far more destabilizing, swamped his mind. What if neither of them had been suffering an ailment? What if a medical diagnosis was uncalled for? Had he got it all wrong? Childbirth, love, marriage had been endowed with so much sanctity that if a woman chose to "unlock her womb" without the necessary ceremonies, she was considered to be mentally ill.

~~~

"I need to make another trip to Varanasi and meet Uma. She has taken total sanyas, which means she has abdicated her right to meet any member of her family," Sameer said with consternation. "I don't know how far the rules and regulations will permit such a meeting, but I can plead with the organization. Uma alone can throw some light on the situation."

"I wonder what Abha had discovered that is so shocking," Vandana interrupted, "maybe that can provide us with some clues."

"See how we go on and on as though we are investigating some great mystery," David said trenchantly. "How does it matter anyway what Romola told me? I am beginning to see some sense in what she said. She had a child, father unknown, she died of her own will, and the child is orphaned today and needs our shelter. Who can give it to him is the only question that matters. Why go in circles? What truth are we looking for?"

"Even if one of us were to adopt Avinash there are formalities to be completed," Vandana looked at the others helplessly, "Are we to be his guardians or his parents?"

"The more I think about this matter, the more angry I feel," Sameer burst out. "Unlocking the womb, what a bizarre idea! Almost obscene when you think of Avinash and the repercussions on his life."

Obscene? The word seemed to dislocate itself from the situation and mock her. Vandana looked at the two men sitting in front of her and wondered why her life seemed inextricably tied to them. She knew her own decision mattered more than anything else, yet how could she make up her mind without taking all of them into consideration? She knew that she was hurting only because they were, like a parasite at the mercy of the host. She felt emotionally drained.

~~~

"I have seen some papers in your bag," Mira said to Avinash. "They say your mother was missing from the ashram and then her body was found in the Ganges. What happened?"

"I don't know," the boy answered sullenly. "I know my mother disappeared in the river. She said she wanted to take me along, but I think she changed her mind."

"You!" Mira screamed in horror, "What kind of a mother was she?"

"She was a good mother," Avinash said doggedly. "She used to pick flowers for the garlands. I helped her pick flowers. One day she told me that flowers had souls, and they cried at night after the birds returned to their nests. I loved Umamasi as much as I loved my mother. She once told me that I had her blood running through my veins for we had the same soul."

"For God's sake, don't talk like that!" Mira scolded. "People would say you are nutty if they heard you. Try telling this to Abhi. He scorns soul talk. He says it is not scientific. I believe you, but I don't want people to laugh at you."

"Let them laugh at me. You laugh too, I know that."

"Swear by God, I don't," Mira shook her head angrily.

'Why should I believe you?" Avinash said cruelly.

'Because I am not an idiot, understand," Mira shot back.

"OK, OK, would you like to see where your soul is? My mother once showed it to me. It is close to where your belly button is. See, there!"

Mira began to laugh softly, trying to peer down at the black hole that was her belly button. "You are laughing, you witch," Avinash gnashed his teeth in rage. Mira felt cold. "No, no," she cried plaintively. "I was not laughing at you! Your head is filled with ridiculous ideas. Abhi says the ashram breeds ignorance. I think he is right. What makes you say the soul is here?"

"The soul is here and here and everywhere," Avinash answered triumphantly. "I have learnt all this from the shlokas that Swamiji taught me. It is you who are ignorant."

"We can ask mother if you want," Mira revealed her last trump card. Normally Avinash was instantly apologetic, but today he averted his eyes, brooding over matters in a quiet way. Mira stepped forward and embraced him; their souls fused in a kind of suffering that went far beyond their juvenile sensibilities.

"My mother used to say that her soul had been locked in a magic box and thrown to the bottom of the river. She said if she could dive deep enough she would find her soul, and then she would come back to live with me, for she loved me."

"Oh, oh," Mira groaned, the sorrow welling up deep inside her. "She did love you. Mothers always do, come what may. She drowned because the currents of the river were too strong and she could not swim fast enough." Avinash stared at the girl with unbelieving eyes.

Rudravasa,
the Wrath of Shiva

CHAPTER TEN

The Inheritance

The house was decaying from within; Sameer could sense that, just as much as he felt the city was rapidly falling to pieces. He was returning to Varanasi after a gap of a few years. In the interim period his parents had passed away within a few years of each other. Now only Chotoma lived in the rambling mansion with her husband and a retinue of servants. Vikram had settled abroad with his family. Despite constant invitations to come over and stay with them, Chotoma refused. "How can I go away and leave Uma so completely?" she asked, and though the logic of her argument infuriated her son, she stuck to her resolution. Uma might have deserted the family, but how could she do the same to her child? With Vikram she felt the bond between parent and child could be maintained over the telephone.

Sameer looked at this ageing woman with her silver grey hair and quiet shuffling movements, and felt that she presided over their grand old inheritance like the embodiment of a matriarch. But she was alert and, unlike Grandma who had metamorphosised into a funny old lady, Chotoma had a quaint, youthful grace about her. She touched Sameer's face with her gentle, soft fingers and traced in its lines the lineage of the Sengupta family. "Look at you. I can see the old man in your face. The only thing that is missing is the frown. But you are so much like your grandfather in his reticence. How are the children and Vandana? You should have brought them along. Who knows whether I shall get to see them at all?"

"Hush, Chotoma," Sameer chided. "Plenty of occasions are still to come. The kids are in their teens and growing rapidly. One fine morning they will be ready to embark on their different goals in life. You have to be there to give your blessings."

Chotoma chuckled good-naturedly. She had got the cook to lay out all the special dishes that Sameer used to enjoy during his yearly visits to Varanasi. He felt happy in an inexplicable way. This was also the first time that he was coming home with all his cards laid on the table; there was nothing that he was hiding from Vandana. Her resilience and quick acceptance of the turn of events surprised him. He was grateful to her for the commonsense she brought into his life. As he relaxed in the presence of his aunt, he felt at ease with himself.

When Abha came over in the evening to meet him, he embraced her readily. He noticed that she too had mellowed with age. Only the round rims of her spectacles seemed the same as before. Her eyes were sharp and brittle, and she viewed him with her usual touch of good humour. The love that they had never openly acknowledged remained in the background, like the delicate fragrance of a perfume that had been used with the correct proportion of restraint. They could feel the heady scent, but neither was willing to sniff loudly or speak about it.

After the usual exchange of pleasantries, Abha paused a second before she said briskly, "I suppose you want to know what I wrote about in the letter. Well, I think I need the right words to say it, otherwise it will sound too sensational. Give me a minute, Sameer. Let me work out the correct way of revealing a secret that ideally should remain hidden. But there is a reason why I feel you and Vandana and David should know the truth."

"Wait a minute, Abha." Sameer stopped her. "I know the secret is top-most on your mind. I read the anxiety in your letter. And I, too, am consumed with curiosity to know what could be so damaging a secret that you could not spell out in your letter. But now, at this moment, it seems the secret can wait. Romola is important, but not more than Uma and this problem that Chotoma has raised."

"A problem?" Abha sounded puzzled.

Sameer felt the weight of family responsibilities. It had been his inheritance as the first-born. "Chotoma tells me that in the share of the family property, Uma has half the claim. Though she has taken sanyas from all material desire, from the legal point of view she has to give up her share for Vikram to inherit it. Will the ashram respect her rights? I will have to approach them and put forward the problem. Naturally Chotoma wants this matter to be resolved quickly, within their lifetimes. What is the matter, Abha? Why do you look so stricken?"

Abha stared at Sameer with growing incredulity. "Dear me," she whispered, "what I have to tell you is far more important in the light of what you have just said. You see, what I am going to tell you has much more to do with Uma than it has to do with Romola."

"No, no, let's not talk about it now. I want to think about things in a focused way. How do we get the ashram to give us permission, and more importantly how do we explain things to Uma? Does she understand matters like inheritance anymore?"

"She has got to," Abha answered firmly. "You cannot

escape from all your responsibilities. It seem as though life
moves in circles! Chotoma did her best in keeping Uma's
inheritance intact. They never cheated her, not in terms of
emotions, nor in terms of material protection. When Uma
left, she did it at her own peril. Then she simply acquired a
mental state that enabled her to sideline all her responsibilities. She continued to receive her family's love without
needing to return it in anyway…"

"Don't say that," Sameer responded quickly. "I think she
did return our feelings in many ways. It was just that the
chain of communication was not so apparent. And I know for
sure that Uma will give up her claim for the sake of Vikram
and his children. It is just that she is not allowed any kind of
contact with the outside world. What do we do, Abha?"

"I will think of some way," Abha said reassuringly, but
she sounded thoughtful. When they parted she continued to
look distracted. He sensed that she was mentally preoccupied with something that bothered her more than she was
willing to disclose. He let it remain at that.

When she had gone Sameer felt whiffs of nostalgia over-
whelm him. He went to the children's room that had once
been shared by Uma, Vikram and him. How do you begin to
divide property, he wondered? How do you give up claims
on your memory?

Uma will sign off her claim, and that will be the point
when she truly leaves the family. And, like always, he would
preside over the moment and see to it that it happens without a hitch. He hated his position as the eldest in the family.
And then a thought that was laughably impossible crossed
his mind. What if he were to abdicate his duties? What if he
turned his back on Vandana and the children? What if, like
Romola, he were to ignore convention. What if he were to

turn to his family and look at them with crazed, wanton eyes and proclaim that he would never return to the fold?

He shook his head ruefully and gave a quick, ironic laugh, aware of his own limitations. He imagined that if Abha had been party to his thoughts, she too would join the laughter, perhaps half-affectionately, half-disdainfully. He had always loved her for those dual qualities she possessed of brutality matched with compassion. 'Loved her . . .' The thought made him pant a little. He lay on the bed that had belonged to him in his younger boyhood days, clutched the bedspread and dragged it over his mouth. He could hear the groans deep down in his throat. His loins ached with desire. When had he and Vandana last made love with real, searing passion? When had they done it without loads of responsibilities weighing them down, so that once their energies were spent, they had gone back to whatever they had been thinking in their own separate, enclosed spaces? But at moments like this, when his life had reached a point of intensity, he was sharing his innermost thoughts with Abha. Was that a mere coincidence? They were together again, and he felt the excitement rush like adrenalin through his body.

He picked up his cell phone and dialled her number. He could hear the sound of traffic in the background. She had not yet reached her house.

"Abha, it's me, Sameer. I had this crazy idea that I was willing to give up everything – wife, children, family – just to be with you. Laugh me out of this thought, please!"

She was silent on the other end for a long of time. When she spoke she was fumbling for words, the tears blinding her and making her hands on the steering wheel tremble. "You can borrow six days of your life and dedicate it to me. We will carry the secret to our graves."

~~~

When he woke up the next morning the sunlight was streaming in through the window. He saw the light grey, lace curtains and his heartbeat began to quicken. Memories of childhood were always so detailed, and in the bland daylight of another day he felt he had all the leisure to go through the nuances one by one.

The madness of his thoughts last night gripped him once again. He had to see her. He checked out his cell. Sure enough, there were several messages for him. He scrolled down until he came to her message. "Fxd appointmnt with Sji. Will pck u up at 11.30". Was he expecting something more intimate? He imagined her keying the message with steady hand, but then the night before he had heard the tremor in her voice. He answered her message. "The night was tremulous. I dream endlessly."

When they sat next to each other in the car he felt tongue-tied. If only they could speak in a cryptic language, without punctuation.

"Did you get my messages?" he asked at long last.

"Yes, and I am scared," she replied instantly. "This is so unlike you, Sameer. Pardon me if I falter with my reactions. What kind of game are you asking me to play? See? The question has sprung to my lips. Please be honest with me."

He allowed his hand to stray and graze her elbow. When she did not withdraw he ran his fingers across the fine, down of light brown hair and the soft skin beneath. She wore quarter sleeves, and his fingers traced the edges and caressed the white, tender flesh of her arms, so smooth he felt his fingers gliding down them. He loved her then in the intimacy of the moment, and the words that tumbled through his lips were on fire.

"Do you believe one can be in a happy marriage and yet love someone outside it? Love without any sense of guilt or shame. I am not committing adultery, please understand that. But this feeling that is gripping me in its vice-like stranglehold is something that is both enabling and wonderful. To deny it would be a kind of death."

She jerked away her hand. "You do not feel this for me at this moment, Sameer. It is the magic of some other, more obscure, turning-point in your life. I am just the vessel that contains the condition of being that you are looking for. Why else would you feel so devoid of moral doubts?"

"I dare say the doubts will come; so will the guilt. But it is worth the price. And make no mistake: I would not feel the same for anyone else."

They were approaching the ashram, entering the narrow road that was impossible to navigate in a vehicle. They parked in the nearby marketplace and began the rest of the journey on foot. The thread of their earlier conversation was put on hold as they discussed the impending meeting with Swami Parmananda.

"Do I lay all the cards on the table?" he asked her.

"Take it as it comes, Sameer. The only risk is refusal. Weigh the pros and cons and then proceed," she answered thoughtfully.

"Are the rules of sanyasins irrevocable? What happens to any property a person might have at the time of taking vows?"

"Good God!" she said in an alarmed tone. "Do you think the ashram can lay claim to it? Not everybody takes vows of total abdication. Maybe they choose their customers cleverly."

They were aghast at the thought. The battle ahead seemed loaded against them.

Swami Parmananda was more inflexible than they had

thought. No one can meet Uma, he said categorically. Papers can be sent in to her, and if she signs it is all right. But the right of decision should be hers. No member of the family can be permitted to influence her.

They returned defeated. From all accounts given by other inmates of the ashram Uma was oblivious to the world outside. Does she remember her own name to sign on any paper, they asked sceptically?

"Look, I am feeling drained of all energy," Sameer said vehemently. "I need a break. Now that I am out in the streets, the city has begun to grip me. Let us go somewhere and pick up some lunch. I am famished."

His mood was infectious. "Yes," Abha chimed in, "let me be your guide! Imagine you are the tourist who comes to this sublime city and is looking for experience that is once-in-a-lifetime. He has a family to go back to, and what he wants to carry home is a basket-load of experiences."

"I have no family to go back to. I am living on borrowed time, and I am making hay while the sun shines. On a rainy day I would like to open my basket and unfurl the world's greatest treasures."

She felt a little breathless, as though some strange madness had gripped them. She stamped on the accelerator and drove to the part of the city she was most familiar with. "We go to the Asi Ghat," she squealed in delight. "To me it is the most beautiful ghat, for it is devoid of any religious paraphernalia. It is picturesque and ancient. And besides, it has got the town's best pizza joint. A quaint little place that even celebrities frequent."

Sameer wrinkled his nose. "I am disappointed in you. Pizza is so modern and Delhi-like! It is just the sort of food that Mira and Abhi like to eat."

"I thought you were unencumbered!" Abha said teasingly. "Believe me, this is pizza with a difference. It is baked in a wooden stove and all the ingredients are Indian. The combinations are so way-out that it is a bit of a culture shock. Only the lasagna is authentically Italian and comes piping hot."

She was like a child in her excitement. It made Sameer feel strangely protective towards her. He must do nothing to break her heart, he swore to himself. Why had she chosen not to get married? Did she have relationships at the university? She was at Banaras Hindu University as a Reader and many of her research papers had been published in distinguished journals from abroad. She had gone briefly to Sussex, and returned having had a book published. She had been regularly in touch with David; during her stay in England she had been his paying guest.

Her hair was glossy black, with just a touch of peppery white near the temple. She wore no make-up, except for a light touch of powder that had caked into white stripes near her neck. She wore girlish round earrings that bobbed up and down when she spoke. It gave her speeches a touch of the comic, and he found himself relaxing in her presence.

They moved up the steps of the ghat, the road having ended abruptly near a turning that suddenly revealed the stretch of the river. The road had a bookshop, Indica Stores, and when Abha waved to the man sitting at the counter Sameer felt a touch of envy at the familiarity of the gesture. The man came out to meet them. They exchanged news about some new book that had just reached the market. She scribbled the name and the references. "I will come next week with money enough to buy," she laughed. The man said he was willing to give it on credit, but she was adamant.

"You must have seen the branch of Indica in the

Gadholia market," she said to Sameer, "but this man has guts to open a book shop here. I am a regular customer. I love the ambiance. It is so far removed from all the religious pell–mell. I am always at peace here."

"There are shops here, the foreign touristy kind. I can see Varanasi has become quite commercial, what with malls and multiplexes. I am amazed at how much things have changed, but the civic amenities of the city are near collapse."

"Don't even mention that," Abha said ruefully. "Have you seen the garbage heaps and the condition of the roads? But why are we talking like this? We were supposed to be experiencing something entirely different, remember?"

Indeed, he was complaining about the city, but his eyes were devouring every single detail. He noticed that many of the huge ancestral houses that were over a hundred years old had been converted into riverside guesthouses. They carried large billboards announcing air-conditioned rooms, hot water in geysers, and sauna baths. He chuckled at the thought of sauna baths in a city that boasted of a river that could wash away a lifetime of sins! But he also understood how second generations in a family found it difficult to maintain inherited property and had to put it to commercial use. As usual, Varanasi had kept pace with the turning of the century.

The Asi Ghat was majestic, and held in its panoramic sweep the curve of the river like a jewelled necklace. The steps leading down to the river were wide and cleaner than usual, because a private household with royal lineage main-tained this ghat. And because the ghat was less strewn with waste products and fruit peels, there were fewer beggars and bulls. The river was turgid green and deep, and the boats that were anchored to the embankment were painted in bright hues of orange, purple and green. The pizza restaurant was built on the steps of the ghat, open-air, under trees with wide spread branches, like canopies to keep away the bright sunlight. The place was uncrowded and they found themselves a cosy corner for two, and as they looked at each other with fervent appeal, Sameer sensed the eyes turning to watch them. 'They mistake us for a married couple out on a second honeymoon, but we are lovers whom destiny has kept apart,' he thought rather dramatically.

"I am a little worried," Abha said, munching the pizza with relish. "What happens now that the ashram has turned down our request? Are you hearing me, Sameer?"

He wasn't. He refused to allow the intensity of the moment to slip by. She looked restless, as though time was of the essence in the presence of the eternal splendour of an ancient city growing besides a river. He sensed that his touristy mood was at variance with her daily negotiation of Varanasi, with its crowded market places and noisy traffic. A branch of the tree nestled close to her face, and the green leaves flicked and shook like fleeting thoughts criss-crossing her mind. He laughed aloud, surprising her.

"You are horribly unromantic," he said playfully. "Moments like this are for you time wasted. I can see why you never found time to fall in love."

"I did fall in love, but I was a little too late."

"You know, Abha, the day you asked me to marry Vandana was the day I had rehearsed a long speech when I would ask for your hand in marriage. Oh, the irony of it! Like some Greek tragedy."

"Or comedy," she intervened. "I prefer to think of it that way. Look at it like this, there is something funny about our situation now."

"You find it funny." He tried to sound hurt. "I think it is wonderful."

Her eyes were sad. "Thank you for saying that. I have never felt so wooed in my life. But this is a bit of a Roman holiday, and once it is over we have to get back to our good old routine."

"Yes, we do, but I will carry these precious moments," he crossed his heart dramatically, "deep in here."

She was openly laughing now, the mirth spilling like the radiance of light shimmering on the riverfront. A bull bayed with full-throated gusto, puncturing the silence. A boatman cleared his throat noisily, and in the background temple bells jangled and reverberated with the fervor of worship. They felt that love was another form of obeisance to life's myriad surprises. They felt blessed, and Sameer marvelled at how much he was at peace with himself. Could he trade off a life-time of associations and responsibilities for this magical moment? The question was out of sync for, sitting on the steps of the Asi Ghat, it seemed to Sameer that both realities could co-exist with ease.

~~~

He returned home that night to find her message on his cell phone. "Meet me 2morrow. Urgent." He dialed her number, eager to hear her voice. It was a while before she came on the line. "Where were you?" he asked impatiently.

"Watering my plants," she said matter of factly.

"At this time?" he sounded surprised.

"This is the best time, after sundown. It relaxes all your tired limbs. After I return home from working in the ashram office I potter around in the garden."

"You have a garden," he burst out. "What happened to that one-room hole you used to stay in?"

"Did I not tell you that I have been living in the university quarters for the last three years?" she said, pleased to have taken him so much by surprise. "A regular three-bedroomed house with a large verandah. My mum often comes and spends a month or so with me. My brother, too, makes it here with his family. His two sons love their spinster aunt. She is ideal for spoiling them. I too have started liking my new role as homemaker. And to further surprise you I have six cats to keep me company. I had just finished feeding them when I heard my cell ring."

"Wow!" he cried out in wonder, "you actually live inside the BHU campus? Remember that's from where you brought home my bride? Oh, our story gets funnier and funnier, almost farcical! It's strange how both you and David settled into lives of gentility, so far removed from your earlier nomadic selves. I used to feel so hemmed-in and straight in comparison. I recall one of the reasons why you felt Vandana and I were so made for each other was because we shared this instinct for home-making, as though it was such an unfashionable urge. I think somewhere deep down both David and you believed that we were made to carve out mediocre destinies. But see yourselves now."

"Please, Sameer, don't speak so harshly," she pleaded. "We don't carry crystal balls, do we, to see into the future? I have lived my life on a day-to-day basis, adjusting to all the changes that it has brought for me. I claim neither praise nor blame for it."

She sounded tired and lonely. His heart ached for her, but much of his feelings sprang from the emptiness of this large, rambling house devoid of familiar faces. He missed Grandma, Grandpa and his parents. Why was he asking Uma to forego her claim on this house? Was there any possibility of Vikram returning to India and staking his claim? What about his own son and daughter? Would they live here? And, even if they were to do so, would the house mean the same to them? Inheritance, lineage, family traditions, all the values that had meant so much through his growing years, how little they really mattered! He felt empty within, like someone whose favourite toy had been snatched away from him.

"Why don't you come over now?" he asked recklessly. "Or maybe I should come over and see the little nest you have created. This huge house of mine, I can feel its decadence on my skin. I have been pacing up and down the length and breadth of the verandah, and except for the crunching sound of my footsteps on the floor, not a single noise has invaded my consciousness. It's like being trapped in a cocoon, like a chrysalis waiting to emerge. I miss you now. I am sorry for my rudeness."

"Sameer, I am worried for you! Whatever is the matter?" she said tenderly. "I have never heard you speak this way. It is quite distressing. You sound so unhappy."

"Unhappy?" he rocked with laughter. "I am riotously happy. I have never felt this way. Really! No baggage to carry, no pretences, no making excuses. For the first time in my life I am expressing myself the way I feel. I am happy."

"Is it so?" she asked unsurely. "Then I am much relieved. But please, Sameer, I cannot permit you to come over to my place. Don't you see? When at the end of the seven promised days you return home, I need an unsullied space to come back to. Home is the only place that can provide refuge. I need to keep it untouched." She said all this without conviction, and he could sense the hesitation in her voice. He felt excited, as though he carried the secret knowledge of her vulnerable point that he could exploit when the situation demanded.

"All right," he agreed. "I am willing to go along with you now, but it is not a promise. The minute I feel the need to break the barriers I will storm in, and believe me, none of this talk about unsullied space is going to keep me away. I should have done it long back, but we were brought up on ceremonies and niceties. We were taught to make sacrifices, as though these were badges we could wear, like stars proclaiming a man's valour. But at the end of the day what does it really bring home?"

She returned to her room, disrupting the watering of the plants. The cats kept scratching on the front door, whining to be let in. She sat heavily on the bed allowing the bedspread to crumble as she gathered the folds in her fists. She felt despair, as she had never felt it before.

"What I am going to tell you will change your life," she groaned loudly. "It will bring mountains of responsibility on you. Will I ever get a chance to see this side of your nature? Will you be happy in the same way? Oh, Sameer I fear for you, and you know what makes all this so absurdly difficult for me, is that I alone will be responsible for sending your world crashing. That is what I dread the most."

CHAPTER ELEVEN

The Midwife

The alley they had entered was so dark, and in such sharp contrast to the bright sunshine outside that Sameer blinked his eyes in amazement. A thrill coursed through his body. At long last he felt he had returned to the Varanasi that had never ceased to fascinate him. Where else in India could streets run like narrow arteries that carried the lifeline of the city? Where else could houses obliterate the sky? He felt he was inside a maze that was both impenetrable and endless, so that once he entered its convoluted interiors there was no going back. And yet it did not feel like a trap or confinement. He moved forward, and wondered at the mystique of a woman who traversed these paths without the slightest hesitation. Abha knew every nook and corner of these narrow bylanes like a seasoned navigator.

Once in a while she turned back to check whether Sameer was well on track. He lunged forward, their bodies colliding. The impact was intense, reverberating through the ancient, rough-hewn bricks and mortar that formed the base of the dwelling places on both sides. Abha felt the blood rush to her face. She noticed for the first time the tiny slits that were doors and windows, and the many eyes glancing furtively at them.

"We have to go further," she said apologetically. But he was hardly listening to her. They moved on at a drunken pace, and Sameer felt the strange urge to pin her down and smother her face with swift, gobbling movements of his tongue. He wanted the taste of her body on his senses, nibbling her ears, neck and the rough stubble of her armpits. In his mind's eye he had undressed her entirely so that she stood before him like a Botticelli painting, naked, luminous flesh. "We are soul mates," he thought intensely, "otherwise we would not be together on this mission."

Why are we here in the first place, he wondered? Why are we trying to track down a woman who holds the key to the secret that Abha refuses to divulge? "Why can't you tell me straight?" he asked roughly. "I have my reasons," she answered mysteriously. Reasons, a lifetime of pursuit to find the right reasons for whatever he had done, seemed to elude Sameer. He was no longer interested in reason. He was following his instinct now as a dangerous substitute.

They stood in front of a door. "She lives here," Abha whispered. "This is the address she had given me. Let me try to go in first. The sight of a stranger may frighten her. It is important that she relaxes in our company, otherwise she will refuse to speak."

"Before we enter through this door I need to clear up a few things," Sameer said forcefully. "Who is this person . . . a woman from what I can gather . . . and how is she connected with the secret you have to tell me?"

"She is a midwife by profession . . . ." Abha began explaining.

"A midwife?" Sameer cried out in horror, his face suddenly dark with concern. Abha recoiled but said with conviction. "Yes, Sameer, she is a midwife. Why should her profession make such a difference? Don't make things more difficult than it is. Now you know this has something to do with Avinash . . ." But Sameer was not listening. He was looking at her with burning eyes, and when he spoke his voice sounded strangulated with pain.

"I am trying to look at things rationally, but there is no end to the horror that opens up before my eyes. I know what you will say. Midwives are still operating in villages in India, and many of them have licences. But you know, Abha, nobody would go to a midwife in a city unless they have something dark to hide. And who knows how competent this one is, whether she has been trained by a medical practitioner or whether she is in this business to exploit needy women. It does not surprise me that Romola would have gone to one. But to meet one myself, and have her tell me secrets. Oh, Good Lord! This is more difficult for me than you can understand."

"I do understand," Abha whispered, "and believe me, I would not bring you here if there was any other way of finding out. But we have to go through with this."

Sameer was staring at the house. It looked so old and dilapidated that he wondered whether it would be safe to enter its portals. He noticed that it was jammed between other houses, equally decrepit and squalid. Outlines of what seemed rooms and perhaps a narrow staircase were visible through a tiny open window. They were the only signs of living space and the possibility that the structure was a home. Abha knocked on the door. As they waited for a response from inside, he grabbed her hand and pressed her fingers to his lips. She looked startled, but did not remove her hand. The small pressure of flesh on flesh felt as potent as the undulating rhythm of the earth beneath the tar-covered streets. The city gripped them from below and sucked them into its vortex.

After what seemed an interminable wait, the door opened, and a young girl emerged from the shadows. She looked surprised at the sight of Abha. "We have come to meet Sakina Bi," Abha said with a fleeting smile. The pressure of Sameer's lips still seared her skin. She felt that the girl's alien eyes had penetrated her secret and were regarding her soiled fingers with disapproval.

"Sakina Bi is ill," the girl replied nervously. "She has stopped meeting anyone. I am sorry." The girl was ready to shut the door in their faces. Abha pressed her hand against the doorknob and said fervently, "Tell Sakina Bi it is the woman from the university. She must keep the promise she made to me."

The girl paused briefly, then she leant forward and whispered in a conspiratorial way, "My mother has guests all the time. Women who need to get rid of their sins. I will tell her, but I can promise you nothing. Will you wait outside, or should I make place for you to sit in the inner room? In case mother agrees to meet you, I will have to change her clothes. It will take time."

"I am comfortable outside. I have another person with me. He has come all the way from Delhi. Please tell your mother I am not returning from this place without meeting her."

The girl vanished inside, shutting the door. Sameer turned to Abha. "I should have known that there is something shady about this woman," he said quietly, 'rid of their sins' . . . is that what she does as a midwife? In modern medicine her role is to help the woman give birth, so what is all this moral talk about sin? Abha, do you have any idea what a midwife without proper license can do? She can kill a woman with her malpractice!"

Abha looked helpless. "We know nothing about Sakina Bi. We have to trust what she has to say."

Sameer allowed himself to be sucked along by the tide. Why was he quarrelling with Abha about a mere technicality? He held her hand. Flesh on flesh and, this time, the pressure of teeth nibbling, making her groan with pleasure. "Stop, stop," she wanted to say, but the words got jumbled in her mind. She felt as though the city was sending out its tentacles to grasp her, to tear off the last vestiges of her modesty. She felt shameless, like street urchins feeding themselves on the offal thrown inside the garbage heap. But she knew that there was no going back from this point. Revelling in the muck and dirt of Varanasi was to touch the point where pure and impure met and fused in abandon. She had been wrong when she told Sameer that she wanted to retain an unsullied space to go home to. Now she wanted every inch of her being to be sullied.

The girl returned, all smiles. She opened the door and allowed both of them to enter the house. She carried a rusty old kerosene lamp. The stairway was steep and treacherous. "Mind your head," she cried out at one point, addressing herself to Sameer, suddenly conscious of this man who was their guest from a distant city.

Sakina Bi was waiting for them inside a room that seemed pitch dark until the girl took the lamp inside. Shadows danced in wild pirouette on the ceiling. "You can put on the light," a disembodied voice spoke from the depths of the room. The girl gave a squeal of delight, and switched on the light. A naked bulb strung on the wall filled the room with a garish, yellow tinge that sucked the shadows from the ceiling. A woman sat on the floor. She looked ancient, like a mummy inside a tomb. But her eyes glimmered and shone, and when she spoke her voice was firm and young.

"Don't mind me," Sakina Bi said. "I keep away from the

prying eyes. A strange disease has shrunk my skin, and makes it look old like a snake moulting. But I have lived only forty-five years in this world, and I have a sharp memory. What you see before your eyes are centuries of sin visiting me. My experience as a midwife has taught me many things. I have seen the most remarkable sights. Life being born, life smothered in the cradle, life aborted, life accompanied by cries of pain, joy and horror. It's a wonder that anybody comes to me. Perhaps we are all afraid of what my vision will reveal. I have much more to say than your soothsayer. He tells lies, I speak only the truth. So everybody is afraid of me."

Sameer was angry. This ghoulish room, and this diseased woman, mumbling some kind of mumbo jumbo about life and sin was the last thing he wanted to hear. Did this woman assist in bringing Avinash into the world? He stared at her in horror, like someone who had just discovered a truth about his loved ones that was more than he could bear. Sameer felt sick in his heart, and that very minute he knew this woman would disclose something far, far worse than anything he had heard so far.

Abha sensed his mood. She felt the world tumbling around her. She wanted then to rush out of the room and take Sameer far away from the truth. But was there a possibility of going back? Gathering all her strength, she moved close to Sakina Bi and said in a matter of fact tone, "Please tell this man what you had told me. Please be brief. We have very little time."

Sakina Bi exploded. Her anger smashed the room into smithereens, sweeping all of them off their feet like a vicious gale. "Get away from me, get away! Why have you come here if you do not have the patience to hear me? Why? You are an arrogant woman who thinks she can order me round. Me,

Sakina Bi! I know your kind. You think I am a disgrace to my profession. So what if I am not a licensed practitioner? I was much in demand in my time. People came to me all the time. They came in the dark and left in the dark, covering their faces in shame. I know why you have come. You want to know what happened on that night. After I tell you the truth, the shameful, horrific truth, you will go back to your respectable lives and carry on as though nothing had happened. You are angry with me because you are angry with yourselves. I do not care. I carry as much anger in me as this city carries in its bowels. Rudravasa, the wrath of Shiva that Varanasi swallowed into its guts."

Abha noticed the vein throbbing in Sameer's forehead, ready to burst. She had never seen him angry before, but then she had never seen him in his present mood. She stretched out her hand as though she wanted to prevent a calamity from happening. Then she noticed the girl in the corner. The girl had allowed her dupatta to slip from her head. She held it over her mouth to prevent the spurts of laughter from spilling out into the open. Her body was wracked with an obscene, riotous mirth so that it jerked and shook like leaves caught in a hurricane. Seeing the look of astonishment in Abha's face, all eyes turned to look at the girl. Sakina Bi's jaws opened and closed like a fish gasping for breath, then she too began to guffaw until the tears poured down her mottled face.

Only Sameer remained silent, the wrath turning his body to stone. He got up to leave. Sakina Bi stopped and said in a gentle voice, "Wait, man. I am sorry for this behaviour. My daughter and I, we have been discourteous, I realize that. You are my guest, and I should respect you. But a lifetime spent in being a midwife has made me see the extremes of emotions. So what seems madness to you is normal for us.

Here, in Varanasi, Rudravasa can turn to mirth or contemplation in the twinkling of an eye. Everything co-exists here. You have to grasp that before you even begin to understand what I am going to tell you."

"Don't worry," Sameer interjected sternly, "I was born in this city, and spent the major part of my childhood and youth here. I know its mores and ways as well as anyone else. Come out with whatever you have to say. My friend was right when she said we do not have much time."

"Really? Then what brings you here after so many years?" Sakina Bi retorted sharply.

Sameer fell silent. He realized that their tussle was leading nowhere. More than anything else, he wanted to leave the room and return to the safety of his own world. The girl re-entered the room with a tray loaded with sweets and lassi. No one had noticed her leave. "Please accept our gracious hospitality," Sakina Bi said, her tone sharp but mellow.

Sameer broke a tiny piece of the sweet and put it in his mouth. The truce had been made, and he waited for Sakina Bi to speak. Abha felt strangely calm. The sweet aftertaste washed her mouth and coated her throat. She allowed the frothy white lassi to pour into her body like a balm.

"I have to make one thing very clear," Sakina Bi said solemnly, "I have no proof for what I am saying. But my eyes have seen more reality than those of the sages. And remember, I bring the child into the world, and I also clean the blood and the entrails. I yield the knife that severs the mother from the child, and I also give the balm that ceases the pain. I have seen too much. My eyes will never tell a lie."

~~~

"That night I was summoned to the ashram because one of the inmates who had been with child was now ready to deliver. The messenger came as was usual, but I was reluctant to go, because I had been ill for over a week with a high fever that made me delirious. It was the beginning of my wretched ailment, but I did not know that then. When I refused he went away. But as I was getting ready to retire to bed, I heard the front door being pounded by someone who was in a great hurry. I opened the door to find the messenger there. He thrust wads of money into my hand and whispered something into my ears that caught my attention. I slipped into my professional clothes, and hurried behind him. I always carry my own instruments. I have certain rules that I insist upon: plenty of hot water, clean towels and clean surroundings to bring new life into the world. A woman deserves that much. I have seen many die from infections when the place is unclean.

"I have been responsible for bringing many a mite into this world, most of them illegitimate, without a home or father to take care of them. Some were given away soon after birth. I hated the sight of the whimpering mother and the empty cradle. Money exchanged hands, but I was never given my due: it was all hush-hush, and I was bundled out of the place in no time.

"They were more systematic inside the ashram. Swamiji was clear that the ashram would take care of those born within its fold; I was always paid well. But I wondered why I was being given so much money for this occasion. It made me wary.

"Believe me, I have never witnessed a birth that is so joyous, so completely devoid of the fear of pain. There were two women in the room, and they shared the experience like twins, joined body and soul. I felt my presence was redundant. We set a fire burning, and as the water simmered and boiled, the woman who was nursing the expectant mother sang a song that sounded unearthly. The refrain sounded like a dirge, but I understood some of the words – they celebrated life's fecundity. The women clapped their hands in glee, and laughed raucously. They asked me to join in. The mood was infectious. The words became more and more vicious, cursing men, women, marriage, and childbirth as a custom. "We spit on you, motherhood!" the two women sang at high pitch. I was shocked, but mesmerized by the power they exuded. I began to sing with them, especially when they satirized the sanitized culture that views motherhood and childbirth as a woman's greatest birthright. It was magical, the power of their words and the utter profanity of their gestures. I had long harboured a grudge against a woman's helplessness when she gives birth without the attendant legitimacy. The secrecy, the shame and the guilt have always filled me with rage. But these two women gave birth without any sense of refinement or the need for ceremony. I say two women, for in reality it was difficult to distinguish the woman in labour from the woman who was pressing the body down and urging the baby to come out."

"I was witness to something that was both utterly profane and sublime. I joined in the cacophony of yelling, groaning and laughing and, finally, when the baby slithered out, covered in mucous and blood, I knew I had participated in a miracle. It was a beautiful boy. I put the baby on the mother's stomach, and all three of us sat and viewed him in sheer joy, like a communion of sorts. Then both the women went off to sleep, their energies spent. And you know what I did? I returned the money they had paid me, though I could ill afford to do it. But I had this sense that what I had done that night was not part of my regular job. For days after that I felt at peace with myself."

"I used to go back to the ashram to find out about the boy. But somehow, once that night was over, things seemed more normal. At times I used to wonder whether it had all been a dream. Then, a few years later, I was told that a woman was missing from the ashram, and that her body had been fished out from the river. It was mentioned that she was the mother of Avinash. I knew the boy's name, and once or twice I got to catch a glimpse of him. He looked like a prince. I was shocked. How could a woman who had such a joyous sense of life die so young? The rumour was that she had drowned herself. I was not willing to believe it. How could she want to die and leave her son behind? What could have gone wrong? So I went to the ashram and begged Swamiji to grant me permission to pay my last respects to her. Imagine my shock when I saw the body!"

"This, indeed, was one of the two women, but she was not the one who had given birth to Avinash. There is no way I could have been mistaken. I knew it, for I had helped the other one give birth."

~~~

"That woman is a bloody liar," Sameer's face was contorted with rage, "are we to believe that Avinash is Uma's son? What a bloody lie!"

They were racing through the city in Abha's car without direction or destination. She felt helpless, as though she was responsible for bringing on a situation that she could no longer handle.

Sameer had simply jumped up on his feet, and walked out of Sakina Bi's house without so much as exchanging another word with anyone. When the girl had tried to block his way, Sameer had flung her aside. Sakina Bi's voice had risen like a screech. "I speak the truth. I speak the truth."

She had grasped Abha's hand in a vice-like grip. "Some remuneration for the truth. From the gentleman's reaction I should be asking for a lot. All I am asking is just enough to buy medicines."

Sameer had turned viciously and thrown money on the floor. Abha had had the impression that the amount was not small. The girl had swooped down like a bat and picked up the money. Abha had run out of the house, afraid that she would lose Sameer in the streets outside. For a minute she lost her sense of direction, but then she had seen his receding figure at a distance and cried out his name in agony. Only when they were inside the car had she begun to breathe normally. She noticed that he was trembling, his hands tensed over his knees like someone seeking to get back his sense of balance.

"My first reaction was one of utter disbelief," Abha spoke out, "in fact, even at the time when I wrote to both you and David, I had this niggling sense that once I discussed matters with you, I would discover how the very idea is preposterous. That is why I wanted you to speak to the woman, to get the truth directly from her. What is the point of flying off the handle as you are doing now? Simple denial can achieve nothing. We have to stay calm, and go over what she said to us."

"You saw the woman with your own eyes," Sameer barked angrily, "did she seem capable of any kind of sanity? You saw the way she asked for money! She is an extortionist, and this is probably what she does for a living."

"No," Abha said firmly, "I have done my own research on her. She did work as a midwife with the ashram. Her name is signed in the register at the ashram, and it says to assist in childbirth. It gives Romola's name. There is no going wrong on the date. I was informed about Avinash's birth. You see, there was no reason for me to want to get in touch with Sakina Bi then. But after Romola died, I was told by one of the inmates that the secret of her death was with the midwife. She told this to me on the pledge of secrecy. She also said that much goes on inside the ashram that will never find its way outside. I ignored her for a long time. But when we decided to send Avinash to Delhi, I was once again gripped by the thought of Romola's suicide. You see, at that point it made sense to plan out a future for Avinash in a foster home, because we thought his mother was dead and under such mysterious circumstances. I felt he should be kept far away from all the gossip and scandal. Besides, one always felt that Uma was in no position to parent a boy. Given these circumstances, I thought I was doing what was best for him. I remembered about the midwife, and decided to get in touch with her. I realized then the enormity of what she was telling me. So I decided to contact you and David."

Sameer stared at Abha shamefacedly. He regretted his outburst, now that she presented the facts so baldly. Besides, how was Abha to blame for what had happened? Whatever be the nature of the story, true or false, the fact was that she had remained the closest ally of the family. She had never done anything to hurt them. He had depended on her at every turn in his life, and he knew that his love for her had grown under these very circumstances. That was why it seemed such an innate part of his being, as though to deny it at this juncture was to be false to himself. He could never part from her in wrath; he could never reject her. He reached out to hold her hand. They entered the premises of BHU campus, and as the avenue of trees swept past them, he knew he was entering a new phase in his relationship with her. He discarded the despair that was in his soul, and replaced it with a blinding, consuming passion.

~~~

The cats emerged out of the garden and nibbled at her toes. She laughed and hugged them one by one. She took him from room to room. He stumbled behind her, like a child searching for a hidden treasure. The rooms were piled with books and discarded clothes. Everything was in perfect disarray, but the windows were bright with sunlight and the greenery outside seemed to enclose them like a bower. He felt secluded, sucked into the secret space where he had made room for his feelings for her. Amazing that through the years of routine- and habit-forming that being a householder entailed, he had kept this space pristine and intact. He understood what it meant when it was said about Kashi that entering her fold was the final act of renunciation. But there was nothing austere or apocalyptic about this moment. His heart brimmed over with a feeling of gratitude. He had to give back to her what this gratitude entailed, love with all the cumulative passion.

He watched her closely, wondering whether she had an inkling of the wild thoughts that crossed his mind. She was flitting from one thing to another. Thus she gathered all the dirty clothes and put them in the laundry basket, she picked up the days newspapers and kept them in a row on the magazine rack, she put the kettle to boil on the gas stove. "Such a mess," she said several times, "but then I never expected to have guests. My clean-up day is only Sunday."

He tiptoed behind her into the kitchen. She was pouring the coffee into mugs. He held her firmly from behind like one would a pet animal. She laughed, spilling the coffee on the cement slab. "Ouch!" she cried out, "it's hot!"

"Stop," he whispered, "You make me giddy with all this feverish activity! Come and sit next to me. Let everything else be."

He led her back into the lounge, both of them squeezing into the armchair. Her hair was luscious and soft and smelt of shampoo. He traced his hand down, from her neck to her waist. She was slim and youthful and virginal. His fingertips plumbed the depths of her supple body. He had never touched anything so wholesome and pure. "Please don't," she cried in ecstasy, "this is all wrong!"

"I have lost all sense of right and wrong," he said passionately, "after what I have heard today! Tell me honestly, Abha, what do you make of Sakina Bi's story? Suppose for a minute we were to take it as true, why should Romola and Uma do what she says they did – swap roles? And how can anyone maintain such a charade? Unless, of course, the ashram was with them in the game-playing. But it makes no sense at all!"

He began to agonize once again, the magical moment of togetherness lost. She sensed his mood and, extricating her self from the armchair, she sat down on the floor. He was grateful, for he needed the distance in order to get back his perspective. And just then the enormity of the truth hit him hard. Avinash! There was little doubt about the family resemblance! He understood why Avinash had struck such a familiar chord with him and Vandana. No wonder Vandana had mistaken him to be the father.

The father? Suddenly the puzzle about paternity took a bizarre turn. If Uma had been with child, then who was responsible for her condition? That wanton look in Romola's eyes, when had it got transferred to Uma? It had often been mentioned that they had been like twins, but how could this situation be explained by what could only have been a metaphor? This was way beyond what medical science described as a mental condition. He felt helpless.

"David was much closer to Romola," he said at last, "perhaps he can throw some light on what happened. I will ask him to come over."

"Yes," Abha agreed, the weight of the situation making her feel burdened, "but in reality the only one who can solve this problem is Uma. She knows the truth. But how do we reach out to her?"

"I will find a way to pierce this veil of secrecy that the ashram maintains," Sameer retorted sharply, "It is a question of the boy's future. If Avinash is Uma's son, then he is family and has as much right over the property as Vikram and his children. He has as much right over Chotoma and Kaku as anyone else. It changes the equation of things. It makes my responsibility towards the boy twice as much. I should have seen it in those eyes! That same look! He has Bela's beauty. I took it to be something he inherited from Romola, but now I know! Oh, yes! There is truth in what Sakina Bi said."

Sameer groaned with the painful realization that truth stretches beyond the pale of right or wrong, even if it cannot be proven. Uma, poor Uma, with all her delusions! Where did they begin? Was it inside the ashram, or were the seeds planted inside the home that became her refuge after Bela left, never to return? How deeply Uma must have missed her mother! But why should she grieve at someone's absence if that person had never been part of her early memories? Another thought, niggling but relentless, crossed his mind. Bela was the never-ending topic for scandal, and who knows how many times the child overheard adults speaking about her? Grandma had never stopped cursing Bela for Grandpa's plight; it was a narrative that was woven into all her prayers, whisperings and her admonishments.

"I know what must have happened," Sameer said in a stricken voice, "Uma was Grandma's constant companion in the prayer room. She must have brainwashed the girl; Uma could not have been spared a minute when she did not hear about her mother's wicked ways. It was the only way for Grandma to keep the child under her spell – by turning her against her mother. Bela's death was the final punishment as retribution. I remember what Uma said about Grandma's reaction on hearing the news of Bela's death, 'The vermin will feed on her body!' Don't you see now? The parent's sin is made to visit the child! Uma kept her mother alive in order to ward off the sin that was her inheritance. Uma must have lived with the ultimate guilt that she was the fruit of Bela's waywardness. She left home in search of her mother. The ashram lured her into believing that she would find release from the burden of her tainted inheritance through renunciation. Oh Abha, how utterly desolate and painful must have been her journey! No wonder she fell so ill, both in body and mind. And then Romola came along . . ."

~~~

Abha was very quiet. Memories of her early acquaintance with Uma flooded her mind. She had been responsible for helping Uma enter the ashram. At that point of time she thought she was helping someone achieve a direction in life. Had she been mistaken? Had she pushed Uma further and further into her state of delusion?

"It's strange!" Abha cried out in anguish, "Uma never struck me as someone who was ill. She just seemed confused and in need of guidance. There was also something austere and pure about her. She was fascinated by the sparse and frugal quality of life in the ashram. I could see that she was drawn towards it, like a bee to a flower. Why should a woman be denied the right to explore an option she desired in life? That was the logic I used. Over the years I noticed that Uma was becoming more and more sick in mind and body. That is why I tried so fervently to help you in curing her. But at the end of the day what did we manage to do to her?"

She was openly weeping now, the tears clouding her specs and making her look ridiculous. He slid down to the floor and held her in tight embrace. He brought his lips close to her ears, and though his words were molten hot and singed her skin, she felt a cold terror sweep through her body.

"Why blame yourself?" Sameer said fiercely, "Guilt and blame, it is all a waste of time! Nothing of this makes sense, does it? It is not meant to. Despite Grandma's best efforts Uma could not be taught to hate her mother. How could she? She was a child then, like Vikram and me, and in all the games we played, we shared a fascination for Bela. It was curiosity that lured us to the room that was forbidden territory, for it was here that Bela had carried Uma in her womb. We used to go there after dark and talk about things that captivated us. It's funny how imaginative we were, and how little we were scared of things like love and hate! When Uma told us that she only pretended to love Grandma, we found the idea of cheating the old witch, as Vikram called her, wildly amusing. Inside that room we were anarchic. It is really strange how far my mind suppressed memories of those days. But today I feel free to explore them. I am beginning to understand what Romola meant when she said they were unlocking the womb. We used to steal the key from under Grandma's mattress and sneak upstairs to unlock the room. We carried torches with us, otherwise we allowed the room to remain dark. I think what Uma discovered with Romola was that space for freedom, for anarchy of the most pristine kind. It is a wonder that they managed to carve out such a space inside an ashram."

"Do you mean to say that Uma regressed into a state of childhood?" Abha asked, the consternation written large on her face. The tears had dried, but they left runnels on her cheek. She looked frightened.

"Possibly not. What she was experiencing was a phase of adulthood that involved breaking free from her childhood nightmares. She found in Romola a ready companion. Romola was naturally wanton, generous and good-hearted. She probably listened to Uma's story, and took her to be the genie trapped inside the magic lamp. Just a rub and the spirit could be set free. Romola must have taught Uma the desires of the body and Uma, in turn, relived her mother's sins through acts of carnal pleasure. I have always felt that the erotic and the spiritual co-exist in easy proximity inside religious places. I do not know how women and men make themselves available for each other, but it must be quite a common practice. We may never really know the truth. When Uma became pregnant, she either revelled in the experience or panicked. Either way, she needed Romola's companionship. What better way to show bonding than to enter into the experience itself and want to share it? If they thought of themselves as twin souls, then it did not matter whose womb was actually carrying the child. But why did the ashram help them keep up the myth? Were they trying to hide something? That is what we need to find out. Was it in any way connected to Romola's death?"

After Abha had heard Sameer's analysis, she shrank back

in fear at the enormity of the disclosures. In the past few days, since Sameer had returned to Varanasi, her own life had turned topsy-turvy. If they were trying to work out a relationship then it was one without any future. She was certain of only one thing: that she would never want to hurt Vandana or the children. Secrecy was the unwritten precondition that both of them had to agree upon. But for how long, and at what cost? Why was the moral issue here drowned out by her feelings? Sameer seemed to be in a far more reckless mood than she, as though he was undergoing some sort of character change. Did she find this new Sameer a little threatening?

He was pottering around the room, whistling carelessly. He looked keenly at some laminated photographs strung across the wall. "There you are!" he said excitedly, "This must have been taken years back. But you don't look a day older. You look exactly as you did then. You are pretty ageless you know!"

'That is a dangerous myth to perpetuate," she giggled, "I am well past my prime!"

'What stereotypes! Let me see," he cupped her face in his hand, "eyes, nose, and mouth and chin, which part is past its prime?"

"The mind, maybe," she ventured, "fuzzy, and no longer in focus."

"Funny you should say so," he said with utter tenderness, "the mind grows and changes with experience. But love is an experience neither of us has shared with the other. We have kept it locked away somewhere. We were deluded to think that a time will not come when we would want to explore that experience with each other. As far as our relationship is concerned, we are in our prime, Abha, and I think there is no looking back for us."

"Come with me," she whispered hoarsely. She led him outside the house, through the garden, and along a path that led to the outhouse. "Most people used it as a servant room. In early days this was the outer kitchen, used by servants who were not permitted to enter the main house. I had it repaired to house my library. It's my secret alcove, where no one is permitted to enter, not even my cats."

She fumbled with the keys as she opened the lock. It was dank, musty and primitive. Books were strewn around everywhere. The floor was carpeted, with cushions thrown here and there. When he mounted her, his passion riding high, he noticed that her left hand was caressing a book lying close by. He wanted to possess her then, in a way that he had never wanted to possess anyone.

CHAPTER TWELVE

Inside the Bower

"Uma?" the voice seemed to come to her in her dreams. Uma got up in a flash as she had been trained to do inside the ashram. Here, there was no scope for procrastinating or dilly-dallying. A year ago she had made her transition to the final phase of her life as an ashramite. This phase was available only to the chosen few, those who had achieved liberation, as Swamiji had announced in the special sermon he addressed to the select congregation. When Uma had made her way into the select body, she felt a strange peace overcome her tired limbs.

≋

"All of you have followed the steep path that leads to liberation," Swamiji had said in his soft voice. He never made eye contact with his followers: it was the unwritten rule of the ashram that each one of the devotees had to abdicate their individuality and listen to the disembodied voice that spoke to the collective spirit. But Uma had felt a reverberation deep inside her that responded to the voice and the meaning of the words. "In a few days from now some of you will enter into the last stage, which is final release. It is not that you will choose your goal; the ultimate destination will find its disciples. You have to listen to your inner voice and discover the moment of truth. When you are ready, we are ready to give you the initiation rites."

Had the moment really come for Uma? "Look inwards," Swamiji had said, and Uma had flinched at the words as if she feared that her tainted soul would be revealed for all to see. But a new excitement had seized her as well: once she underwent the initiation rites she would enter the final bower, where no one could pursue her, and she would break free from all her desires and mortal ties. As a sanyasin she would be protected by the ashram, and no one would be able to see her or meet her or communicate with her.

≈≈≈

"Uma," the voice repeated itself in anguish. She felt the pain sear her body. She turned her face away from its direction.

It was easy to bend rules inside the ashram. Romola had taught her that. "For every sin that you commit, there is a small penance that you can do," Romola told her in her usual intriguing way. "The penance can be a mere token like one missed meal or one additional prayer to the almighty to forgive you, or it can be something from deep within. Oh, they are fools to demand so much from us!" The words replayed through her mind and made her tremble. She had convinced Swamiji that her state of mind had reached the final pinnacle of purity that defined liberation, and she had been given the final nod to enter the state of the sanyasin. Then why were these voices bothering her so much?

She went through the early morning rituals of the purifying bath, cleaning the precincts of the temple, weaving marigolds into garlands that would be placed at the feet of the deity. The sanyasin lived in the midst of the community inside the ashram, but she had to be invisible. She never looked at the sky or the horizon so that her sense of bounds was replaced by knowledge of infinity. She had to drain her mind of all memories, good or bad, so that her face carried a beatific smile. She never shed tears or broke into laughter, her chest was not to heave, nor her breath to exhale in a sigh. Her hands were not to stroke or touch any part of her own body or anyone else's. Her mind was to turn only within in a sea of tranquillity. No wonder very few inmates could ever hope to achieve this final stage of liberation from worldly ties.

≋

The day Swamiji had initiated Uma into her state of liberation, he turned his eyes just once to look upon her. He did this against the rule, but of all the disciples she was his personal favorite, and he always felt her presence in a benign, affectionate way. Her delusions empowered him with a sense of commitment to his vocation. On the day he had discovered that her womb carried life he was struck with a fierce sense of mission. He understood why the portals of the ashram were kept wide open for lost souls like Uma. She, more than anyone else, needed what the ashram offered, a refuge from where there was no return. He had not been mistaken in the faith he had reposed in her as his most ardent pupil.

Apart from that little aberration in the form of Uma's devotion to Romola. That had been a mistake that the ashram could hardly have afforded. He thought of Romola with a strange sense of foreboding, as though even her death had not laid the matter to rest. But, he thought, the death had been natural retribution, with the Mother Ganges seeking her own kind of justice.

Swamiji's practised gaze discerned the torment in Uma's eyes, but he feigned ignorance of it. He would do penance for this. The only way to keep Uma free from all the scandal that would surround her, should her story became public, was to initiate her into the ultimate rites of seclusion. That would seal her lips forever, and her secret would go to the grave with her. He poured the sacred water over her head and chanted the words with fierce intensity. The sound reverberated in her ears and dulled her anguish. When the rituals were over she was smiling, at peace with herself. Swamiji felt the tears prick his eyes, but he was happy deep within. At last he blessed her, and asked the woman elder to take Uma back to her room.

Swamiji decided that it was time for him to make his annual trip to the mountains. In the seclusion of the icy caves he would communicate with his soul and ask for answers to the many queries that plagued his mind. For the time being he had managed to leave matters simmering. If Uma's story was heard outside the four walls of the ashram, the media would hound him, he knew.

≋

Sameer woke up early in the morning and, as was becoming his habit, he thought of Abha. Initially he had felt a lot of guilt. Not because of the intimacy that had developed between them, but for the simple reason that his mind no longer dwelt on Vandana. He was very sure of one thing: he had not ceased to love her. In fact, infidelity had deepened his love. He recalled in vivid detail all that he had shared with Vandana, and he was grateful for the fact that he could communicate all this to Abha. But there was no urgency or intensity in his love for Vandana. There was gratitude and a lot of tenderness. He spoke to her every day on the phone. Did he sense a distance in her? She was there with David, her long-lost love, and the irony of the situation startled him. For once he wished that some sort of spark would rekindle between her and David; there would be poetic justice in that. But he knew her well: she was nothing if not moral, in a severe and almost naive way. Nothing could quite make her cheat on him and the children.

Was he really cheating on his wife and children? He buried the thought and moved on, with a self-indulgence that now bordered on a kind of obsession. What he felt for Abha was not quite love in the conventional sense. He felt an emotional dependence on her, a sort of dedication to an idea of love that had much to do with the fact that they had been parted by fate. He built in his mind a possibility of what might have been, and what had been denied to them.

As for Abha, what were her feelings for a man whose destiny she had helped to shape some twenty years back? Did she know her feelings then any better than she did now? How strange that love had been granted to her, but in a manner that was far removed from what she really wanted. She felt helpless and yet enamoured, as though life had its unique way of offering chances that one had missed. She did not feel anything less than awe and gratitude to everyone, Vandana, Sameer, Uma, Romola, everyone who made this turn in her life possible. This is how it had to be, she told herself again and again. But what made her shiver was the premonition of the parting, and the thought that the vacancy in her life would remain to haunt her. Could they keep up this relationship forever? Could they love each other without disturbing the equanimity of all the other relationships that hung in the balance, waiting to make their claim? She had no easy answer. She lived from moment to moment, filling in the in-between hours with routine work – feeding her cats, watering her plants and washing the car with a long hosepipe. When they met they embraced passionately and proclaimed a lifetime of loving. The danger hung in the air and made them desperate.

But both of them were conscious of another responsibility. There was a little boy back in Delhi who was waiting at a crucial juncture in his life for certain decisions to be made. That alone would determine his place within the family. Sometimes it shocked Sameer to think how closely people's destinies were tied up with his own. He had to make up his mind sooner or later, and he knew that Abha could not figure in his life in any way. He was confident of the fact that, given Vandana's sensitivity and social conscience, Avinash could be assimilated into his family. As for Abha, could Vandana ever understand or forgive him for forging this relationship that was essentially illicit? He knew with blinding clarity that in this game of lost chances Vandana had played no part: he alone had to take responsibility.

He begged forgiveness from Vandana in all his waking hours. But he did not pause to consider what her reaction might be. He did not imagine her suffering the consequences; his mind had space only for the new love that consumed him. This feeling was real, palpable, intensely true. For the first time Sameer felt he was taking matters into his own hands and experiencing life, not in the realm of speculation, but as it had to be lived, with immediacy, fervour and conviction. He felt happy in a way that he had not felt in a long time. The secrecy of this happiness made it alluring.

~~~

When Uma got the summons from Swamiji's office, a tremor ran through the rest of the inmates. Normally Swamiji's office was out of bounds for women. It was a place where administrative decisions were taken on matters of great importance. Only members of the Executive Committee were invited to attend such meetings.

Uma tried to go about her daily chores in her usual manner, but her mind churned like a spinning whirlpool. She felt at a loss. Why did she allow these waves of panic to invade her, throwing her out of gear? She had just about begun to gather the mutilated pieces of her life and shape them into moments of piety and renunciation. "It is of the utmost importance that you swallow the rage you feel," Swamiji said in one of his sermons. "Shiva's rage destroyed the world, turning it into a charnel of matter without beauty or soul. But Shiva's might enabled him to transform that rage into a cosmic dance that exuded the energy of creativity. We as mortals can expel our anger by allowing the healing power of love to touch us. Anger and love are entwined in us to create the most melodious feelings."

It was this harmony that Uma tried to achieve in all her prayers and waking hours. But today something else compelled her to go back to her room and rummage through her belongings. The room was bare except for a tiny bag that contained all her worldly goods: her two sets of saris and her prayer beads. A bucket, a cake of soap and a coarse piece of cloth to dry her body were her only other possessions; before she had taken the vows of a sanyasin she had been permitted to have pictures of gods and goddesses in her room if she so desired. The room opened into a small patch of land where she grew her flowers. But now nothing was permitted to enter, be it fragrance or touch.

She sat in the midst of the vacant space, closed her eyes and allowed the flood of memories to swamp her. And then she began to feel the rage, slowly, slowly, in the way Romola had taught her to feel it. It grew in her entrails and began to poison her body until she felt her skin prickle, her ribs quiver and knock out her breath. She allowed her back to scrape against the wall and, as she hit the back of her head with a dull thud, the hollow brick resounded with her cries. But nobody heard it because she lived in quarters distant from the rest, and her cries were soft, lethal, like nails tearing flesh.

She undid the folds of the sari kept inside the bag and saw the little bundle tied in a knot at the end of the pallu. This was the only way inmates could keep some personal belongings without them being noticed. Romola used to tuck little knick-knacks between the cleavage of her breasts. Uma took out her possessions. It was a strange assortment, and nobody would understand what it meant. A lock of hair, a bead bracelet and a tiny butterfly pendant. Her memories grew vivid, and she knew why she felt the need to take out these objects and hold them to her lips. The salt taste of tears made her suck in her breath. The body odour of people who were dear to her permeated her being. She knew then that Romola had left behind traces of herself, like morning dewdrops lingering on leaves that have begun to wilt under the sun's rays. This was a lock of Romola's hair before it was shorn by the barber as part of the rituals of widowhood; the bracelet and pendant David had given her as tokens of love. Uma knew that before entering Swamiji's office room she needed to communicate with her inner spirit of resistance. "Your body is your own. Do not allow them to confiscate it from you. They can only see the outer layer of skin; what lies beneath is the murderous, surging flow of life-blood in the veins."

These were Romola's words, and now they filled her ears. As she walked to the office with the young novitiate who had been instructed to direct her to the room, Uma looked picture perfect in her demure bearing. But the rage was dancing within, like Shiva's cosmic dance of destruction.

~~~

"I am wondering whether Swamiji will give her my letter," Sameer said to Vandana over the phone, with consternation in his voice.

"How much longer do you have to stay there, Sameer?" she said in response. "The children are getting a little restless."

"I cannot give you an accurate date, Vandana." He sounded tired. "How are the children? Mira and Avinash, how are they?" He was about to ask whether Abhishek had finished with his exams, but Vandana spoke, evidently not quite listening to him. "Abhi has his pre-boards soon. He has no time for anything else. He is giving his IIT prelims as well, you do remember don't you?"

He felt a little annoyed with himself for not anticipating the implication of what she was saying. He sensed the friction in her tone. It made him tense. These telephone conversations were becoming a little remote. He would have liked to see her face, so that he could gauge how much of his mood was rubbing off on her. Sometimes the truth could communicate itself simply by a gesture of the hand. He knew that about Vandana: she was intuitive in a way that took you by surprise. Years of marriage had taught them the art of communication without words. He realized that he missed this quality in Abha. She was verbose and direct, never mincing words. But as a rule he avoided comparisons. He felt it as a betrayal of his wife. Come what may, she came first in his life.

"You have no idea what these past few days have been like,

Vandana," he said forcefully. "Things will become clear to you once I tell you what I have discovered about Romola and Uma. In many ways it is beyond your imagination. I cannot speak about it on the phone. Besides, I have to get the picture clear before I can disclose it to you or David. Trust me in this matter. Sometimes I am terrified by the turn of events."

"Terrified?" she sounded puzzled. "You speak differently, Sameer. Something is the matter. Look after yourself well. With mother not being there, I hope you are being taken care of."

He put down the phone. Terror? Yes, indeed, he was experiencing life from an entirely different angle. He thought of Uma and Romola and the terrifying charade they had lived through. Did they feel frightened? And now, what would be Uma's reaction on reading the letter? How strange that he could not think of them as real flesh-and-blood people, as though they existed in some make-believe world, where standards of morality did not matter. But Avinash was real enough, and both he and Vandana had certain responsibilities towards him.

The next thought that passed through his mind made him shiver a little. Would he have a responsibility for Abha as well? In a few weeks from now he would be in another city and they would be communicating by telephone. Would she inundate him with similar questions? Would the distance between them seem insurmountable? At the end of the day he could measure his life in terms of the several responsibilities he had had to shoulder. How many times had he been called upon to bear the weight of a secret he had to keep? He was never permitted to break rules, or step beyond the family fold. Had he transgressed all the rules in loving Abha? Why else did he feel so weary and hemmed-in?

When he rang Abha he discovered she was in college and would not be free until late afternoon. He changed his plans to have lunch with her. He decided to invade Bela's room, unlock its dark interior. His mother often spoke about the correspondence that Grandpa had had with Bela. He felt a strong urge to unravel family secrets and burrow deep into the heart of the matter. Suddenly he felt energized, seized by a sense of mission. He switched off his mobile phone so that nobody could disturb him.

~~~

Swamiji handed Uma a sealed letter and said to her in a stern voice, "This is from your brother. I have not asked him to disclose the contents, but he did hint that it was some sort of property paper that you would have to sign. I think it is better you do it. You can open the envelope in the privacy of your room. It is important that you face this situation all alone. It is the last tie with your family that you need to sever. Anyway, in the final phase of renunciation you need to give up everything, especially property. But you realize that in permitting you to open and read this letter from a family member I am breaking every rule of the ashram. I have given you too much leeway, sister. Another occasion and you will be excommunicated."

Uma sat with her eyes downcast. Not a word escaped from her lips, but the rage tumbled inside her, sending shock waves through her body. She had not felt like this in a long time. Not since Romola's death. When the news had reached her, she had remained calm. It was a pact they had made with each other: that they would share every single emotion that they felt. The sight of the still body, the white alabaster skin and the eyes closed, as though she shunned every kind of human touch, had made Uma recoil deep within herself.

This was the stillness of death. How could Uma mimic it while she was still breathing? Her rage brought the pain to the surface, making every sinew of her body taut, but her heart went on beating at an even pace.

She did not stretch out her hand to take the letter. The young novitiate placed it on her lap. "You may leave now. I ask you to return the papers by tomorrow morning. Do the needful," Swamiji said, pleased at the training he had imparted to his disciples. She left, the fire burning her bare feet.

She went about her usual meditation before she opened the letter. The pages fell out one by one: property papers, stamped and authenticated. Then she saw it. A thin white sheet, soft and a little crumpled by the rows of sentences written in ink. She felt the tension from top to toe. She had entered the forbidden zone of experience, as she had often done with Romola. She wanted to howl with joy as animals do in heat. The rage became the cosmic dance. The sunlight dappled the floor of her room, a quick breeze ran its course through the narrow crevices of her window.

She opened the letter and as she read it through she felt neither shock nor surprise. "Dadabhai," she muttered the name with the love that accompanies a sense of belonging.

Dearest Uma,

I do not know whether this letter will reach your hand. I am praying that it will, and that you will understand the meaning of what I am saying. Your son Avinash is now with me in Delhi, and we beg you to help us reach certain decisions about his future.

You must have had the best of reasons to keep this fact a

secret. I am not asking you to disclose anything, but I
think you owe it to us to tell us what the reality is. It
would make my task easier: I have a certain responsibility
towards your son who will then bear the family name.
Just one more question Uma, and then I will seal this
letter. If Avinash is your flesh and blood, then why did you
abandon him? You of all persons should understand what
I mean when I say that the sins of parents should not be
made to visit the children.

Yours truly
Sameer

~~~

For a long time Uma held the letter to her chest. She read it
again and again. She signed the papers and put them back in
the envelope. She lay prostrate on the bare floor. She
touched the dappled sunlight with her fingers and began to
croon a lullaby. The sweet smell of the fecund earth invaded
her nostrils, like rose petals floating in the milk inundating
the Shiv linga. She heard the temple bells and voices, the
body pressing her down and spilling the seeds of life inside
her. "Let us exchange roles," Romola was telling her. "You
will nourish life and I will bear the stigma and the shame.
Nobody need know about it."

~~~

Sameer paused a bit before he began rummaging through the
chest of drawers. His mother had always been a meticulous
woman who believed in preserving things. She had mentioned something to him about letters exchanged between
Grandpa and Bela, and how she had thought of destroying
them. "Have you seen their content?" Sameer had asked her,
but he knew her answer even before she replied. His mother

had no time for things that did not matter. "What can old letters tell you?" she chided him. "Can they change the reality of anything? Can they bring back Uma or give us back all that we have lost? Let your grandpa's soul rest in peace."

"And yours as well, mother," he muttered under his breath, suddenly glad that the house was emptied of its folk, and there was no one left to judge him. A chapter of the family history was closed, and now the mantle had passed on to him and the generation to follow. Only Kaku and Chotoma were left, and they too were in the evening of their lives. He realized with a sense of relief that his secret love-life with Abha had to be kept away from fewer people. Whoever said secrets grew and became cankered like over-ripe fruits that no one had consumed? Inside the four walls of the room he felt safe.

Why was he here, searching out letters that did not matter to anyone any more? Was it because his mind was constantly dwelling on Uma and what her reaction would be once she read his letter – that is, if she got to read it in the first place? He was surprised at the alacrity with which Swamiji had agreed to give her the papers to sign. "It is best this matter is laid to rest," Swamiji had said wearily. "The quicker Uma is released from all her worldly ties, the sooner she will adjust to her new life."

"Yes," Sameer had lied. "However difficult it is for us, we have to set Uma free from all her ties." He had looked uneasily at the envelope. It contained the truth about the only tie that Uma could not give up. Why did you abandon your son? It was the single most important question that had to be asked.

Was he waiting for her answer, or was he seeking out an answer amidst the mounds of memories that lay scattered in the room? It was locked as usual, and to open it he had to search through a whole drawer of disused keys. The room felt oppressive with stagnant air. Everything was covered with white sheets. So much like his mother to take care of matters even after she was gone. The room felt funereal.

Everything was intact, including the chest of drawers and the bundle of letters, kept in a neat packet, marked and labelled. His mother had this quaint way of putting everything in its rightful place. He had found that soon after she had passed away; the will, the insurance policies, the property papers were kept in separate files along with photo albums and letters written by the grandchildren. This was the only part of Grandpa's life that had had to be kept far away from the rest of the family.

They were routine letters. Bela had wasted no time or effort on anything personal: just a few lines about her inability to return to Varanasi, her recovery from a bout of influenza, and concern for her elderly husband's delicate health. In one of her letters she seemed to indicate that he was dying, and that it would change everything about her life. As Sameer read through the letter he felt shocked. How could a mother mention not a word about an infant daughter left in the care of others? What was Grandpa's response to all this he wondered? What did he write to her?

And then, in the midst of the pile he found the single letter that made him tremble. It read as follows:

"I am writing this letter to you with great urgency. Please, consider what I am suggesting to you. I know I have no right to make any demands on you. I have let you down at every stage, and I have no complaints when you tell me that you are ashamed of me. But think, I have never demanded anything from any of you, not from Ma Baba, nor from

you. I have carried this cross on my own shoulders. I have
broken moral codes and loved a man who was not to be
mine. I carried his child and gave birth to her without
making any claims on him. Yes, I have abandoned her,
but at the cost of suffering alone for my action. But I think
a miracle is about to happen in my life. He has agreed to
acknowledge my child and me. Let me know what you think.
Do you think I can make a life with him and with her?
The very thought fills me with untold fear . . . my child
has started visiting me in my dreams . . ."

Sameer searched frantically for some indication of what
happened after that, but the letters seemed to come to a full
stop at this point. What did Grandpa write to Bela? Why was
there no follow-up? Or was it that Grandpa never acted on
the suggestion? Why is it that his parents, or Chotoma for
that matter, never spoke about any such possibility?

The possibility that Uma could have returned to her
rightful parents, and the fact that it had been a matter under
consideration, sounded so preposterous that Sameer felt his
heart beating furiously. He looked at the date on which the
letter had been written. It disclosed nothing but the fact that
in the eleven years that followed the date, before Bela died,
not once was this matter brought up before the family. All he
had heard as he was growing up was that Uma had been
abandoned irrevocably by her heartless mother.

Was it possible that Grandpa never mentioned this letter
to anyone? But why, since he never really seemed to care
about Uma? His mother, for sure, had not known, nor had
Chotoma. How would they have reacted if they had? They
only spoke about Uma's well-being. Perhaps they would
have thought Bela unfit to bring up a young girl, but surely

they would have given Uma her chance to make a choice. Or would they?

Sameer found himself staring at a new reality about Bela that no one had ever spoken about. He re-read the letters avidly, and somehow another woman, so pathetically different from the one he had always known, appeared before his eyes: Bela pleading, entreating, asking . . . Bela dreaming of her newborn child, suffering the consequences of her actions and begging to be understood. This was not the same person. And Uma, did she ever know her real mother?

A thought more terrifying than anything he had ever experienced flashed across his mind. If Bela had claimed her child, Uma need not have entered the ashram or suffered her delusions. This was the possibility that never came about, like one of those fatal errors in life that no amount of effort could ever rectify. Sameer put back the letters, but not in the neat pile his mother had left behind. He shut the drawer firmly, as if the sight of all the disarray was unbearable for him.

He went back to his room and sat there, staring vacantly at the empty space all around him. He picked up the family group photo, taken after he came home on receiving Uma's urgent note, and discovered with a sense of panic that she was not in their midst. We should never have let her go, she was too much a part of us, he said aloud to himself. But the words, the tone, sounded false. Ultimately, they had had to let Uma go.

He picked up his cell phone. There were seven missed calls from Abha. Could he share this secret with her? Should he confront Chotoma with the truth? He suddenly remembered that he had rushed out of the room, leaving the door ajar. He went back and locked it firmly.

CHAPTER THIRTEEN

The Original Sin

The sins of the parents should not be made to visit the children.
This line returned to haunt Uma. She had ceased to read the
letter but each word was imprinted in her mind. Had she
abandoned her son from the beginning, when she allowed
the world to know that it was Romola who was with child?
Why? *You of all persons should understand . . .*

"My angel, you live a borrowed life," Romola was teasing
her as usual, but the truth stung. "Why did you enter the
ashram in the first place?"

"Hush, Romola," Uma replied, the creases of worry
deepening on her forehead. "You are not meant to ask this
question. It is a matter that gets settled on the day your initiation rites are over. Otherwise you will have to do penance."

"I am asking you the question. It will remain within
these four walls. You can keep a secret, can't you?"

Uma nodded her head affirmatively. Her throat felt
parched. She could not remember the reason why she had
come to the ashram. It was not that her life was unhappy.
She was loved and cherished and pampered within the large
household, and she knew that in her own quizzical way
Grandma was dependent on her. Chotoma adored her, and
the man whom she knew as her father was also kindly and
caring. In all fairness they had made her motherless predica-

ment absolutely transparent, so that Bela remained the absent presence in her life. It was not so much the question of missing her mother's presence, but of knowing that all the love that came her way was in compensation for something that was missing. It was a moral void, and anything she suffered as a consequence seemed vaguely deserved.

On her birthdays the family would gather and shower her with love. "Poor motherless child," Grandma would say in a hushed voice, but loud enough for the others to hear. "Chotobouma has been an exemplary mother."

She had no idea why she wanted to distance herself from such a family. There was something about the precincts of the ashram that had appealed to her. There was peace and a kind of serenity. Uma had stayed on in the ashram because it made certain demands on her to follow the path of abstinence, sacrifice and the forsaking of selfish love. Here the only love that was permitted was towards God and the needy.

"Why did you enter the ashram, Romola?" Uma asked.

"I have not given the reason any thought. But now that you ask me, let me see. I wanted to break the ties with my past life. But why an ashram? It is the last place where I can get the freedom I was looking for. Perhaps all I needed then was shelter, and David brought me here. But then I met you, and now the only reason that is valid is the love we share."

Uma laughed. "Hear yourself, sister! It is sinful to talk like that!"

"You laugh but you recoil. They fill your head with a lot of bunk. You heard what Swamiji said today in his sermon? Forsake worldly love to achieve spiritual truth. What is this spiritual truth, I ask you? What is any truth that you cannot feel?"

"Oh, Romola," Uma cried out, "can't you feel God in you? Can't you feel the rhythmic beat of the universe? Every morning when I go down to the ghats to bathe, I feel the water act like a salve over my tired limbs. It is then that I feel the power of divinity."

"I feel the power of divinity too, but only in the love I feel for you," Romola intervened forcefully. "We are only meant to love our own kind. To hanker for divinity is presumptuous on our part. There is a wide gulf that separates us mortals from the divine!"

"Why would you love me as much as you say you do?" Uma queried, part teasingly, part seriously. "You hardly know me!"

"I feel I have known you all my life," Romola replied feelingly. "Besides it is not so difficult to love you. Have you seen yourself? You are like a rare pearl inside a perfect shell that has been drawn from the deepest ocean. I love your refinement. Believe me, I have known nothing of it in my own family. We come from a typical trader family, money-minded, penny-pinching and full of traditions. I have hated all that. I was married off at such a young age to a man old enough to be my father. Another kind of trade-off, done for reasons I could not understand. He wanted an offspring right away. Imagine his shock when he found that I would have problems in giving him children. I became a curse then. He was soon very ill, and I was told that he might be dying. I didn't know how to react: whether to feel very relieved or devastated. And then he decided he wanted to die in Varanasi, as if it is possible to buy yourself a place in heaven. Death does not come according to your whims and fancy. We stayed on in this city for months, our resources soon diminishing. Then we met David and I think there was some kind of trade-off, I do not know the details. When my husband finally died, my in-laws decided they had no need of me. In the few months that I had been here in Varanasi I had seen the widows and I knew what was in store for me. Have you ever been to the Widow's Ghat and seen these women? I was soon to be one of them. I told myself. But the ashram has offered me something else: a sense of security, four walls within which I can belong, and more than anything it has given me your companionship. I have found my god."

≋≋≋

Uma felt an overwhelming sense of warmth as she remembered Romola's words. "Do you have any idea what you meant to me?" she mused. "You never ceased to puzzle me. I had never met anyone like you. For the first time I experienced a love that was not borrowed or in compensation. It was all-consuming, and only giving, asking practically nothing in return. In the beginning I was a little scared to be loved like that. What if we were discovered and I was asked to pay a price for it? What if the ashram were to separate us as punishment? But you were cunning, Romola, and our tiny deceptions became an elaborate game we played all the time. How much we could communicate through mere eye contact, how much we spoke to each other in the dead of night, how wonderful were the stories we wove! The river was a perfect setting for our charades. In the early hours of the morning we bathed and prayed, and in the evenings we watched the lighted diyas floating away with the tide. I could tell you everything. The rage I felt at my mother and Grandma. The hankering I had for Grandpa's attention, all the secret childhood desires and the many heartaches that I had kept hidden from everyone. You listened in a way that nobody else had ever done. You did not judge me, or push me away."

~~~

The signed papers were delivered to the Sengupta house-hold. Sameer wondered whether there would be some kind of communication from Uma. But there was none. Had he expected anything different?

"The fact that she signed the papers is her own way of communicating with you. She is saying that she has under-stood that you know her secret," Abha explained. "She does not have the means to write back to you, even if she wanted to."

Sameer nodded his head in agreement. His job in Varanasi was over. He must now return to his family and take up his responsibilities. They went about the rituals of parting with-out looking into each other's eyes. Just that slight stretching of time by prolonging every move, saying things not once but twice over: avoiding any kind of finality of gestures or words.

"You understand what this signature means?" Sameer spoke sadly. "In Swamiji's language it means Uma has severed her final ties with her family and must go on with her life as a mendicant."

"But her family now includes a son," Abha cried out in distress. "How can she sever ties with her family?"

"Well, becoming a biological mother does not mean you have formed lifelong ties with your children," Sameer said emphatically. "She gave up her child from the time of con-ception. Why else carry on with the charade? There is much in this case that we will never know. Not why it happened, or why Romola died. Was it really suicide or just an accidental death by drowning? The question that comes up now is what future for Avinash? Do we let the larger family know his real identity, say Chotoma and Kaku? Avinash is their grandson, and maybe now they would give him his rightful share of the property. I wonder how Vandana and David will react?"

"Yes, David especially." Abha looked intrigued. "Will it be that the woman he loved finally gets absolved, or will he be filled with a renewed sense of regret?"

"Who said life is a simple equation of cause and effect? Sometimes we do things and marvel at what life has to offer in return. Are we meant to live for the moment? I wonder at times."

They sat in silence, the words echoing ironically. They wanted to hold back the sense of sadness, as though that would make the parting final. A pause or just a shift in focus was what they could at most easily accept about their situation. The cats had grown very familiar with him. He fed them milk in their tiny bowls. He was going to miss them. He was going to miss the greenery of the campus. Memories came flooding in: her feeble attempts to botch together a hurried lunch; the elaborate washing of dishes; and listening to the churning of the washing machine doing its round. As she hung the clothes on the clothesline, he felt there was something lonely about her self-sufficiency. He had never before watched a woman do her household chores with any kind of attention, since back in Delhi, this kind of task was a drudgery performed by Shantabai.

Sometimes he felt guilt at what he had unleashed. He could see the dark rings under her eyes, and that tight-lipped manner in which she discussed their future. "Let's talk of something different," she would say in a dismissive manner, but he knew that her late hours at night, after he had left for home, were spent in thinking of nothing else. In the morning she would look drained of all colour, her cheeks blanched and white.

But he also knew that Abha was too pragmatic, too caught up in her own work to brood for too long. Perhaps, out of sight would mean out of mind for her. Besides, she gave too little importance to relationships that were dependent on others charity, and he knew with what distaste she viewed women who gave too much importance to their men. "It bores me to think that people consider falling in love the most significant event of their lives," she had once said to him in her heyday. "What paucity of imagination!"

Had matters changed for her? He tried to find out. "Do you think falling in love is a significant event in one's life, however hopeless the situation might be?"

"Significant yes, but not the be-all and end-all of life," she answered snappily. "Don't worry, Sameer, I won't do anything drastic in your absence, if that is what you are worried about. I have nursed this feeling for you for many years now. I am comfortable with the status quo. But I am warning you about one thing. There are no guilt pangs, and I have every intention of keeping this lamp of love lighted. And I will make sure that you, too, will feel its warmth."

"If that is a threat, then I embrace it heartily," he said intensely. Is it something about this place, he wondered, that despite its strict religiosity Varanasi filled you with a sense of masti, and breaking of all barriers? Like the ghats, where veneration and commerce co-existed without flinching, and able-bodied men lay prone in states of indolence, while the place vibrated with the sights and sound of devotion.

≋

Uma felt the memories pressing in on her. She allowed them to unfurl one by one. It was the day the inmates of the ashram were permitted to meet their relatives and friends. Uma could see that Romola was excited, for in a while she would get the summons to meet her guest. David would be there without fail, and Uma would experience the pangs of jealousy, more real in many ways than love.

Why was Romola so unmindful of her feelings, Uma wondered? For the past few weeks she had not stopped talking about David. "Davie is wonderful. You must hear him speak about the Ganga! He says it is the world's most mystical river. He knows all its legends by heart. I can listen to him for hours on end. And to think he is not even an Indian! I have asked him often what brings him to our country, and you know what he says? Your women folk! They are as mysterious as the river, so fragile, so strong, so commonplace and yet so unique!"

Uma refused to meet David. "Isn't he the man who was meant to marry Vandana?" she asked sceptically.

"He is. But who cares about marriage? There is always an element of convenience in marriage. Every relationship has its reason, don't you agree? What about ours? Have you ever given it any thought? I think our relationship makes sense in this city, and in this little bower of ours. In Varanasi difference does not matter. See how close Manikarnika Ghat is to other holy ghats, as if there is no difference between life and death! I was brought from one such ghat into this arbour. I think you were waiting here for my arrival. It was a moment in our destiny that foretold our love. We just had to find the strength to accept it. I like Davie because he sees me for who I am."

"He will take you away from me. I am afraid of that."

"No, no," Romola cried out, her voice tender and full of compassion. "Is that the reason why you look so forlorn? Oh, my darling! Fear nothing. Only death can part us, and that too temporarily. I will reach out to you from wherever I am. I will swim aeons of distance to touch you."

Uma stared at the void of the morning and wondered whether the gap between the living and the dead could be overcome. But Romola had been correct. She felt safe in the cocoon of love that surrounded her. This bower was magical. She read the letter again. Yes, the secret was out, but that is how it was meant to be in the first place.

"Don't worry about Avinash," Romola had told her. "He is safe either way. We are both his mothers, and what matters who is known to the world as the true mother. Is giving birth what matters? What about carrying him in the womb of the universe? If there is original sin in the world then surely there is original expiation as well. How does one pay for original sin?"

≡≡≡

"Here is something that I had kept aside for the children and for Vandana," Abha said to Sameer, handing him a small packet. "I have kept it small so that you have no problem in carrying it back."

He looked at the packet, surprised by her gesture. "It is nothing," she continued, "just a small token of . . ." She stopped, floundering for words.

"May I ask you something?" he said rather quizzically. "If you had to do a re-run of your life, would you still pair me off with Vandana? Or would you take your chance with me?"

She laughed, a tiny laughter that broke against her chest like a tremor. "A re-run? What luck! If I knew then what I know now: what would I have done? Let me see. My anxiety to settle Vandana with you would have been much less. But at the end of the day, if I saw her distraught because her life with David had no future and you were the most eligible man around for her, I would still have given her a chance with you. You were made for each other at that stage in your life. I don't know that I would have been willing to give up Varanasi and settle down in Delhi. A life of gentility did not seem a viable option for me then. I had my work in the ashram. Uma needed me, as did many of the other women. I would have chosen them over and above you."

"If you had asked me to give up my career in Delhi and stay here in Varanasi what would I have done?" Sameer asked. "I really don't know. It would have fitted in so well with what my family expected me to do: step into father's shoes and look after the family clinic. But I was looking for greener pastures. I could have made a happy life with you, Abha, there is no doubt about that. But this hankering would have remained."

"Stop! Stop!" she cried out. "I am happy things turned out the way they did. Our relationship is inextricably tied up with Uma, Romola and Avinash. I became their guardians, and in fulfilling my task I made my own claims on you. Believe me, once David is here, I will pick up the thread from where you have left off and complete the task. That is a promise."

He looked at her earnest face and an overpowering feeling of love made him move close to her and hold her in a tight embrace.

~~~

"What is the matter, David?" Vandana cried out, aghast at
the expression on the man's face.

"Oh, I have been such a fool," he almost wept from the
sudden agony. "I paid no attention to what she told me that
night sitting under the banyan tree." Then seeing the look of
extreme bewilderment on both Vandana's and Sameer's
faces, he tried to gather his thoughts and explain to them all
that had transpired between him and Romola.

It all sounded so strange and out of place in the bland
daylight of a Sunday morning in Delhi. Sameer was just
back from Varanasi and, after the usual getting back into the
feel of the place, he called the others to the privacy of his
bedroom and blurted out the truth about Avinash. Vandana
looked at him without so much as blinking an eyelid, but her
chest was heaving rapidly as though she was trying to keep
her equanimity in balance. How many more secrets would
tumble out by the end of the day, she wondered? David
allowed his breath to rush out of his bosom in a low whistle
that sounded like a scream. But he did not utter a word or
ask anything more from his friend. The rush of memories
was more than he could bear.

≈≈≈

He had brought her a tiny butterfly pendant. Romola grasped
it in her hand with laughing eyes and said to him, "If Swamiji
sees this object he is going to confiscate it and punish me. An
entire week of penance. Jewellery is meant to increase our
vanity. I don't know why they say that. The world is filled with
things that are ornamental. Look at flowers, colour, smell and
our taste buds! All around us we are being tempted with thing
that are in excess of what we need. Uma gets worried all the

time. She believes in austerity and denial. I tell her it is against the wishes of God. He would have made a different world if that had been the case. Think, if man had not committed original sin, what kind of world would we live in?"

David looked at this woman with a knot of pain growing in his chest. How did she survive in a place like this? Did he do right by sending her here? Was there any way in which he could rescue her from it? He offered her a home, a place in his heart, marriage. He had no idea how he would make all this happen, but he felt the need to surround her with assurances. She seemed unmindful of his caresses, spoken through tender words, for touching was strictly prohibited here. Only once he told her how much he desired to kiss her, run his fingers down the slope of her face.

"I know of a place where it is possible," she said mysteriously. He was taken aback by the simplicity of her proposition. If such a place existed in the ashram it had to be secret, yet at the same time widely known.

"I don't believe you," he countered, suddenly alarmed. But she had that mystical look on her face that she often put on when she was teasing him. But their meetings were too brief and regimented for him to prolong these moments. He had to let them slip by, so that he could pack in more things that he wanted to share with her. The matter rested there for a length of time, until one day they wandered off to a part of the ashram that was less frequented.

It had been one of those days when David thought his meeting with Romola would not take place. To begin with he received a message that she was unwell. He felt distraught, for returning without meeting her meant a week gone by without a sense of focus. He realized how much he looked forward to every Thursday and the routine of just being with her. Over the months these meetings had become almost repetitive, so that they often sat without saying anything to each other, except for a few anxiety ridden queries on his part about her well-being. Increasingly she looked preoccupied.

He was about to leave when he saw her coming towards him. He waited for her, his heart beating rapidly. She beckoned him, and then, as though in slow motion, she crossed the large stretch of greenery to a part of the ashram where he had not previously ventured. She led him to a large banyan tree, and sitting under its ancient roots she said to him, "You can touch me now. You remember I told you about the place where people meet and touch and kiss each other. This is it."

He was astounded. "This is the place? But how? There is no privacy here. The whole world can see us." Her body was burning with fever. "You are not well. Have they shown you to a doctor? Have you taken medicines?"

"Nobody can see us. These roots act as curtains. Haven't you noticed something? This tree faces the back of the building and there are no overlooking windows. This space is totally blocked out from anybody's vision, unless you are standing on the terrace. But at night it is too dark and no light can penetrate these roots."

David stared at the thick canopy with a strange feeling of misgiving, as though he was standing on forbidden ground and witnessing a crime. He saw her then, her body rooted to the tree, her eyes roving through the branches as though she wanted to pluck and eat the fruit that was furthest away from her. "Don't you like this place?" she asked, her voice hushed and full of wonder. "Uma and I often come here in the dark. At night the soft, shivering sound of leaves caught by a gentle breeze is like the music of the spheres. We watch the moon, looking like the belly button of the night witch, so naked and shameless. The brambles scratch our backs and the rotting moss on the bark fills us with its heady smell. We are drunk with the magic of being alive. I wonder why they never teach us this lesson in the ashram? Inhale, exhale are the two exercises that we are taught, but under this tree we feel the pulse of the universe, beating without pause."

Then Romola said something that puzzled David. He was not to understand its meaning then, but he remembered mulling over it long after he had gone back to England, when the news had just reached him about Romola's drowning. She moved his hand over her face, and as the fever burnt his fingertips she brought the middle finger close to her lips, and cooled it with her wet tongue. David had felt that his soul would burst with the simplicity of the gesture and its sheer madness. "I want a child, David, though God has forbidden my body to have one. I have the longing in me. I think maternal love is the original sin that God planted in the world, for it is the only feeling that carries the shame of unbridled desire, pride in self, a sense of mastery and sacrifice. I treat my state of chastity with disdain. It is not the way God wanted the world to be. I tell that to Uma very often. But she is too possessive about her body; she treats it as something to be kept unblemished. She tells me that her mother had been the centre of all kinds of scandals. She hated her mother for bringing her into the world and not taking responsibility. 'I am that unbidden fruit,' she often told me, 'unwanted, left to ripen after the tree has shaken it off.' But I tell her, you have no idea how much your mother must have yearned for you, just as a simple expression of her maternal instinct. In wanting to have you she loved you, and the reason why she abandoned you has nothing to do with her want."

David stared at Romola, the words as inexplicable as the touch of her lips. Her eyes were candid and burning with the desire to seek clarity in the moral labyrinth that surrounded them. He was acutely aware of the fact that they had strayed into a part of the ashram that would involve punishment if they were discovered. The place reeked with spies. She was unmindful, but there was that slight hesitancy that accompanied the confidence she was seeking in him. He sensed a tension in the way she looked at his face, demanding total attention. Her voice was pleading, and years later David was to know that in that single gesture of pouring out her heart Romola had made her secret public.

"You know why I have brought you here? I want you to sit under this tree and feel its power. Uma has begun to see this power for herself. Last night we spoke at length and she has pledged to give me something I desire without shame or limit. She will have a baby. Her womb becomes the unblemished vehicle. I bear the burden of the original sin. We live out our surrogate roles through each other, and in giving we love. But what if one of us breaks the promise, we ask each other? As God is my witness, I am certain of one thing. If ever Uma wants to claim back her womb, I will seek release in the bosom of my mother, the river Ganges. She will wash away our sins."

≋

They sat in silence, David's words hurting them with their intensity. "You have to tell me what I need to do now," Sameer asked the others, allowing the statement to dangle in mid-air. Was anyone equipped to give him advice?

"What do you mean 'do now'?" Vandana asked, "There is nothing that we can do to change the situation. We have to learn to live with the truth, that is all. Yes, now I know why Avinash seemed so much a part of the family. The resemblance is uncanny. But where does he grow up? Chotoma and Kaku are too old to take up his responsibility. We have to ask Vikram and his wife, surely. Avinash can live here, but it is not simply a question of giving him a place to stay. What do we tell the children?"

"It has to be a collective decision, I know," Sameer said sharply. "But we are talking about a child, and these are decisions to be made with a lot of understanding and love. We cannot dole out responsibilities."

Vandana got up to leave. "I will have to think this through," she said stormily. "You cannot ask me to make up my mind instantly. I have a lot of responsibility on my head already. Abhi is growing up. He is an intelligent kid, and he finds this change in our lives a little difficult to come to terms with. I have to take care of his feelings. As for Mira, she is sensitive and very, very vulnerable in many ways. I have to think about her as well."

"Please, Vandana." Sameer felt helpless. "Sit down and talk it out with all of us. If need be we will include the children as well."

"No, Abhi has his IIT entrance from tomorrow. This is the last thing he needs. Uma and Romola could fancifully abandon their child, but not us."

David watched the couple with a sense of despair. Why were they quarrelling at a time like this? Was there a wedge between the two of them, he wondered? He had sensed a certain loneliness in her that he could understand the reason for. But she never spoke about Sameer with anything less than deep affection. She did not complain about the state of her marriage.

In the few weeks that they had spent together alone in the house, he had sensed her detachment from him. "I have done right by coming back and living out this impasse between us. Sometimes we leave things undone, and its very loose-ended quality holds out as a promise. This has been my way of saying goodbye to Vandana. She is a woman of such sterling quality that I would have given anything to make a life with her, but it is better this way." David typed the words in his computer. He was beginning to write his experiences in the form of a book. Not a research treatise, but a novel perhaps. He had no idea what shape it would take. But he knew he would write it.

As he recounted the words Romola had spoken to him, David felt the inadequacy of language. Could he create the magic of touch, that brushing of mind against the stillness of air, the invisibility of thoughts other than the ones that are given shape, and the slight quiver of the heart that nurses a secret desire? Romola was talking about wanting to be a surrogate mother because God did not permit her to become one. What did she mean by that? How was Uma given such permission?

"I wonder what she meant by that?" David asked, puzzled.

"I think I know," Sameer interrupted him. "My medical experience tells me that this is what a woman says when she is biologically unable to have a child. The onus is put on God. It is one way of shifting the sense of inadequacy from ones self to a bigger, unquestioned authority. If it becomes a psychological state then we have to explain how the problem is only medical."

"Yes, that sounds like a plausible reason," David agreed. "So the pact between the two women was simply to help each other. In this case, it was an expression of extreme love, and sense of giving."

"But how did it help Uma?" Vandana asked skeptically. "Did she have her own reasons to accept such a pact, as you insist on calling it?"

"I wonder," David said with conviction. "Was it a kind of tug of war between the two women? Did Uma feel threatened by Romola? Was Romola, with all her wantonness, and quaint ways in which she broke every rule of the ashram and challenged all its norms, the kind of woman Uma had wanted to know in her wayward mother? She had never been given a chance to make her mother love her. So she must have felt the need to keep Romola happy. To give her that one thing that Romola could not have. A gift of love that was also a guarantee of gratitude. I do recall how Romola used to tell me that Uma was jealous of my friendship with her. 'She is brooding now that you are with me,' she used to say. It used to make me nervous, as though I had to win this girl's confidence against all odds. She was committed to God and Uma, and there was no way I could break that balance. I was the third person, and soon enough I knew I had no chance to win Romola away from the life that she was committed to. Even as I am saying this to you I am filled with the kind of despair I used to feel then. And the final blow came when I heard she was pregnant. How terrible that I was not to understand what had really happened!"

"Abha and I were wondering what your reaction would be." The words simply slipped out of Sameer's lips.

"Yes, Abha," Vandana butted in. "Strange that she had not been taken into confidence. I thought she and Uma were very close. But then, what am I saying? Uma has been in her deluded state for so many years. Where was there a chance

for her to share her secret outside her own world? Oh, the
misery of it all! You know something? I am willing to believe
all the reasons you are giving, but the bottom line is that
Romola exploited Uma. She was not in her proper frame of
mind, and she was led to believe that what she was doing was
correct. I shudder to think what this pregnancy would have
entailed. Why did the ashram permit such a thing to happen? And why did they keep it a secret? I am horrified.
Sameer, you have not said a word about Abha. How is she? I
feel so guilty. She is living all alone, isn't she? We should
have seen to it that she got married. But I have been so
wrapped up in my own world. And I have always been a poor
matchmaker!"

"Abha is happy in the university. She lives on the campus
with her cats and her books. She has sent something for you
and the children. It was lovely being with her after so many
years." He allowed the moment for making amends slip by.
He knew he would never have the courage to tell her the
truth, though what he was doing was wrong. He was simply
slipping back into their relationship as though nothing had
happened. It was this moral gulf that he would have to learn
to live with.

"I will meet her when I go there," David said, suddenly
happy to hear about a dear old friend. Abha would help him
in his secret mission. He was going to meet Uma for the first
time since Romola died and, if possible, get to hear the
secret of what happened between the two of them. Vandana
was correct when she said there was something shady about
the whole matter. Had Romola exploited a woman who was
not in her right frame of mind? But at some stage things
must have changed. Why did Uma want back her son or
'want back her womb' as Romola described it? And why did

Romola choose to let Uma have her way? It was a question whose answer would make it possible for David to leave India for good, with no regrets or sense of things left undone. As he packed his luggage to leave for the mystical city that had lured him to distant shores, David felt a strange sense of anxiety enveloping him.

Kashika,
the Luminous One

CHAPTER FOURTEEN

The Family Circle

David had been examining his feelings about Varanasi. As the train brought him closer to his destination, he began to write. "I am entering this city after a gap of many years. An excitement grips me and I am prepared for any eventuality. Will I feel at home or will an overpowering sense of alienation drive me to despair? I see that I have not got over my earlier habit of using strong words when I need to describe Varanasi. I look out of the train window, and I see only a dirty station milling around with travellers who are embarking on a journey that brings or takes them away from home. For me, home feels very distant, but the memories of here are vivid. I lose my sense of time. I know now what coming back to Varanasi means: it is to bridge the gap between past and present without losing one's sense of self. I, David, stand at the very spot and raise a toast to my youth and its obsessions. I feel vulnerable, rootless and full of dread. But I know I love all that I see before me with the intimacy of someone who reunites with his or her beloved."

He embraced Abha with an urgency that made her laugh. "Dear me, I realize now what Sameer meant when he said you have changed." She spoke with deep affection. "You look middle-aged, prosperous and very English. But you are here in response to my plea. So something in you has not changed!"

"Nothing and everything," he responded, "like each one of you. But I can see that you have changed the least. Oh, I am so glad for that! You will make me relive my Varanasi days without any sense of time past. I cannot wait to meet Uma. Tell me, is that possible?"

"As a matter of fact, yes," she said eagerly, "something that would have been impossible a few months back. But I have come to know something very important. Uma has given up her life as a sanyasin. Is it in response to Sameer's letter, I wonder? In which case, it is a very significant development. It seems every sanyasin is given a time period within which she can revoke her position. The ashram accepts this. As an inmate of longer than 20 years, Uma is at liberty now to meet her near and dear ones, if that is what she wants – our asking for it will not do."

"I wonder whether she would want to meet me," David said doubtfully. "She used to see me as a threat. Maybe she thinks I will blame her for what happened to Romola. How do I quell her misgivings? You will have to help me, Abha."

~~~

Uma tried to keep sleep from invading her eyes. Since the day she had made her decision to quit the status of a sanyasin, sleep came heavily and encircled her. She felt it as the oblivion she had sought for many years now. For the second time in her life she was summoned to Swamiji's office. It was obligatory for members who broke rules to serve some kind of penal task. In her case she had to work in the garden for a month. It was heavy labour but it made her happy, connecting with the raw earth, feeling its slippery wetness run through her fingers. Since Romola's death she had hardly communicated with people. She went about her task like someone sleepwalking, but her mind was alert and deep in thought.

Swamiji had spoken to her in a soft voice, but she could sense its coldness. Why are you doing this to me was the unsaid text, after all that I have done for you? "This is God's will," he said with great diplomacy. "We are all putty in his hand. But I have to punish you for breaking a rule of the ashram. You entered into something without the proper frame of mind, which is sin. You lied to me. I am disappointed in you, sister."

Though he did not turn his head to look at her, he waited to feel the tremor in her body language. She had always been his most obedient disciple, so young and impressionable on the day she entered the ashram, severing her ties with all her loved ones. He had become her parent. It was Swamiji who had inculcated the values in her. Today, she was a woman past her prime, and he was in his declining years. He felt the pride of a patriarch who was leaving behind a legacy. He alone had looked deep into her tortured soul and seen its dark secrets. He, better than the others, knew why she had come to his abode to live under his wing. It gave meaning to his mission, and however much he was able to convey his sense of goal in the many sermons he addressed to his believers, it was Uma who quelled his self-doubts. Her refinement, her fine sense of being, the purity of her soul pleased him.

When she had begun to slide into silence he had not really been worried. Silence was one of the golden rules of the ashram. Inmates were encouraged to look inward and to meditate; communication was permitted only in small measure. In the women's wing silence was tied up with virtues of modesty and austerity. It was in his ashram that Swamiji experimented with the family fold, and though it was a very small group it found a prominent place in his scheme of things. A productive householder was always a good disciple.

But such a title could only be bestowed very selectively. Single parenting of children was permitted but personal ties and bonding were discouraged. Children and wives were given community tasks to perform, and everyone had to take part in the times that were set side for prayers.

When had he known that things were not going right for Uma? That she was sickening with her delusions? It had been the first time that Swamiji had become fraught with a deep sense of failure. His prayers did not heal: they pushed her deeper and deeper into the rut of her disease. He had thought she must be dying. That is when he had sought help from her brother. Had he done right in all that? A certain despair made him feel numb to his very toe.

Suddenly he remembered her presence in his room. There was no tremor in her body; only a tensile strong calmness that caused his own heartbeat to quicken. He could not break this woman, neither bit by bit, nor with one blow. For the first time in his life Swamiji felt his diminishing power. "David the Englishman wants to meet you. He was Romola's lover. You can go back to your room and ask yourself what you want to do. If the answer is 'yes', then send me a message." He looked at her with piercing eyes, his voice deep like rumbling thunder. "Maybe you should ring the temple bell that I have kept for the summonses, I would like you to announce it to the world. You can step out now."

She touched his feet as usual. It brought tears to his eyes. Then she slid out of the room on silent feet. Swamiji closed his eyes to get back his equanimity. Just then he heard a sound. The harsh clank of the bell vibrated through his brain. He thought his breath would stop entirely.

≈≈≈

If there was one fatal mistake that Swamiji had made, it was to accept Romola into the ashram. That woman had spelt trouble from the day she arrived. Strangely enough, he had had no misgivings when he first saw her. Her youth and her beauty had taken him by surprise, but the story of her abandonment had a familiar ring to it. He remembered the first time he had seen her in her widow's garb. He had been touched by her innocence, as though she was wearing borrowed clothes that she would soon have to discard. But she continued in them in the days to come, wearing them with indifference. She strung garlands of marigolds for the puja time, and as they hung on her knees they obliterated the white of her clothing. The red vermilion stained her feet.

He soon realized that she had an Englishman under her spell. Swami Parmanand was not fazed. He knew that the rules of the ashram were well-observed. Anything illicit or immoderate would be summarily dealt with. Most women took the wrath of God seriously. All he had to do was burden them with a task that severed them from their gods. The utter loneliness that seized their souls made them penitent. He rarely had to punish them twice. But in Romola's case he had discovered that he was mistaken. She left the tasks undone, and any sense of severance she felt from her god did not seem to hurt her. It puzzled him deeply. He thought of ways to chastise her, but a fear of failure made him wary.

She was happy and spirited and spread cheer all around the women's wing. She never did anything that was overtly forbidden, but like a rain-laden cloud she brought the storm in her wake. She communicated all the time, in words, in snatches of songs, in the way her eyes danced and her feet skimmed over the bare grounds. Once in a while Swamiji saw a gaggle of hens skipping behind her as she worked in the fields. As she stroked the flanks of the cows and goats they would nuzzle close to her. She would scatter seeds amidst the pigeons and sparrows, making a low clucking sound with her tongue. It was as though she had uncovered the magic of his sermons and countered it with her own unwritten, unspoken text.

He hoped the Englishman would lure her away from the ashram, and that she would return to the world outside. But he had been woefully wrong. She had never loved David. She had loved Uma, and in a way that made no sense in Swamiji's world. He understood the enticement of the body. He understood illicit passion across caste, creed and gender. But the meaning of feminine solidarity eluded him. How could two women call themselves twins in mind and soul? How could they share dreams and visit each other in their thoughts? How could they build a world apart from the one that gave them shelter? He was shocked by Romola's power. He searched the scriptures for its meaning, but even amidst gods he read about dissonance and womanly squabbles, sacrifice, and renunciation.

Only the Mother Earth had the all-encompassing power of compassion. Her fecundity carried the seeds of death, therefore Shiva Shakti embodied creation and destruction, rage and laughter. The mountains of ancient knowledge weighed heavily on Swamiji's head. He began to falter in his sermons. He went away to the Himalayas, but for the first time in his life he felt that the ashram was unsafe in his absence. He hurried home to discover that the blighted tree had spread its roots into the mind of his favourite student. Uma was pregnant.

The shame of it! He felt as though the blessed deity had been sullied by hands so impure, so evil, that his body trembled at the very thought. He gnashed his teeth and broke his head against the wall until the blood ran down his bare chest. Who was responsible? He did something he had never done before. In the dead of night he visited Uma in her room. Romola came in through the night, the moonbeams splashing on her face. Pinpoints of light danced in the pupils of her eyes. He was afraid of her.

He began to sob like a man vanquished. "How did this happen? Who? When? Where? You are like my child, Uma. I trusted you. I thought of you as the unsullied river, untouched by the serpents that coil Shiva's head. Which one of them sank its fangs in you?"

It was Romola who spoke: "The child is mine. I have just placed it in Uma's womb."

"You are a lunatic," he shrieked. 'Do you understand what you are saying? It goes against nature's process."

"Why should it? Have you not read your scriptures correctly? Mother Nature lends us her seeds when she wants to sow life. She planted desire in me, the first seeds of motherhood. My own womb is broken – it cannot bear new life, but Uma is healthy and she shares my dream. We have made this thing possible together."

"I will punish you, Uma," Swamiji said in a harsh tone, the anger spilling out of him. "You have broken all the rules of the ashram. This child is the result of illicit passion. I will call for the management and ask them to pronounce a punishment. And you will be punished too, sister," he announced to Romola.

"I have promised Uma that I will protect her with my life. I am willing to be punished. I am willing to bear the stigma. Let the world not know that Uma is with child. This child is mine anyway; I will face the shame and the scandal.

We will live incognito for the next ten months and then, after the child is born, the secret will be with us till the day we die."

Swami Parmanand had agreed. He knew that this was the only way he could keep Uma's image untainted – and it was the only way his failure would remain under cover. So that the scandal would not escape the walls of the ashram, he decided to collude with the two women. That night, as he crept back to his room, he felt utterly broken in body and spirit. Years of meditation, self-discipline, and keeping to the most difficult of vows in order to gain unchallenged power in his kingdom, had been negated by two, delusive, insane women. Poor, poor Uma, her delusions had broken through the dam of compassion in his soul. All these years he had loved her as one loves an injured bird with broken wings. But that night he saw something that made him shudder. Even if she had been led by Romola, this time her delusion had become her cure. Uma had recovered in mind and body because motherhood had liberated her, allowing her to spread her wings and soar.

≈≈≈

Time hung heavy for David. "My life has been transformed into a state of animated suspension," he wrote. "I am still waiting for confirmation from the ashram. Will Uma be willing to meet me? Meanwhile I devour Varanasi with all my senses. In the years that I have been away the city has grown in a haphazard way. Newer colonies that look no dif-ferent from any other Indian metropolis have sprung up, especially near BHU. but I am not interested in them. For me Varanasi resides in the majestic ghats and the myriad rituals; the sound, smell, the feel of an ancient city; the river, as seamless and mystical; the devotees, as frenzied and spellbound. There is nothing familiar about this place, yet it tugs at my heartstrings as though my distance from it has been a breach of trust. I return to it with the passion of one who returns to his beloved.

"I think of Romola all the time. I know that my meeting with Uma is nothing more than an attempt to retrieve the last vestiges of my memory of Romola. If the two were twins, then surely I will see glimpses of her in Uma. Even Abha seems part of that mystic circle, more complex than a family. We have spent evenings reminiscing, our hearts full of love. Something tells me that Abha has found her peace of mind. And I am happy for her. I never ask her any questions; she is not secretive or cagey, only quiet about things that matter to her. I respect her for that.

"I am suddenly aware of the fact that here in India everything has to be viewed in a holistic way. Each part depends on the others for its existence. Varanasi teaches me this mammoth lesson of unity in the midst of fragmentation and dissonance. Divinity, mortality, the here and the absent, worship, trade, the vulgar and the pure, the ascetic and erotic are all part of that mystic circle. I can return to it at any point and feel the serenity of its oneness.

"I can so easily believe what Uma and Romola did together. There is nothing too strange about their story. The fruit of it I have seen in Sameer's household, a fine boy who inherits twin souls. And what makes things so marvellously logical is that I can see him grow up in Vandana and Sameer's care. In India families spread across cities, branch out in different directions, and yet belong to a tight-knit circle of kinship. Does Abha fit in somewhere? I believe she

does. Do I fit in somewhere? I believe I do. Maybe that is
why I come back again and again. I realize now that I have
not come here to bid farewell to this city and this country: I
have returned to find my space in this family circle.

"Yes, yes, yes! I am to meet Uma in a few days time. I am
like a man possessed. I cannot sleep, eat or do anything without feeling the blood rushing through my veins. My heart
pulsates and throbs. I go to Manikarnika Ghat to feel the
ashes slip through my fingers. I close my eyes and Romola
emerges from the river, the green algae cling to her body.
She is hollow-eyed, but I can see the soft heaving of her
chest and the slight parting of her lips: she is still breathing.
I cry out to the bystanders, but they look past me. The crowd
is growing in number: I can hear the rumble of people, even
as the fire crackles at a distance. Then the drift of the river
is carrying her away from me. I stand there, my feet rooted
to the ground; a strong undercurrent is sucking her into the
bosom of the river. I hear the last splash, and just before she
vanishes I see the curve of her fingers raised in my direction.
I look for symbols but I find nothing."

~~~

The meeting is scheduled, as usual, for a Thursday. "I can
take my leave," Abha says gently. They have found a space in
the midst of the milling crowd, but there is a sense of seclusion, for the trees are thickly branched like an overarching
green arbour. The surrounding voices fade away.

"No," Uma stretches her hand to hold Abha back. "You
can stay. It is better that you hear what I have to tell you. For
me you are more than family: you gave me a sense of direction when I needed it most."

Abha felt the lump grow in her throat. The Uma sitting
in front of them was lucid, in control of herself. "If only

Sameer could see her now," she thought, gratitude coursing through her body. "And, yes, Vandana as well." This was the inner family circle, and she felt an expansive power reaching out and drawing each one of them in. Had she sullied that space by falling in love with Sameer even as he was married to her best friend? But then, here was David sharing that same space, looking at peace with himself. And what about Romola? It was her story that was going to unfold itself now – she had been the invisible link that had brought all of them together across cities and continents. They say Varanasi is the one pilgrim spot that straddles time, space and distance. Kashika, the Luminous One that holds in one single circumference the confluence of all paths. Who knows at which point all paths meet, why hearts beat in unison, why memories are shared, and why the mighty river flows seaward and then changes its path to seek its source? People come from all over India to find holy release in Kashi. But the gods could never abandon this city. It is this single, luminous truth that makes Abha reach out and touch Uma's hand.

CHAPTER FIFTEEN

A Gift of Love

"Yes, Avinash is my son. I gave birth to him. Romola and I had made a pact that the world would never know the truth. But maybe it is better this way. You must be wondering why I have chosen to talk to you? I got a letter from Dadabhai; it changed the way I looked at things. He said the sins of the parent should never be made to visit the child; Avinash deserved a secure future, and that I of all persons must understand what it means to abandon a child. How could I do the same to my own flesh and blood?

"I went through childbirth like in a dream. It was my gift of love to Romola. Motherhood was what she wanted. Before she came to the ashram the doctors had told her that she was barren. It was the source of the trouble she had with her husband and in-laws. They saw her as incomplete. I think two things made Romola feel whole again. The love we shared, and the love that David gave her. The love of God was secondary to her. Most of the time I was afraid for her. I thought, what if the gods get to know her secret? What if they peep into her heart and see the lack of devotion? But when I shared my fears with her she simply laughed and called me a baby. God is smothered with love, she said, he can do without love. Love is what we poor mortals need, because we have this worm inside us that is always wanting to be loved and desired.

"She often asked me this cutting question that made me tremble with fear. Why did I leave a home that cherished me so dearly? Was I running away? Did the ashram offer me something that I had missed out on at home? Yes, I told her. It has taught me the value of unselfish love; it has taught me the lesson that I must love without possessing. Grandma, Chotoma, Kakima they all loved me, but they wanted gratitude in return. They wanted me to purge my lawless mother from my life. They wanted me to feel motherless. It was the price I had to pay for their love. I came to the ashram because I wanted to understand the meaning of renunciation and sacrifice. I told myself my mother had left me because she had good reasons. She was not an evil woman.

"But away from home I felt lonely. I ceased to be a person here. Love meant only giving, without expecting anything in return. My mother ceased to exist here. There was only the goddess, the universal Mother. She combined wrath and love, she held weapons in her hand and she sat on the lotus. Her eyes were fierce, and her nostrils flared with the fire of the elements. I could only bow my head in obeisance at her feet. If this was love, then it brought little solace to my soul. In the ashram I came to understand the reason why death carries such a sense of finality with it. Death is the final parting from loved ones. My mother, whom I had never seen except in faded photographs, had deserted me so completely that I could not fill the vacuum with any other love. I began to shut my eyes to keep away the sun. I did not want any sound to invade my ears. I wanted to die, like my mother.

"When Dadabhai came to cure me I should have known what family means. Both of you were here for me. But I was lost to all of you. I remember one moment with great intensity: the day I reentered my childhood home, and felt the presence and absence of loved ones. I remember Chotoma's ceaseless crying as though her heart would break. Do you know what I felt then? A sense of retribution. I think my heart had turned to stone then. I felt I could fill up the vacuum in me only with pain, and I wanted everyone else to feel the same pain. I know, today, that it is the worst state of mind. But believe me, nothing that Swamiji ever told us in his sermons gave me a clue as to how to deal with my pain. Even my prayers were empty. All the idols had turned to stone; they were death-giving. My mind became a prison.

"But a miracle was waiting to happen. Don't you see? My story is only possible because I lived through it. I did not die. Sometimes I think Dadabhai brought the miracle home to me. He made me understand that my mother had died physically. But death carries its own rituals of forgiveness. Romola often said that she rose like the phoenix from my mother's ashes. Do you think my mother really abandoned me? Or did she resurrect herself in the shape of a woman who opened the floodgates of love?"

~~~

David asked himself many questions. "This is a story about two women. For many years now, I could not begin to write it. I made notes but they remained incomplete, and I thought that, once again, I would fail to finish what I started. Is it something about this country? Will the mystique of India always elude me? I have acquired a laptop. It travels with me everywhere. But the words I want to put down seem inadequate, without life, so that a story as delicate and formless as the one I am going to relate cannot quite be captured on paper. As I press the keys the letters dance before my eyes and I cannot make sense of them. I marvel at the fact that Uma had no problems in relating her story. I wish I could capture that look on her face. How do I describe it without making analogies?

"Her eyes reflected the profound and luminous beauty of someone who had found the key to happiness. I had always balked at the conventionality that surrounds the lives of women here in this country. What kind of freedom do these women have really? They are tied down by invisible shackles that they have been required to love. I once told Sameer that I marvelled at the way Indian women lived lives of sheer compromise. But that was before I met Romola. And now in that green arbour that acted as a shield from the wide world outside, I have met her twin soul.

"I believed every word of Uma's story. I believed her description of how freedom and empathy go hand in hand. Though Uma was grieving for Romola, she recounted events with a flamboyant joyousness that would seem obscene to anyone who did not know this country. I realized that Abha had trusted me a great deal in making me part of that mystic circle. I thought of Vandana and the ups and downs in her life. How she had discovered a rhythm in the midst of chaos. Was this compromise, I asked myself? There were no easy answers."

~~~

Sameer and Vandana did what they had not done for many months now. They sat in Sameer's chamber late into the night. The neighbours, especially Mrs Chopra, saw the light peeping out from behind drawn curtains. Mrs Chopra muttered a small prayer under her breath.

The Senguptas were good people, and they were liked by the families that lived around them. Avinash had fitted in well with the children. His strong resemblance to the rest of the family made it easy for strangers to think of him as belonging. He had lost the initial awkwardness of one who had been brought up in a different world. He was quick in picking up on his studies; and much to Vandana's delight he had a natural flare for mathematics. That aroused Abhi's interest in him. Soon the two boys were doing crosswords together and sharing information in physics. "His foundation is pretty strong, Ma," Abhi said encouragingly. "I was afraid that the ashram would fill his head with obscure beliefs. But he has a natural ability to be rational. See how little he indulges in soul talk anymore!"

"Do you think we should tell the children who Avinash really is?" Vandana put the question to Sameer.

"Let us wait a bit longer to find out what Uma has to say about it," Sameer answered swiftly. "Maybe she has wishes of her own that we would need to respect."

"Poor, poor boy," Vandana said, her eye moist with tears. "Motherless and fatherless. Sometimes I wonder what kinds of confusions go on inside his little brain. Have you noticed how he clings to me? He even developed sibling rivalry with Mira, and I had to work hard to wean him out of it. I paid equal attention to both of them. I am glad there was no resentment in Mira."

Sameer stared at his wife with a tight knot at the base of his chest. He had wronged her in a way that seemed inexplicable now that he was sharing her bed and room. It seemed so natural to feel tenderness for her. The phone calls to and from Abha were regular, but there was the urgency of events that made communication necessary. He did not have to stop when Vandana entered the room. He could easily pass on the call to her, so that he heard the two women exchange pleasantries with a great deal of affection. Strange how the family circle seemed all-inclusive. It made him feel both less and more guilty. He would tackle it later, he told himself firmly. His responsibility lay somewhere else, and the question of whom to love seemed self-indulgent. He pushed the thought away, and continued to stare at his wife with renewed admiration for her instinctive understanding.

"You have been my pillar of strength," he said to her with complete honesty. "I would not have believed in the strength of motherhood if we had not gone through this terrible crisis."

~~~

"When Romola first came to live in the ashram I did not like her presence," recalled Uma. "She was everything that I was not. She was full of life. And all that I wanted was the emptiness of denial. I felt angry. I had never been so angry in my life. And do you know what Romola told me? 'Do not bother to expel all this anger from your body. See what they tell you about Shiva's wrath, it churned honey from poison.' I refused to listen to her in the beginning. But then one day I began to talk about myself. I wanted to tell her that I had an identity of my own. Romola was fascinated. She told me that my stories were stranger than anything she had ever heard. So we built our friendship through our story telling. Soon we had so much to share. We began to do what storytellers always do: we began to spin imaginary tales.

"We became sisters: twins who had got separated in childhood. Our mother was the evil princess who had put us in two separate baskets and allowed the river to carry us to Varanasi. Our father was a powerful King who had abandoned us because he had to rule his kingdom. Our souls had been locked up in silver caskets and lay at the bottom of the riverbed. Who had the keys? Our stories became stranger and stranger. We had to find a way to unlock the souls and fuse them together. When this happened the spell that kept us apart would dissolve. I began to laugh and cry for the first time. The anger had begun to sift the honey from the poison.

"But unknown to me, Romola had found her Prince. When I got to know about David, I cried, for the first time all alone. I can never forget how alone I felt. As though for the first time I was missing out on my mother, brothers, aunts, uncles, the family I had known, the family I had never known. I promised myself that Romola would never get to know my feelings. But she did! And do you know how? Through my stories. She turned her face away to hide the tears. And then one day she told me that she did not have the magic wand that would take away the distance between us. It was the first time I understood the meaning of separation between two people. We had to cross the bridge from two different ends. Our meeting points were never the same.

"From that day onwards we had different stories to tell each other. You could say our relationship had grown. I ceased to feel jealous of David. Romola would hear about my childhood and compare it with her own. She told me how she was brought up in a conservative family where girls were always in the background. Her education was incomplete in many ways. She was never allowed to pursue her dreams. The only games she played were the ones that were part of her growing up. So she played with dolls, and made homes that she had to clean and keep tidy. She decorated her toy house with little beds, chairs, tables and cupboards. Her dreams were tailor-made to fit into what her family wanted for her: a reasonably well-off husband who could give her healthy children, and the security of a home. But everything went wrong for her. A series of family misfortunes made them dependent on relatives who saw her as a millstone around her mother's neck. Marriage proposals came easily because she was good-looking. But another obligation made the family agree to a proposal that was not at all suitable. Even then, it was not the difference in age that mattered. She was soon to discover that her husband was very, very ill. The marriage had been a way of keeping away the evil eye. But Romola learnt that if there was any shortcoming it was in her. She was barren. It brought the wrath of the family on her head. She became the evil eye. Her in-laws wanted to get rid of her.

"My story was very different. But the one thing that fascinated Romola about my story was the forbidden room. I told her how as children we went into the room after we had unlocked the door with the secret key. We stole the key from under Grandma's mattress. Inside the room we became devils. We talked about things that would shock the elders. I used to believe that my mother lived inside this room. She was invisible, and I used to pretend that I could see her. We played planchet and tried to communicate with her soul. We lit candles in the dark. The furniture would move with a creaking sound. We held hands and prayed to all the evil spirits in the world. I prayed that Grandpa would die and his soul would go to hell. Sometimes when I was angry with Grandma I would spit into the candle and watch the light flicker. I told the others that this was death, blowing out her life.

"Romola would listen to my stories and tell me that I was lucky to have had a forbidden room. Your anger was churning the poison into honey, she told me. Today I look back and think to myself, yes, inside that room the family had come full circle. In keeping that key away from me both Grandma and Chotoma wanted to protect me. Like Grandma's prayer room it was secluded. Not everyone could enter. But forbidden spaces teach you the important lesson of learning to break

rules in order to enter. You learn that you are alone in this
world. The anger and joy you feel, they belong to you alone.
Every door opens and closes for you in different ways."

~~~

David realized he was in great awe of Uma. "I search for
shades of Romola in her. My mind begins to play tricks with
me. Bit by bit the woman I loved comes alive in front of me.
It is as though Uma is the conduit through which Romola's
story is unfolding itself. I look around to take in the ambi-
ence of the ashram. The years have changed little here. The
building has remained the same. The trees, the green foliage,
the temple with its flying pennants, the ghat, and the narrow
lanes leading to the ashram look the same. Only the commercial buildings in the neighbourhood have changed. The
shops have bright neon-shaded hoardings, colourful plastic
furniture and glass panes. They sell coke, finger chips and
Baskin-Robbins ice cream. They have pictures of pop stars,
Bollywood stars and cricketers. The gods and goddesses are
still there in the alcoves carved inside tree trunks, but the
tourist can easily miss seeing them.

"What fascinates me about Uma is how ageless she is. She
is dressed in the white sari with blue border. Her hair is closely
cropped; the fine line of her chin and forehead gives her a chis-
elled look, as though a sculptor's hand has moulded her face.
She is thin and gaunt but her arms and shoulders are rounded.
Her eyes have lost their downcast look. Her lips are parted and
her voice has a soft, clear timbre as though she is happy to
speak out. She can choose to be silent, and all she has to do is
to allow her undulating breath to pause. But she goes on speaking like someone possessed with inner strength. We listen to
her in total silence. My mind is busy recording all that she
is saying. Sometimes I feel I can hear overlapping voices,

especially when she fills in details about what Romola had said to her. Her voice becomes animated then. Her eyes begin to dance. At times she changes the inflection in her tone. Then she sounds teasing, like someone who is trying to get as close as possible to an experience that is deeply private. We are the outsiders, intruders into the inner sanctity of her mind. She reaches out to us, but with a sense of our distance from her experiences.

"Was this the sick Uma we had known? My heart was spilling over with joy. If story-telling could empower a woman to such an extent, then why was I wasting my own ability to write? And that too about experiences that were so fascinatingly far removed from what my own countrymen would ever live? Perhaps that is the reason why I had come to India in the first place. I was in search of my vocation. My vocation that is tied up with the length and breadth of my experiences. It suddenly seemed that the job I held in the university was only ever a stopgap arrangement. I had settled into a lifestyle that was dull and routine. It made me feel commonplace. All that I had experienced in Varanasi, was it only meant for writing a thesis that would gather dust in an archive? Listening to Uma I felt as though I was being liberated."

~~~

"Has Uma spoken?" Sameer was on the line to Abha. He was whispering into the telephone, his fingers curled around the receiver. The voice that floated across space was so clear he felt he could simply extend his hand and touch her.

"Yes, she has," Abha answered in a hushed tone, realizing how difficult it was to convey the sense of what she and David had heard. She paused, groping for words, trying to get her feelings under control.

He waited, and then when he spoke he sounded harsh.

"Well, what did she say? Any clue about what exactly transpired? What is her state of mind now? How does she view the whole change of circumstances? I am waiting, Abha."

"Look, I cannot answer all your questions. All I can say of her mental state is that she is no longer sick. She sounds in control of herself and her emotions. For David and me this is the biggest miracle. As to what transpired, it is difficult to put it into sequence. The two women shared a relationship that did wonders for Uma, that is very clear."

"I have to be blunt," he interjected. "Has she said anything about how she got pregnant? Or who is the father?"

Abha held her breath. Why did the questions sound so out of place? Why were her answers so inadequate? Normally she was never at a loss for words. But for the first time, she wished she was not having this conversation with Sameer, or that David could be here to deal with him. "No, she hasn't, and I do not think it matters. If you listen to her, Sameer, you will know that the question of paternity does not cross her mind. Maybe she does not know who the father is. According to her, she only lent out her womb; the real experience of bearing a child was undergone by Romola. It is possible, you know, for a woman to carry life in her womb and not to relate to it at all. Motherhood is a sensibility that comes from something more complex. I have seen that in my own experience of doing social work with downtrodden women, particularly with women who are pregnant against their will or are victims of violence. But what makes this story so remarkable is that it is a joyous one. I wish I could convey its sense of jubilation and celebration. Am I making sense to you?"

"Frankly, no. Why do you call it a story? Is she making it up?"

"No, no," Abha said emphatically. "I believe her. She is no longer deluded. She said to us that is was your letter that changed her mind about meeting us. Sameer, Uma has taken a big step in giving up her life as a sanyasin. You understand that it took a lot of courage on her part. I think she is thinking for herself for the first time. And I believe her when she tells us that this strength is Romola's legacy."

"Yes, we have to keep that in mind," he agreed with her. "This is her own decision. Perhaps, it is the first sign of her recovery. In that case we have much to celebrate." He sounded in a happier mood. It brought back her sense of longing for him.

"Do you miss me?" she asked half-playfully.

"I am there with you all the time, sharing the intensity of what you are undergoing. You are my soul mate, I realize that far more when I am away from you. But I am committed to Vandana, not just because I am married to her, but also because there is a lot of love and regard in our relationship. I can never disturb that balance. But there is a great deal that is missing. The responsibility for infidelity is mine. My inability to clear the air between us is entirely my fault. It is a distance between us that I can never hope to overcome. I will live with this guilt for the rest of my life. Though she is here with me, I miss her more than I miss you. It is this hollowness of loving without fulfilment that I cannot remove from my life. Do you understand what I am saying?"

"I wish my answer was no but yes, I understand."

~~~

"If Romola taught me one thing it was to love my body," Uma remembered. "She told me that love is always selfish. It is like looking into the mirror and loving your reflection. I asked her, what about renunciation, what about giving?

Wasn't that the great lesson taught by centuries of wisdom? What she felt for me, wasn't it unselfish love? She always laughed at my questions but never in a hurtful way. She thought about everything I said to her, and sooner or later she would come up with her answers. Our discussions were endless, as though to talk and communicate was the secret spring of our happiness. I had never felt so fulfilled in my life.

"But nothing that Romola had told me prepared me for motherhood. It was as though my body acquired another dimension. The intensely physical nature of the experience left me exhausted. Romola bore the entire brunt of the scandal that followed. Nothing seemed to daunt her, the whispering campaign, the wrath of the authorities, or David's sense of moral outrage. Ten months went by in seclusion. We became twin souls in the real sense of the term. We shunned all company. Only Swamiji was permitted to meet us. I saw the fear in his eyes. He told us that the ashram would be destroyed if the secret went out into the world. He never mentioned the wrath of God. He never asked us to pray for souls in peril, which had been the routine punishment meted out to those who broke rules. I sensed that he wanted to protect me. Inside the ashram it was the news of Romola's impending childbirth that spread far and wide. Nobody spoke of it except in a whisper. But I think they found the whole episode as inexplicable as the ways of the gods. It is strange how we all like to talk of our individual destiny without really wanting to take responsibility for it. So nobody blamed her for what had happened. It was just the punishment for her blighted fate that people spoke about in a hushed whisper. And what made them shudder in apprehension was the fact that a new life was being brought into the world. People pitied Romola more than blaming her.

"How wrong they were! The last thing Romola needed was pity. This was the happiest time of her life. She wanted to experience every stage of childbirth with me. Once again I became the storyteller, except that I wove every strand without the help of words. It was touch and feel and moods. For the first time I felt the intricacies of my body. Everything about the body – the heartbeat, the inhalation, the exhalation, the hunger I felt at the pit of my stomach, the sleep that descended on my eyes and the gentle ache that made my limbs heavy – was tied up with the power to create that swamped my being. It was this miracle that I tried communicating to Romola. She revelled in it, but at times I caught the sadness in her eyes. It was my gift to her, but our bodies were separate entities. The distance that separated us could not be covered.

"As my body burgeoned with life, hers grew pale and emaciated. Only her eyes were luminous and contented. I asked her why she looked so thin? Had she stopped eating? She said her body did not matter any more, like the arid fields after the harvest; they were now barren but the granaries were full. She felt little hunger; my body cried for nourishment. She was wakeful all the time; I slept long hours of the day. She moved swiftly like the wind; I was slow and lethargic. As the baby grew to full term in my womb, and the final hour of delivery loomed near, a strange desolation descended on me. Then one day I told her about my feelings.

"Hardly had the words slipped out of my lips than I realized how selfish I had been. I wanted to give her this gift of love, but not before I had made my own claims on it. I told her the strangest possible story. It had come to me like a fleeting vision, disturbing one of those noontime naps that I took regularly. The baby inside me stirred. It opened its large, saucer like eyes and whispered into the hollow of the cord that tied us together. I heard a voice cry out 'mother' inside me. The dreams became more persistent, coming to me unbidden. Once, I thought I was wide awake. The vision was so clear that I found myself perspiring heavily, my breath coming in short gasps. I was walking through long, empty corridors opening into nothingness. But then I saw a locked door at one end. As I moved towards it, the two panels slid open with a slight creaking sound. Inside the room it was dark and a little misty. A gentle breeze blew against my face. I saw an open window and outside, the sky was inky blue with a large red moon. The colours were so brilliant that I drew in my breath in sheer surprise. Life stirred inside me, vibrant, pulsating, little kicks that made me hold the largeness of my girth with grasping hands. I was laughing happily. Then I saw her, and though I have no living memories of my mother, she stood before me in her full likeness. She was so beautiful that I felt a tremor run through my body. 'Uma,' she called out, and the intimacy of her voice shocked me. 'Do you want this child?' Before I could answer I woke up."

"For the first time I saw the laughter slip out of Romola's eyes. She looked stricken, and the only question she asked me again and again was what answer I had given. I had given no answer. But I knew then that love was selfish, and that in a strange way my desire to experience childbirth was a desire to relive the circumstances of my own birth. Had I really done this for Romola? I did not know then. I know the answer now, but you will have to wait before you hear it from me. There is much else that had to happen before I knew for sure.

"Had I forgiven my mother then? I knew for sure that I had, and the years of guilt, despair, rage simply slipped out of my body. We spoke about my dreams for great lengths of time. Romola was intuitive; this is something that is rarely spoken about her, but I want you to write about it, David. She was compassionate and wise and almost clairvoyant. She saw into things. I know she would not commit suicide out of despair or the lack of will to live. The river must have summoned her. Very often she spoke about things that happened because you listened to an inner voice. But why did her inner voice draw her away from the people she loved?

"According to Romola, my vision meant that I had understood the single most compulsive reason that drives us towards what is creative. I had become a mother not because I was misled or compelled by forces outside my control: I had made a deliberate choice. Avinash is the expression of my love. Please tell Dadabhai that when I gave away my baby it was out of another choice. Renunciation is selfish. It is often done as an act of self-expression, the simple way of being true to oneself. But there is untold love in it for others; though it is a way of loving that can hurt terribly until the time we understand. Romola had shown me the path of that understanding, and I am ever grateful to her. It was she who had planted the 'want' of desire in me. She taught me the art of taking responsibility for what one seeks to have in life. She released me from my delusions, that forever running away and seeking places that had been my way of coping. But it took a while before I understood all this. When we discussed my dream I was still distressed by Romola's answers to questions that I refused to reply to. My dreams continued to trouble my waking hours for great lengths of time. But however hard I tried to silence it, the voice inside my womb continued to call out my name. 'Mother,' it whispered again and again."

~~~

Abha spoke to Sameer explaining to him all that Uma had recounted. "I should have been there," Sameer said ruefully. "So much of what she is saying makes sense to me."

"No, it is better this way," Abha demurred. "She talks to David because he is the vital link with Romola. It is strange how we are all part of a mystic circle, those present and those absent. It is like living out life within the wide, enmeshing web of circumstances, layers of consciousness, time past, present, and memories. It is this completeness of being that comes through her story. You understand now why I call it 'a story'? Not because she was making it up, but because through it we can see that we are all a part of it. What better word to describe those myriad twists and turns that brought us together or severed us apart? It is her story, our story."

He could feel her passion bringing them together across cities. "It is not just our story, Abha. It is the story of two cities, and what ties them. The year I chose to live in Delhi and not Varanasi was also the year I met Vandana through you. You chose Varanasi. I chose to return there and I met you again. Romola came to Varanasi. Avinash was sent to Delhi to live with us. It's amazing isn't it?"

"I could not agree with you more," Abha cried out with suppressed excitement in her voice. "I used to tell David very often when he was doing his research on the Ganga. You call the river mystic, but it is not beyond history. I think he can understand what I meant now. He tells me that the Ganges brings him across continents, as though it is calling out to him. I am once again sitting by its banks, he says, and listening to a story that makes my hair stand on end. He is planning to write all this, you know. He will probably give up his teaching job and become a full-time writer. I am encouraging him all the time. The river Ganga as the backdrop, flowing through an ancient city, and the point at which our lives meet each other, and its mystic core. It is a book worth writing, don't you agree?"

Death in the Bowers

"Do we have premonitions of death seconds before we die? I think not. I think all accidental deaths are sudden, like slipping away in the flash of an eye. Why else would Romola not say goodbye to me or to her son that morning before she went down to the ghats? She said in her usual way to Avinash, 'Will you come down with me or do you prefer to stay back with Umamasi?' Before Avinash could answer, she was climbing down the steps.

"For a time I felt at peace with myself. The boy was growing up fine. He had my family face, but he inherited his mother's temperament. She nurtured him and taught him all the rudiments of knowledge. She asked Swamiji for the best teachers for him. She made him read the scriptures. He worked in the fields with the other boys. He knew each plant and tree. He knew the names of gods and goddesses. She told him all the folklore, taught him songs, and under her guidance he learnt to distinguish the seasons.

Inside the ashram he was part of the community and his tasks always brought him in touch with the others. We loved him, but without any display of possession. He called Romola mother, 'mai', but it was only a name. He uttered the word 'masi' with as much reverence. I think he saw us as sisters who mothered him in different ways. I was happy with this arrangement and I believe we would have gone through life without anything upsetting this balance. But it was not to be.

"One day Avinash asked Romola where was England. Was it there on the map that hung in Swamiji's room? 'Swamiji said my father lives in England.' We were taken aback. Swamiji had broken the first rule of our pact. There would be no questions asked, and no answers given.

"I saw the consternation on Romola's face. Neither of us were prepared for this. We knew that people whispered about an English father. They were simply putting facts together and arriving at conclusions. Romola had learnt to accept this. In many ways it made things easier for her. I understood its logic and why it was better this way. But for the first time in my life I wanted Avinash to grow up with the truth, or what seemed an easier version of the truth. 'Your father is not an Englishman,' I interjected. 'He is the Lord Krishna. We are all wedded to him.'

"I broke the spirit of the pact. In many ways, mine was the betrayal. An invisible tussle grew between us. It was not so much over Avinash or whom he belonged to; it was more insidious and cruel than that. It became the worm that gnawed away at the fruit of life. Its rich exterior hid the canker that grew slowly but steadily. For the first time, we stopped communicating with each other with our stories, not in words or in gestures. The silence tore us apart. But we did not quite notice it, because we were so caught up with the boy who had just begun to string together his first sentences.

"Nothing is worse than the silence you can hear in your waking hours. We were each hurt by the other, each waiting for the other to break the silence. There were times when I felt the need to tell her my feelings. I had no one else to turn to. She must have felt the same. I wonder what kept us from making the first move? If Avinash sensed the growing distance between us, he never let us know. But we were always vying for his attention. Who puts him to sleep? Who gets to feed him? Who oversees his bathing hours? In a family unit parents do share tasks, but ours was an unusual household. Two mothers seeking their son's attention. I guess I was being selfish. I should have known what I was doing when I had agreed to the pact. It had been my conscious choice. But as Romola never failed to tell me, love is selfish. I looked at the boy's face as one looks at a mirror, and I wanted to see my own reflection. For the first time in my life I wanted to call this relationship my own. It belonged to me by the sacred rights of motherhood. I had put in much effort to earn this right. I felt the calling deep inside my body. Every sinew, muscle, flow of blood strained to possess the object of love. I felt paranoid at the thought of losing him.

"One day I woke up to find both Romola and Avinash missing. There was nothing unusual about the situation. The two of them often went down to the ghat to see the early morning sunrise. But that morning I felt waves of panic, like someone who has the premonition of something terrible about to happen. I left all my morning tasks undone and ran through the fallow fields crying out for the boy. Nobody could tell me where he was. They looked startled to see me. Then one of them said very firmly, 'What is the matter, sister? I think I saw Avinash with his mother. There is nothing to worry about. So long as he is with his mother no harm can come to him.'

"I went back to my room, but something must have broken inside me. I knew then that Romola had the rights of

motherhood by social sanction. To the world at large Avinash
is Romola and David's child. What if tomorrow she decides
to leave me and go away with the boy, to claim her rights
from the man who loved her and had wanted to marry her?
Who would give credence to my story? Would Avinash
believe me once he was a grown man? What would I tell him
anyway? That I had abandoned him, my own flesh and
blood. And that I had swapped roles with Romola as though
we were playing some sort of a game? I was appalled at what
I had done. I felt the kind of moral outrage that David felt
when he first knew about Romola's pregnancy. I realize now
that the sense of sin is something we borrow as a matter of
habit from being told how to look at things.

"I could not think in any other way. I felt tainted, sinful.
I did something I should not have done. I went back to
Swamiji and confessed my state of mind. He looked at me
with withering eyes. "What did I tell you?" he said to me in
his authoritarian voice. "I knew you would return to me one
day. You are made of different stuff. The family tradition
that runs through your veins is refined. It can never let you
down. I knew it from the day I set eyes on you. You have
committed a grave sin, but what matters is your penitence.
The river will wash away your sin and restore you to your
state of purity." I felt grateful, then, for a system that can
give back what you have lost.

"I went back to my prayers, the ascetic lifestyle, the emp-
tying of mind of all worldly desires. Romola was intuitive.
She knew the direction my life had taken, and she knew the
reason why. We talked about it only once, a few months
before she died. I will tell you exactly what she said to me:
'Do not punish yourself in this way. Why must you listen to
them? What they tell you is born out of centuries of oppres-

sion and exploitation. They have taken away your right to speak, to think, to use your body in whichever way you want. Don't you see what they have done to you and me; they have made us into vessels that can be used as properly or as savagely as they choose? Swamiji says he is your protector, you will feel safe within his fold. He lies to you. I knew one day he would get to you. I should have anticipated this and protected you. But I was too busy pouring out all my attention on Avinash. Forgive me, Uma, I have let you down. Please listen very carefully to what I am telling you. It will enable you to live life your own way, even if I am not there to help you. Avinash is your son because the seeds of desire were planted in your body. You may not have realized it when it happened, but think of what your dreams have been telling you. In the ten months that your body pulsated with new life you felt the single want that brought back your health, body and mind. No one can ever take away that gift from you. Listen to what that want in your body is telling you. If to want is to sin, then God has not invented a penance for the sin.'

"I look back on those days and realize that I had gone deaf and blind, and was so misled. Why else would I be appalled at what she said? I noticed that she said something about not being there to help me. Was she planning to go away, and would she take my son away from me? The very thoughts filled me with despair. I realized how much that want had dug its roots in me. It was the first time that I wanted something for myself. I did not want to share Avinash with anyone. I wanted the world to know the real story. I went to Swamiji and begged him to come out with the truth. He froze me with his gaze. I think this was the first time that he looked at me directly. There was something in his face that made me cringe.

Was it exultation or a sheer display of power? 'Let her go,' he raged, 'she has only brought you suffering. She is not meant for this ashram. Sooner or later she will leave us. Don't you see what she has been doing to you? She has been using you as a weapon to fight her battles with me. All my years of meditation and trial by fire has been reduced to dust. You must let her go before she poisons your son's mind against you.' It was the last blow for me. I felt my world crumble.

"I should have understood what Swamiji was doing to me. He had sowed the seeds of suspicion deep inside me. I felt cold towards the world. But I was lonely without her, as though all the colour had drained out of my life. The austerity I now practised hurt every sinew of my body. My mind was in great turmoil. My prayer times did not bring a sense of peace to me. I felt divorced from my god.

"Like in earlier times Swamiji took me under his wings. He had mastered the art of possessing your tainted soul and preparing it for salvation. He gave me tasks that drained out my energy, body and soul. I completed them as acts of penitence that filled me with shame. He asked me to expel Romola from my consciousness, and cleanse my memory of her. Only then would I feel complete again. But Swamiji was wrong. I did not want to lose her. She was my twin soul, and together we were mother to Avinash. To lose her was to feel distant from the only identity that mattered to me.

"One day Romola chided me for not fulfilling my responsibilities as a mother. 'See yourself,' she said with great conviction, 'you are lost to us. What is the matter, Uma? When did you last feed the boy? When did you last take him to the ghats and see the sun rise? When did you last sing a song for him? You think you can be a mother only in name, without the hard work? Giving birth is just the passage into this world. Unlike other animals, human beings are weak, and dependent on the parent for a much longer time. We experience motherhood only when we nurture and keep our children safe and happy. Do you think I could let you take Avinash to the ghat without fearing that he might do himself some harm? You are so unmindful.'

"Was I sickening again? I wondered at times, and the very thought sent waves of panic through my body. I should have known then that what Swamiji was offering was a trap. My delusions were the only way he could keep me in bondage within the four walls of the ashram. It was not Romola's going away that he feared; it was mine. He knew that neither of us would really leave the ashram physically, but there is a sense in which the rules of the ashram become the binding force that keeps us in a state of obedience. He was pushing me deeper and deeper into my sickness.

"I believe that Romola knew what was happening to me. You might ask me why she did not do anything to save me? I have sought an answer myself, but the riddle only becomes more mysterious. One day she said something that shook me deeply. 'This is a battle you will have to fight alone. I went to Swamiji in desperation, and asked him to release you from his clutches if I promised never to come in his way. You know what he said to me. I will win, come what may. You see, in this tug of war your son is in the middle. One of you will have to give up in order to save him.'"

~~~

"It was like any other day, hot and humid, especially after the quick showers that beaten down on earth, making the depths of the river turgid and treacherous. The steps leading to the ghats were slippery. Romola was making elaborate preparations to give her offerings to the river. She was teaching

Avinash the rituals of prayer and, though it was for him nothing more than a game, there was interest in his eyes. Memories flooded my mind. I was back in Grandma's prayer room, watching her light the diyas and blow the conch shell. The sound pierced the quiet of the afternoon. She asked me to shut the door because she did not want to wake up Grandpa. I did things dutifully, except that I left a slight opening in the door, and when it was my turn to ring the bells I made it jangle with a harsh sound. I knew the sound would travel to Grandpa's room and disturb his drug-laden sleep. It would often make his body convulse. To me these convulsions were like death throes, and I secretly wanted him to suffer. After so many years I felt the same hatred course through my body. I should have known then what divided loyalties could do to a young mind. But Avinash was the object of my love, and I wanted to possess him fully. But please understand, I never wanted Romola out of my life. I never wished her death, or pain for that matter.

"Was Romola's death of her own choice? Was it suicide, as Swamiji declared to the police? I think not. When she talked about leaving me alone she meant that my struggles were my own. Once before she had taught me this lesson of loving, and shown me that we were two separate people. We were caught between the system and our individuality, the tug of war as Swamiji described it. But this battle is age old, and we were in it because we were discovering the selfishness that lies at the heart of all loving. But loving has its own rules of giving as well. Swamiji should have known this power of renunciation. He should have described Romola's death as an accident, in the same way as life and death is an accident. The causes are too many, and some of the reasons are beyond our control or understanding.

"I had absolutely no misgiving when Romola left for the ghat with her plateful of offerings. I promised to send Avinash after a while. When he came back without her, I had no premonition or fear in my mind. He, too, looked happy and excited about all the things he had witnessed. He carried the prasad in a leaf plate, one for me and one for him. As we ate the pieces of God's food I felt a sense of blessing run through my limbs. When I asked him when his mai would come to join us, he said, 'Something strange happened today. One of the diyas fell into the river. When mai stretched out her hand to bring it back, the river rose and carried her away. I kept waiting for mai to come back. She always told me that one day she would go down to the bottom of the river and bring back the two souls that are kept in a casket. She said when the two souls are fused together we would never be separated. She asked me not to be frightened.'

"It was the receding tide that brought home her body. I did not let the boy see her. She will return one day, I told him. He lives with that belief. I do not want to break it. Please tell Dadabhai that I do not want the truth to be known today or any day. Avinash is Romola and David's son. I have asked Swamiji to give me visiting rights. I will not abandon my son. Nor will I allow the sins of the parent to visit him. I think the two of you can do the best for him."

CHAPTER SIXTEEN

Postscript

I have been living in Varanasi for many years now. I write full-time. I took a decision to give up my teaching job in England. This country gave me my vocation. It was a conscious choice I made, because there was no way I could stop myself from documenting the many stories that I had gathered in the course of living here. I wanted to put each one of them into words. The process of writing seemed ceaseless. But there was another, more amorphous reason why I stayed back. I used always to think that I could negotiate the vast alienness of India by remaining a tourist, someone who refused to put down his roots here. I fell in love with the streets, the music, the language, the literature and the women, but I was not ready to make this place my home. At every crucial point in my life when I had to make a commitment, I would buy a plane ticket and turn my face away from my loved ones. But Romola had other plans for me. She left behind a family for me to take care of. If there was any way in which I could make amends for my past mistakes, here was an opportunity that I could not pass up.

I remember the moment Uma held my hand and said to me, "I will keep my trust with Romola. I will carry the secret to my grave. I know this is one moment when I can seize what is mine; Avinash is my son, Dadabhai will certify that I have recovered from my illness; I alone can get his custody. But this is not what I 'want'. You can help me, David. Romola the mother has died and he is orphaned. He can get a foster home. I know Dadabhai and Vandana will not turn their faces away from what they will see as family responsibility. I know both of them well. But to do that would mean Romola's right to motherhood is erased. But nobody will deny that the father has natural custody of his son. You can exercise your right as a parent, which in everybody's eyes you share with Romola. It will give Avinash the stability he needs. He thinks his mother will return one day with her twin souls, and both will fuse to create the perfect family. And he waits for his father to return from England. How can we disappoint the boy on both counts?" As she spoke, I felt the presence of the other woman shine through the feverish glitter in her eyes. I knew the strength of sacrifice was something she had imbibed from Romola. In a split second I made the decision to change the direction of my life. It did not feel as though I was giving up anything: it felt like a homecoming.

So Avinash and I moved into that sprawling Sengupta ancestral home where he rightfully belonged. This year he turned eighteen. I think Romola would be proud if she was to see him today. He is preparing to follow in the family foot-steps. He has gained admission to one of the leading medical colleges in Delhi, in fact the very institute that Sameer stud-ied in. We are a very proud family.

I believe that one's link with a city is symbolic. Avinash has three homes that he knows he belongs to, the one here in Varanasi, the one in Delhi where his closest family stays, and the third in distant England where my kith and kin reside. He straddles all three places, and the difference in culture has helped to shape him. He has in many ways helped to unlock all those secret doors that would exclude us from the mystic circle.

It has made Avinash sensitive to the idea of what is a family. If there is one thing that I have been able to give him it is the sense of 'looking for roots'. He has always wanted to know more about his 'mai' and his 'masi'. That has kept him in touch with the ashram. It has opened up a world apart for him. He has read all my writings on the Ganga, and that makes him curious about the confluence of realities which is the core of Varanasi. But more than anything else, it is Bela's mystery room that has been unlocked. It is here that Uma spends a few days of the month when she is away from the ashram. Swamiji went away to the Himalayas and took his samadhi there. The ashram runs on the same rules and conventions, but the new age has crept in. The relationship that Uma shares with Avinash is a special one. They share stories, as Uma relives her life in them. I know that it is her way of preparing Avinash for the truth about his mother's death.

Abha has retired from the University. Once again we work on many of my writing projects. Sameer and Vandana have grown old together, gracefully. I am told Avinash and Mira share a special bond, and much of his heartache he is able to communicate to her. The family reunites every summer for one occasion or another. At such times Abhishek makes it a point to come home from the US. There is much rejoicing and going down memory lane then. To this day, the Indian sense of the family reunion has never ceased to fascinate me.

All relationships are fragile, especially when they are held together by norms not set by society. As my book is ready to go to press, I am afraid. It has taken me many years to write it down as truthfully as I could. If there are gaps, it is only because I could not make sense of the truth then. With hindsight, a lot of things seem crystal clear. Sometimes, I am afraid that the truth will hurt Avinash, but then I wonder if that would be the case. All novels are both fictional and autobiographical. Mine is a simple story about two women who shared a single dream: to love without shame or fear. How can such a truth hurt?

Glossary

bidi tobacco wrapped in tobacco leaves; a poor man's cigarette

brahmin the highest caste in the Hindu caste system

chaste Hindi pure Hindi in its Sanskrit form, spoken by scholars

chauki a small wooden table of low height

diya an earthenware candle

gali lane

ghat river bank

ghatiya a priest who conducts prayers and assists in cremation rites on the ghats of Varanasi

Gita the Hindu Holy Book

handi a circular utensil used for cooking

householder those who have chosen to lead a married life and have children; in an ashram, the stage before leaving the family to become an ascetic

IIT acronym for Indian Institute of Technology

Kailash Yatra journey or pilgrimage to Mount Kailash situated in the Himalayan Ranges

kurta a long shirt worn by men and women over pyjamas

linga phallic symbol associated with the Indian god Shiva

mai an affectionate variation of the word mother

masi maternal aunt/mother's sister

masti mirth and laughter celebrating the spirit of the carnival

Matador brand name for a 24-seater minibus

moksha liberation or release from life cycle

panch koshi and **tirtha sthan** pilgrimage sites; the five paths for those undergoing pilgrimage in Varanasi

prasad offerings of fruits and milkcake made to the gods inside a temple. Once the food has been blessed by the gods it is distributed to the devotees.

pujari priests who offer their services to conduct prayers inside the temples

rajanigandha strongly-scented white flowers

samadhi taking one's place in a grave, or choosing to die by starvation

samagri the items that are offered in prayer to the gods

sambar lentil soup; a southern Indian dish

sandhya arati evening prayers with lighted diyas

sanyasi an ascetic; one who renounces all worldly ties and desires

sanyasin a female devotee who has renounced the world

schloka sacred hymn

sevika a woman who serves within a household or a religious order

shamshan a cremation ground

shiv-linga a bisexual symbol associated with the Indian god Shiva. It is shaped like the erect shaft set in a circular base or seat. It represents divine energy as combination of male and female sexual potency

shudra the lowest, untouchable, caste

sindoor red-coloured powder worn by married women in the parting of their hair, at the front of the head

tempo a three-wheeled vehicle used for carrying cargo

Veda a holy scripture – there are four Vedas in the Hindu religion